Stella & Dane

DEANNA ROY

casey shay press

Stella & Dane

This is a work of fiction. All the characters, organizations, and events portrayed in this novel are either products of the author's imagination or used fictitiously.

A huge thank you to Aunt Kay, a former prison nurse, for amazing information on how prisons work on the inside. And especially to former Missouri State Penitentiary guard Brian Kostic for information on the prison when it was still functional. You can now tour the MSP, including ghost tours at www.missouripentours.com.

Casey Shay Press
PO Box 160116
Austin, TX 78716
www.caseyshaypress.com

ISBN: 9781938150036
Also available in as an ebook: E-ISBN: 9781938150029

Library of Congress Control Number: 2012912343

Other books by Deanna Roy

Baby Dust: A Novel about Miscarriage
including more of the story of Stella and Dane

Jinnie Wishmaker
an adventure for 9-12 year olds under the name DD Roy

Dust Bunnies: Secret Agents
an iPad story book app for children ages 3-9

Learn more about the author at
www.deannaroy.com

For Kurt

May all love stories be as passionate as ours

PART ONE: *Collision*

1

WATER TOWER CLIMB

Fall 1984

STELLA should have known not to climb the water tower in plastic shoes.

When her pink jelly slipped off the ladder, she managed to clutch one of the rungs. Her knee banged against the metal as she scrambled to hang on. Hell of a way to go, falling four stories to her death.

Janine screamed below, and that really got Stella's blood pumping. If she somehow managed not to die, her friend was going to get them both caught.

Stella felt around with her foot and planted the flimsy shoe squarely on one of the bars. She hadn't planned on scaling the tower in jellies, but the gorgeous fall day had inspired her to take a risk.

"Please don't yell," she called down. "Old Lady Springer has been looking for a reason to call the sheriff on me for years."

From this height, Janine resembled a Rainbow Brite doll in a purple dress with yellow leg warmers. "Why are you so crazy?" she shouted.

Stella twisted around to face out on the ladder, the soft shoes curling around the rung as she grasped the bar and leaned forward. The whole town could have looked up her miniskirt, if it hadn't been so tight. "Only way to be in a town like this."

Janine covered her eyes. "Please don't hang like that."

"I've done this drunk at midnight."

Her friend peeked between her fingers. "I know."

The sun blasted off the aluminum roof of the shed at the base of the tower. The morning fog had burned off, and she was late for work. But, walking along the block, Stella couldn't resist the urge to climb the silver dome. After twenty-two years of living in its shadow, scaling it in the middle of the day was just about the only thing she'd never done. Seemed like something to check off her list before she left for good. Should've had Janine bring a camera. Get a shot of her underneath the giant black letters that read "Holly," the town's ridiculous name.

Stella whipped back around on the ladder. Just one level to go until she reached the platform that encircled the massive water tank.

"Hey! I'm going to get docked. My boss ain't like yours." Janine backed away from the base of the tower, crouching to duck through the section of the chain-link fence that had been cut decades ago by high school seniors seeking to spray-paint the side of the dome. Stella herself had added a blood-red "Seniors '81" a few years back.

Stella waved down at her and scurried up the last segment of the ladder. She reached the platform and pushed through the narrow opening, grasping the bar that served as an ineffectual rail. As far as she knew, nobody had ever fallen off the darn thing, and she wasn't going to today. She wouldn't get caught, either.

Plenty of people had been up there before her. The entire circumference of the tower was defaced with "Mark loves Ellen" and hundreds of other couplings, many crossed out and amended. Stella had warned the boys never to put her name up there. That was a deal breaker, certain to seal the doom of her latest fling.

But one had disobeyed, Carter something-or-other, a Montana boy who moved to Holly when his dad started working at the bank. He was full of himself and his shiny Camaro. He'd been after her, thinking he was doing something romantic by dragging an eight-foot ladder up the tower to inscribe "Carter & Stella" higher than any of the other graffiti.

Stella followed the platform to the other side, facing downtown, where a huge black splotch covered his transgression. Being on the short side, she'd had to drag a TEN-foot ladder up the damn tower to get rid of it. And, after blotting out his mistake, she emptied the rest of the spray can on his little red hotrod. She had a temper, and she knew it. It caused her a world of grief.

He'd known she had done it, but the small town was good at closing ranks to separate the born-and-bred from the newcomers. Carter's dad didn't want to make waves in the community, so her lawlessness had been ignored. They hadn't stayed even a year in Holly.

Standing on the tower in the daytime was a completely different experience from all the nighttime jaunts. Why hadn't she done it before? She peeked down at Janine's purple form hurrying along the block, heading to the grocery where she worked as a cashier. Janine stopped suddenly and pointed ahead of her without looking up. Stella followed her arm, puzzled, then saw the sheriff's car cruising into view.

A trespassing ticket would dip into the fund she'd put together to get the heck out of Holly. She needed that money, and she'd planned this escape for years.

The sheriff's car coasted along the broken pavement. Stella kept her back to the tower until the squad car passed, glad for the silver lamé shirt to help her blend in. Once he'd turned the corner onto Mulberry, she stepped away from the wall to look out on her soon-to-be ex-town.

The school. The track. The athletic fields she'd never stepped foot on, not once.

Houses filled a few blocks, then the highway snaked through town, the artery lined with what few shops attempted to make a profit. She'd worked at a few, even the convenience store for two weeks, until Old Man Jenkins took to showing up in an overcoat, barelegged in black socks and dress shoes. Her mama made her quit before her purity got stained. Ha.

Stella could just make out the roof of her grandmother's house, almost smack in the middle of town, a few streets off Main behind the courthouse. It had been empty for eight long months, other than those hours Stella visited, dusting Grandma Angie's favorite things while Johnny Mathis crooned from the record player. She would call Grandma's number at the nursing home from the pink rotary phone in the bedroom, although she rarely got an answer.

Even though Stella didn't like the facility, its smells and long corridors, Grandma was always out and about, painting sunflowers or making leather key chains. So it had to be good for her. No one would really explain to her why Grandma had made the move, especially since Branson was twenty miles away and Stella didn't have a car.

But Stella knew about the cancer, and sometimes she steamed open a hospital bill before her mother got to it, to see if she could glean any news from the payment information. She could tell that more chemo had been happening, but Grandma was a fighter.

With Grandma Angie gone, Stella didn't have much keeping her in Holly. Her sister, eight years older, had married off and split at the first opportunity. Her parents were no reason to stay and, in fact, her overbearing and always disapproving mother was every reason to go.

The wind kicked up, and the temperature dropped a notch as clouds passed before the sun. The humidity was going to wilt her carefully sprayed bangs. Stella leaned way over the bar, spotting her shiny purse with its can of Aqua Net inside. She could repair later. Part of working at the perfume shop was your appearance. Beatrice always approved of makeup breaks.

With her belly bent so far over the rail, she could do a somersault, just like on the monkey bars as a kid. And why not? She picked up her feet and rushed forward and down, her necklace hitting her nose, and the world whirled as she spun around the thin bar.

She was a little too tall, so her calves smashed into the sheet metal. She lifted her feet to find the platform, lightheaded. Stella laughed out loud. Janine would have had a fit. The rush of it felt good, so she did it again, this time tucking her knees a little higher.

The metal shifted against her stomach. Panic zipped through her as she realized the rail couldn't quite hold her weight and had begun to bend. She lost momentum and hung with her head down. The town below was a blur of green and gray.

God, she was going to die after all. Blood rushed to her face, her stomach hot and sick. Her hair brushed the platform, and anytime she moved, the bar bent even more.

Stella hung on, eyes closed, trying to control her fear. She could hear her grandmother, when Stella had gotten stuck in a tree, saying, "Don't let fear win, Stella. Beat it."

She kicked her legs to force her body the rest of the way around. The metal had pinched in enough that when she made it full circle, her lower back grazed the platform. She clutched the bent rail, feet dangling, trying to figure out how to wiggle her way backward and up to safety.

Her shoulders screamed with the effort of hanging on. Stella looked down, imagining her body smashing onto the roof of the shed below. Good God, what had she been thinking? She swung her legs from side to side, zinging anew with fear as the metal bar scrunched again, until finally she caught the lip of the platform with her heel.

The flimsy plastic of her pink jelly snapped, and the shoe flipped upward, balanced on the edge of the platform, then fell below. Stella watched its descent as it banged against a leg of the tower and tumbled end over end until it landed in a tree beside the shed.

She grunted and brought her other foot up onto the platform. She ducked beneath the bar and rolled toward the tower, not stopping until she lay against the wall. Her breathing came in great huffs, her lungs sucking in air until she choked.

Stella curled against the metal, feeling each rivet and seam. Death had moved in close, and she'd cheated it. Yet, she still had to get down. She turned her head slightly, but even the glimpse of trees and rooftops set her to shivering.

The drainage mesh in the center of the platform bit into her bare legs and foot. Down below, drum taps and tweets of a flute and whomps of a tuba filtered upward, happy and light. The marching band must have left the school, probably heading toward the practice field just beneath the tower.

A cymbal crashed, startling her. She inched her way to the edge so she could see, forcing herself to accept the height again. The kids were lined up below, the percussion only a few yards from the chain-link fence that cordoned off the base of the tower. She hadn't factored in their arrival, even though she knew they practiced right after lunch. Now she was good and stuck with no way to call her boss and explain why she was so late. Losing her job, now that would be a crappy addition to her day.

One of the kids climbed a rickety stepladder and shouted at the others. They stood still, poised and perfect, expectant. When the kid clapped and lifted his arms, they raised their instruments in unison. After a four-count, the band bellowed the first bars of a marching song.

Stella laid her cheek against the metal and closed her eyes. Just forget everything. Listen to the music, blow off the job. Something would come along. Life would move forward, one way or another.

* * *

She awoke to a sprinkle on her cheek. The band was gone, and her watch read 2:00. The sky had gone gray, and the first light raindrops were spilling across the face of the tower. God, she was late. She peered over the edge of the platform, her stomach rumbling. The pink shoe still hung in the tree. A maintenance man squatted by the wheel of a bus. One hour until classes let out. She had to get down before then.

She crawled back to the opening that led to the ladder. Maybe if she didn't stand up at all, just slid right through to the rungs, she'd be fine. Don't look down, don't think about where you are. She'd done this so many times. Maybe dark was better. You couldn't see where you'd land.

A voice, thin and tinny, came from below. "Stella?"

She couldn't see who it was from the hole. Stella drew a deep breath and moved nearer the edge, grasping not the thin rail, but one of the supporting legs.

Beatrice, her boss. Good Lord.

"You okay, Stell?" She looked up at her, blond hair tuffed just so, shoulder pads so wide she looked like a linebacker. The black and white checks on her jacket were big enough to be a chessboard even from this height. Stella could almost catch the waft of Chanel No. 19, but probably that was just memory. Beatrice would get wrecked in the rain. Her coiffure didn't hold up well to the elements.

"I'm fine. Sort of," she called. At least she wasn't fired, it seemed.

"Janine stopped by on her break, saw you weren't there. You need me to call the fire department?"

God. "No! I'm coming!" Stella forced herself to slide back to the hole and stick her legs through. Her bare foot caught the rung, so she eased down to stand on the ladder.

Her pink jelly immediately slipped, and she gripped the platform so hard her bracelet snapped against the metal.

"Careful, honey!"

Stella huffed a few stabilizing breaths, then scraped her heel against the rung, knocking off the shoe. She was better off without it. It thudded below, probably landing on the shed.

She pulled her hand back to grasp the top of the ladder, grimacing at the wet, and inched down another two rungs. The bracelet pulled loose—too loose—and slipped down her arm. No!

The amethyst beads glittered as they moved into the crook of her elbow. The birthstones! Grandma Angie had given Stella the bracelet last May. Stella couldn't bear to lose it.

The wind bit into the tears at the corners of her eyes as she tightened her arm, trying to keep the bracelet from falling. She let go with her left hand, hoping to catch the beads, barely daring to breathe. The rain came in earnest now, and she wondered what Beatrice was doing below.

Her fingers clutched what bits of the bracelet were still trapped against her body. Others rolled off, hitting the roof like hail.

Her skirt didn't have any pockets, so she stuck the beads and bits of metal in her mouth. Down, down, down, she knew she had to hurry now. The ladder would get increasingly wet and treacherous. She descended the first tier, trying not to breathe too hard, or she might swallow the beads.

Her foot reached tentatively for the second ladder, a short gap that felt like a mile. Her foot slipped again on the wet bar, and she gripped hard with her toes. She chanced a look down. Beatrice was obscured beneath a *Vogue* magazine opened over her head.

Stella transferred her weight to the other ladder, feeling her foot slip again. Her tall bangs hung in her eyes now, dripping down her face. If she got down, she swore she'd leave this godforsaken town tomorrow. And grow up. Time to do that.

The storm responded with a flash of lightning. Beatrice screeched down below, and Stella moved quickly now, sure-footed as she descended the second tier. Just one to go.

The last jog was a bigger stretch, but the towering elm tree that held her shoe had protected the metal from the worst of the rain. The beads rolled against Stella's tongue, and she had to let saliva dribble out the corners of her mouth to keep from swallowing. What a sight she had to be. She could taste hair spray. The blue eye shadow and violet mascara no doubt lent her a freakish appearance.

She reached out with her foot again, transferring to the last ladder.

"You almost got it, hon!" Beatrice called, her voice muffled by the drum of rain on the metal shed roof.

A bead tried to make it down her throat, and she almost gagged. But she tilted her head forward to slide the bits toward her lips, where she could hold them tight.

No distractions. Her feet moved swiftly down, down, down, her hands grasping the rungs with fierce intensity. The last few feet required a jump, but she was barefoot. She looked below at the gravel and weeds, slick with rain.

Beatrice rushed forward, holding out her arms. "I got you, sugar doll. You can let go."

Stella worried the jolt would cause her to swallow the beads, so she spit them into one hand while hanging by the other, then released the rung. She fell on top of Beatrice, and they tumbled together onto the wet stones. Stella saw a sparkle by her elbow. Another bead! She snatched it up, scrambling along the ground to spot any more.

Beatrice stood with a grunt. "What got into you, girl?"

"I've climbed it a hundred times." Another jewel. Stella snatched it up.

"In the rain?"

"It wasn't raining when I went up."

Beatrice brushed gravel from her knees. "I guess we both have to clean up before going back to work." She grimaced at the caked mud. "Maybe we'll just close up for the day."

Stella snatched her purse from where she'd hidden it behind a rock, dropping the beads inside. The loss of the bracelet hit her hard now, her nose running madly. "I have to get on the shed."

She set the purse down again and stumbled across the gravel, looking for a way up. The water came down in sheets.

Beatrice grasped her arm. "What is with you? You nearly died at least twice up there."

She'd cheated death again. There would be payback, she knew. "My grandmother's bracelet. It shattered." She held up her empty arm, scratched and bleeding.

Beatrice squeezed her shoulder. "I know how much it means to you. Maybe we can find the beads tomorrow, when it's not wet. The rain will wash them off the roof."

Stella collapsed against the wall of the shed. "I hate this town."

Beatrice rolled up the soggy *Vogue* and shoved it in her oversized bag. "Stella, this town's got nothing to do with you nearly falling off a tower."

"It's time for me to go." Stella pushed away from the shed and grabbed her purse. "I've overstayed my welcome."

"Stella, no. Don't." Beatrice followed her, keeping up easily as Stella picked her way across the gravel with tender feet. She grabbed Stella's arm. "I have to tell you something."

Stella jerked around. "What now?"

Beatrice pressed her lips together. The rain had totally deflated her bottle-blond hair, now a sticky helmet plastered against her scalp. Stella knew she looked just as bad.

"It's your grandmother."

Stella stepped back, wincing on a sharp rock. "What is it?"

"Your mom called. I didn't let on you weren't there. I figured you'd show, right up till Janine came in. They've moved your grandmother out of the nursing home. She's back home."

"But that's great. She's doing better, then?"

Beatrice's face crumpled, her own mascara streaming from her lashes. "Not exactly, honey."

Stella whirled around. When her feet hit pavement, she broke into a run. She'd known there would be a reckoning, just not that it would come so fast.

2

Visiting Grandma

"STOP. Stop right there."

Stella halted in the doorway to Grandma Angie's house, footsore, wet, and hurting in forty-seven places. "What?"

Vivian, Stella's mother, blocked the foyer. "You look like a whore on a bender. What were you thinking, walking in, makeup down your face, soaking wet—and where are your shoes?"

Stella tried to push past, but Vivian stood firm. "I'm serious, Stella. You are not going to upset your grandmother with your appearance. Surely you weren't at work this way."

"I got caught in the rain coming here."

Vivian sighed. "Go home and fix yourself up. Grandmother doesn't need to see you like this."

"What's going on? Why is she home?"

Vivian grasped Stella's arm and led her to the kitchen. She snatched a paper towel and wet it at the sink. "It's home hospice."

"What does that mean?"

Vivian held Stella's chin and began wiping her face like she was three years old. "So much mascara. Good God, child."

"What is home hospice?" Stella tried to pull away, but her mother persisted, rubbing the rough cloth under her eyes and down her cheeks.

Vivian set the paper towel on the counter. "It means she's come home to die."

Stella turned to the kitchen table and sat on one of the straight-backed chairs that had been there since before she was born. She ran her fingers along several teeth marks in the wooden seat, left by her sister. "No one told me she was dying."

"You knew she had cancer."

"She seemed fine on the phone."

"She didn't want you to know."

Grandma hadn't told her. Stella hadn't seen her for a couple of months, but still, she'd seemed mostly the same, well, maybe a little thinner. "Why isn't she fighting it? Why aren't they doing anything?"

"She's been fighting. She lost."

"Before she went to the home?" Her head buzzed. She'd been utterly betrayed. The home was supposed to be temporary, for her to do rehab and get strong again.

"No, she kept the chemo going. She was too weak to get around."

"I would have taken care of her."

"She knew that. She wanted you to live your life."

Stella gripped the table, angry at herself. She should have taken Grandma's car keys and driven there, talked to the doctors herself. She had been so stupid. She should have gone. "How long does she have?"

"A week, probably. That's what the nurse said when they arrived." Her mother wiped the counter absently. Dust coated everything. Not that it was clean before. Grandma felt people were more important than a spotless house. Stella was firmly in her camp on that.

"Where is she?"

"In the living room. The nurse is arranging her bed and an oxygen tank."

Stella stood up, but Vivian stopped her again. "Your hair," she said, trying to arrange the sticky strands around Stella's face.

Stella pulled away. "She isn't going to care."

Vivian turned back to the counter. "She was always soft where you were concerned."

Unlike Vivian. This was the longest conversation they'd had in a year, and that's the way Stella liked it. She padded out of the kitchen and into the darkened living room. She couldn't see anything for a moment, but the changes hit her anyway. The ever-present aroma of Grandma's baking, lemon and vanilla and browning pie crust, had been replaced by something medicinal, antiseptic.

As her eyes adjusted, she saw a woman in pink scrubs bend over the controls of a metal hospital bed. A motor whirred, shifting the angle of the mattress, and Stella made out the form of Grandma Angie, slender under a thin blanket. Stella rushed forward and grasped a frail, chilly hand. Grandma's eyes were closed, the thin lids fluttering.

Stella dropped to her knees and leaned into the mattress. "Hey, Grandma. You're home."

Grandma opened her eyes. "Stella, my girl." Her voice was ragged.

"So we can go partying again, right? Now that those buzzards at the nursing home aren't circling?"

Grandma smiled. "Only if you brought the right tequila."

"You hate the cheap stuff."

Grandma closed her eyes again, drawing a shallow breath and letting it go with agonizing slowness.

"She might go out on you," the nurse said. "Just started a morphine drip."

"Is she in pain?" Stella clutched the fragile hand.

"Not now." The nurse tugged a second blanket up over Grandma Angie, tucking it under her arms.

"Can I talk to her?"

"All you want." The nurse patted Stella on the shoulder and left the room.

Stella leaned her head on the bed, her own breath coming in long shudders. "I broke your bracelet."

Grandma squeezed her hand. "That's all right."

"I'll find all the beads. I'll fix it."

"You'll make something even more beautiful."

"I'll try." Grandma had taught Stella everything about jewelry making. They'd started when Stella was just five years old, stringing pony beads on fishing wire.

Vivian walked into the room and scooped up a box labeled "Angelica Sutton" filled with pictures and knickknacks that had been at the nursing home. She clomped away, her flowered dress hitching up on one side, caught by the box. "Don't tire her out," she warned.

When she was gone, Stella asked, "Do I tire you out?"

"No, child."

"You can't leave me."

Grandma fixed her ice-blue eyes on Stella. "My girl."

"I'm expecting you at my wedding. So you better hang in there."

Grandma's mouth opened, but no sound came out.

"And there's no one on the horizon. So it might be, like, twenty years still."

A small smile. Grandma squeezed her hand.

Stella's heart ached. She laid her forehead on the bed again. Why hadn't she gone to Branson more often? What had been more important?

Grandma's hand suddenly went limp. "Grandma?" Stella asked. "Are you okay?"

The nurse reentered the room and lifted Grandma's free hand, fingers pressed against her wrist. "She's asleep now. The morphine has kicked in."

"Why are you putting her out like this?" Stella wanted to talk to her. She had so many things to say.

"She's in some pain now, sweetie." The nurse laid Grandma's hand back on the bed and marked something in a notebook.

"What sort of pain?"

"The tumor is putting pressure on her lungs."

Stella looked down at her grandmother, who now breathed in shallow gasps. It seemed like she was dying before her eyes.

"What will happen?"

"Well, either her lungs will fill with fluid, and that will end things, or she'll get too weak from not eating."

"She doesn't eat?"

"Hasn't for a while. Eating prolongs it. It's hard, dying."

Stella gripped her grandmother's hand more firmly. "Hard on everybody."

3

GOOD SCENTS DISTRACTION

STELLA pushed through the door to Good Scents the next day, heavy and tired. She spotted bits of Beatrice through the glass shelves built into the counter that held the cash register. The boxes of high-dollar perfumes shifted around as her boss made room for new inventory. A half-dozen unopened cartons lay scattered across the store.

"Hey, Stella doll. How is your grandmother?" Beatrice asked.

Stella shoved aside a velvet curtain that led to the storeroom and dropped her purse on a table. "I just left there. She's mainly sleeping."

"You sure you want to be here?"

Stella pushed a box toward the display wall. "I can't really talk to her now. They have her so drugged up." She picked up a box cutter and slid it along the line of the sealing tape. "I need something to do."

As she opened the flaps, the perfumes inside wafted out. She sneezed.

Beatrice settled on the stool behind the counter. "The cheap stuff? That always sets off your allergies."

Stella laughed through a cough. "My one true gift. Identifying crappy perfume."

"Girl, you have many gifts."

Stella sat on the floor, hoping to concentrate on work for at least a few minutes. She knew Grandma would not approve of moping, especially over her. She pulled a pink bottle from the box. "What is this junk you've bought? Something called 'Eau de François'?"

Beatrice heaved herself from behind the cash register to weave her way through the pink-draped product tables. Today she wore a bright green pantsuit, much too flashy for her weight. She looked like a watermelon in a wig.

Stella passed her the bottle, shaped roughly like a heart. A sparkly topper covered the spray nozzle.

Beatrice aimed a light spritz into the air. She sniffed. "Ugh. This is the four-dollar stuff, right? For teens?"

Stella cut the invoice from its plastic sleeve. "Yep. $3.89 per. Retails at $8.99."

"It's a cute bottle." Beatrice turned it over in her hand. "Make a little display with that pink tissue paper with glitter in it. We'll sell it to the kids."

Stella wrinkled her nose. "People will buy it, and I'll have to smell it."

Beatrice set the bottle back in the box. "We haven't talked about yesterday."

Stella walked to a shelf, moving a case of bath beads aside for the new display. "Nothing to talk about."

"You. Water tower. Rain."

"Just an impulse." Stella rapidly pulled out pink bottles, calculating how many would fit.

"You still planning on blowing out of Holly?"

"And leave you?"

Beatrice paced the store, adjusting the perfumes lined up on the window displays. Her ample silhouette was almost eclipsed by the glare of the light. The floor-to-ceiling glass ran the entire front of the shop, the morning sun setting all the colored bottles aglow. "You're the best salesgirl I've ever had."

Stella picked up the box, now partially empty, to carry to the back. "You're lucky to have me. But I'll stick around a bit. I can't leave Grandma Angie now."

A motorcycle roared up to the curb, and they both turned. The man wore a black T-shirt with the sleeves cut off. His jeans were tight, and the belt stood out as definitely not from Holly, black with silver spikes. He pulled off his helmet, and his profile was masculine—sharp jaw, scruffy beard. He didn't buy into the current trend of rattails or boy-perms. His black hair was traditionally cut, with a wave in it, but gelled into submission to be sleek, almost wet.

He swung a leg over the bike, hooked his helmet over the handlebars, and strode toward their door. Stella perked up, but Beatrice waved her on back. "Go find the pink paper. I'll handle this one."

Stella frowned, but shrugged. The last thing she needed was a complication. Grandma Angie was the only thing holding her here. She certainly didn't need a man.

But another glance at him as she passed through the curtain to the stockroom changed her mind. A stranger. A dangerous-looking one. She set the box on a table and tiptoed back, pushing the red velvet aside just enough to watch the man with Beatrice.

"So tell me about the girl," Beatrice said, eyeballing his outfit, sizing him up for a price range. She could separate the big spenders from the cheapskates. And not everyone was as obvious as you'd think. Sometimes the high rollers in fancy suits wouldn't spend much at all. And a teenager might bring in a fifty to impress some girl. Beatrice always knew, and Stella was pretty good at pegging them by now.

The man shrugged. "Kinda flashy. Wears lots of color."

Beatrice reached beneath the glass counter at the register and pulled out Beautiful, Obsession, and Opium. Mid-range stuff. The man fingered the boxes, and his strong, dark hands kept Stella rapt. She could already imagine the places they would go.

"Passing through or new to Holly?"

"Just got in town a few weeks ago."

Stella wondered where he had lived before. Something about his nose seemed familiar. Maybe somebody's cousin.

"Where from?" Beatrice asked as he pushed one of the boxes toward her without smelling any of them.

"Texas. Near Houston." He leaned on the counter, his butt jutting out. Stella gripped the curtain a little tighter. She definitely needed to learn more about this one. She didn't care about the girlfriend. Half her exes had already been in possession of girlfriends. She did, though, leave the married ones alone. She wasn't that kind of home wrecker. But otherwise, she figured she was showing the other girls the true colors of their men, ahead of the white dress and diamond ring. They could take that knowledge or leave it.

The man fished a wallet out of his pocket and paid for the Obsession. Not a half-bad choice for someone unwilling to sniff the actual product. Beatrice didn't carry a whole lot of junk, though, other than the kiddie scents.

"Is the girl local?" Beatrice was asking, stealing a glance at the curtain. She knew Stella was there.

"Yeah. Name's Darlene." He stuck the change in his wallet, tossing the coins in the little dish by the register.

Beatrice took her time wrapping the package. "Darlene Woods or Darlene Pittman?"

"Woods."

Stella grimaced. God, she hated that girl. Good-for-nothing. Back-roads whore. What was this guy doing with the likes of her?

"And you are?" Beatrice handed him the pink box.

"Dane. My brother works down at Joe's. They needed a bike mechanic. So I came up. Seemed like a good change."

"Holly's a nice little town. You treat that homegirl right, you hear?"

Dane laughed a little, the gentlest hint of color crossing his cheeks.

The image of him and Darlene going at it made Stella's stomach burn.

He turned and walked out of the shop. His motorcycle fired up again, his chiseled jaw disappearing in the helmet.

"You done gawking?" Beatrice asked.

Stella stepped through the curtain. "That one was worthy of the gawk."

"Agreed. But taken."

"No one stays with that two-bit floozy for long."

"She'll hang on to this one, if she knows what's good for her."

Dane circled out of the spot. His thighs filled the jeans just so, black boot perched on a silver bar. She had to track that boy down and get him out of Darlene's clutches. "Her bleach jobs last longer than her relationships. And she's a gold digger."

Beatrice stuck the duplicate of the sales receipt on a silver spike. "She grew up poor. That can do it to you."

"Yeah, well, I wasn't exactly rich."

"You always had food on the table."

Stella moved back to the curtain. She ran her hands along her hips. "Too much, maybe."

"You're a skinny little mite, and you know it," Beatrice said. "Talk to me when you're my size."

Stella passed through to the stockroom, searching the shelves for the pink paper. That would never happen.

As she unfolded lengths of the sparkled tissue for the display, she thought about Dane again, and how they might meet. Grandma always seemed pleased when Stella met a new man, saying, "You never know which piece of coal is a diamond in the rough." Maybe talking about it would make Grandma come to a little, give her a little spark.

He worked at the garage. Certainly someone had a car that needed a little service.

4

PREPPING FOR DANE

"I think this is a super-bad idea. One of your worst." Janine capped the hot-pink nail polish and blew on her fingers.

Stella snatched up the bottle and shook it. "You're just not as adventurous as me."

"Nor as stupid." Janine flung herself back on the bed, holding her hands in the air. "Darlene is going to attack with fur flying if you go after her man."

A floorboard squeaked outside Stella's door, and both girls silenced. Janine propped herself up on one elbow and whispered, "Your mom?"

Stella nodded. That stretch of hallway had saved her more than once. Vivian was an eavesdropper. "Hot pink is a great color on you."

Janine sat up. "You doing your toes?"

Stella opened the bottle and applied a brush of color on top of the old chipped version below. "Yes, I like them pink."

The floor squeaked again. They paused, waiting.

"She's gone," Stella said.

"You totally have to move out." Janine stood to look through the makeup on Stella's dresser. "You're too old for mama to be hovering."

"I couldn't save money as fast if I got a place on Renters' Row. I don't want out of this house. I want out of this TOWN."

Janine spritzed herself with Obsession. Stella grimaced. "That's the stuff he bought for Darlene. Don't come anywhere near me with it. I don't want to smell like her."

Janine pointed the bottle at Stella threateningly. "Then promise you won't leave me."

Stella set one foot on the floor and started on the other. "You know I can't do that."

Janine stepped forward again, aiming the nozzle at Stella's throat. "What am I supposed to do in this town without you?"

"Your boyfriend."

Janine set the bottle back on the dresser. "Thank God for him."

"Y'all going to get married?"

"Eventually. Mama says we might as well wait. Plenty of time later to get sick and tired of him."

"I never do."

Janine peered over Stella's shoulder at the polish. "You never stay with anyone long enough to GET sick and tired."

Stella capped the bottle. "Yeah, well, I saw that sort of misery up close and personal." She frowned at the door, the only thing that kept her parents' unhappiness at bay. "You can keep that perfume. I'll never wear it."

Janine turned back to the dresser. "Wow. Thanks."

"Just don't use it around me."

Janine plopped back on the bed. "Darlene is nobody to mess with. If she's sunk her claws into this guy, she's going to fight."

"We've known Darlene since we were kids. She never wins."

"True." Janine picked up the polish and shook it. "But that brother of hers. He's a problem."

"I can handle Bobby Ray."

"Like you did in his trailer?"

"Doesn't matter. He didn't get anywhere." Stella moved to the mirror, tugging her hot-pink shirt off one shoulder just like *Flashdance*. "This too much?"

Janine came up behind her. "Not on you." She fluffed Stella's hair out another inch, sprayed into an airy puff just above her shoulders, blond as gold. "He's not going to be able to take his eyes off you."

"Except for these." Stella lifted her hands up to reveal nails ragged and chipped despite pink polish. "Not much that can fix this. Color makes them look worse."

"I have just the thing." Janine opened her purse and plucked out a package of Lee Press-On Nails in bloodcurdling red. "Every girl needs her daggers when she's going in for a catfight."

* * *

Grandma Angie's white Mustang put-putted down Main Street, occasionally spewing a cloud of black from the exhaust. Vivian had forbidden Stella from taking the family car.

But Grandma Angie had always wanted Stella to have hers and even gave her a set of keys that Vivian didn't know about. Stella never used the car, though, as one of Vivian's ex-jerks was the sheriff, and he took to pulling Stella over whenever he spotted her. So usually she walked.

But not today. She patted the vinyl seat. "Thank you, Grandma."

She only had an hour while Vivian was off at Bible study, and of course the car hadn't started. Stella called Janine to have her boyfriend come and jump it. Stella knew how to attach the cables, but the nails would fly off at any pressure, and she was too anxious to get to Joe's to deal with putting on a new set.

Stella could, in fact, change her own oil, rotate her tires, and clean a carburetor. She wasn't into being a helpless nit, and besides, boys liked it when girls knew the difference between a Chevy big block and a Ford 302.

She punched the button to turn on the radio, hoping something suitable would play before she drove up to the garage. Maybe it could be her and Dane's song. She got so enamored with the idea that when she found nothing but commercials and "You Can't Hurry Love," she drove around the block a few times, hoping for something else. Grandma's car didn't have a tape deck, so she couldn't force a mood.

The opening drum licks for "Maneater" made her mad. Stupid fate. "She Blinded Me with Science" wasn't exactly ideal. She was about to give up and just shut the damn thing off when she found another station. "It Might Be You." A little cheesy, but yeah. Why not?

She passed the gas pump and pulled up to the bay doors. Hopefully it'd be quiet, and she could spot Dane.

Old Joe stood just inside and waved her in, tugging a rag from the pocket of his navy overalls. Stella frowned, peering into the dim light, hoping he wasn't alone. In the back corner, two men leaned on a workbench and laughed. She almost missed Joe's signal to stop and slammed on the brakes, embarrassed by the sudden squeal.

The two guys looked up, and her heart caught. Dane. And another guy—what was his name? Ryker. That's right. He'd moved to town a year or so before. Joe had hired him out of semi-desperation after knee surgery, when he couldn't crawl under cars for a month.

Stella hadn't run into Ryker very often. He liked his women older, and she liked her men her own age. He was probably thirty, maybe more.

But now she recognized the nose. That's where she'd seen Dane's before. On Ryker. He must be the brother Dane had mentioned to her boss. She could see it in how they laughed, the shape of their heads when they turned to her.

"Stella?" Joe was leaning over, tapping on the window. What little hair he had stood out like an electric shock.

She shook her head. The song! Damn! It was nearly over, and she'd forgotten to roll the windows down. And now it would play for Joe! She turned the volume down.

Joe opened the door. "Taking Angie's car out for a spin?"

Stella tried not to look at the corner to see what Dane was doing. "Yeah. Hasn't had anything done to it for quite some time."

Joe stepped back so Stella could get out. Her shirt was all cockeyed and wasn't even falling off her shoulder anymore. She tugged at it self-consciously, and a fake nail popped into the air. Damn it!

Joe reached in front of her to release the hood. "Needs oil, no doubt. Maybe a filter. We'll take a look-see."

He moved around her again, walking to the front of the car. "You can hang around here or come back in half an hour. Unless there's something major wrong, we'll have her ready."

Stella walked carefully toward the front, glad for flat shoes. The floor was gritty and strewn with bits of rubber tire and loose nuts. Joe's didn't have a recessed pit like the commercial shops. He jacked cars the old-fashioned way or rolled underneath on a creeper.

"Hey, Ryker," he called over his shoulder. "Bring me a couple quarts of basic Penn."

Stella watched Ryker head to a storage cabinet. Finally Dane moved toward them.

"What we got, boss?" Dane asked, eyes on Stella, not the car.

Stella thrust her chin out. That was more like it. She cocked a hip, holding his gaze.

Joe stepped up, wiping the dipstick on a shop towel. "Nothing major. Fluids. Filter. Check the tires, will ya?"

Dane tugged a gauge from his hip pocket, still watching Stella. This was going so much better than she'd hoped.

Stella leaned against the car, right beside the passenger-side front tire. "This one might be low."

Dane knelt by her bare leg and twisted the cap off the valve stem. The pressure gauge popped out as soon as he pushed it in place. "You're right," he said, looking up at her. "Could use a little something." The light crested off the perfect waves in his black hair. His jaw could have been made of steel. Damn. Boys like him didn't come through Holly too often.

"I'm Stella."

"Dane."

A snort behind them broke the mood. "This looks like a set-up for bad porn." Ryker set four yellow bottles on the roof of the car.

Dane stood, elbow landing soundly in Ryker's belly. "Sorry, man. Didn't realize you were so close."

Ryker backed away with a rush of air, but laughing. "I'll get the film crew."

Stella's face radiated heat. What a jerk.

"Ryker," Joe called. "Get down there and drain the oil." He shoved a creeper with his foot to roll it in the brother's general direction.

Stella and Dane exchanged a conspiratorial grin as Ryker grimaced. Dane moved to the next tire, and Stella turned to watch, loving the shift of his arm muscles in the sleeveless shirt, the curve of his back. She so wanted a piece of that.

Footsteps approached, a crunch on asphalt, and Joe cleared his throat. They all looked up at the same time.

"Yoo-hoo, Dane, boy. Where are you?" The voice came from a figure, backlit as she entered the garage, quickly morphing into Darlene.

Stella stiffened as the girl glared at her, then leaned down to Dane's level, forcing his head around for a kiss. Darlene wrapped her fingers around his neck, showing off red nails. Stella hid her mismatched fingers behind her back.

Darlene stood, as tall as Dane in neck-breaking heels. Her black miniskirt was tight and so short that it barely even existed. She wore a red halter and matching red balls for earrings. She passed by Stella, too close. "Like the perfume?" she asked. "Dane said he stopped by your shop. Did you sell it to him?"

Stella faked a smile. "He has good taste. In perfume."

Darlene strutted around the car. "So, Joe, baby. You going to let Dane go? Doesn't look busy at the moment."

Joe turned the shop towel over in his hands. "I reckon he can head on out."

"You're a doll," Darlene said. She wedged herself between Dane and Stella. "I believe you were going to take me to dinner. If, you know, we can wait that long."

Stella sidestepped her, circling to the other end of the car. She'd let it go for now, but not without a parting shot. "Don't bother with the meal, Dane. She goes for much less than that." She waved at Joe, avoiding Darlene's angry glare. "Joe, I'll be visiting Grandma Angie. Give us a ring? Tomorrow is fine. No hurry."

"I'll lock it up," Joe said. "Why don't you drop by first thing, before Beatrice opens shop?"

"Sure." She waved to Dane. "Nice meeting you. Thanks for checking the tires."

Stella felt Dane's eyes on her as she walked away and headed back to her grandmother's house. That had been a bust in the end, but still, the hook was set. Up to him to actually spit out the other girl's bait.

5

DANE MAKES A CHOICE

DANE bought himself some time by checking the other tires. He didn't want to look Darlene in the face, afraid she might misinterpret anything she saw. She'd been all right for the few weeks since he'd come to town, and he'd made a show of keeping her with the gift. But her claws were out, and after Stella's obvious interest, no doubt she'd try to sink them into him.

Joe seemed to understand, and instead of releasing him as Darlene had suggested, asked him to vacuum the car before he took off.

Darlene rolled her eyes and settled in a chair in the waiting area. Dane attached the wand to the vacuum, taking great care in cleaning the creases of the already immaculate seats. He didn't put too much stock in women, overall. The one love of his life had run off inexplicably, and not even for another man. Pam had just…gone. Didn't want anything to do with him.

Dane shook it off. Five years gone. Screw her. Too immature, or messed up, or whatever. And if Stella made him think of Pam, then that was one hell of a sign. Run the other way, fast.

He glanced at Darlene. She'd been all right, not too clingy, just fun. He didn't blame her for reacting sort of strongly to Stella's intrusion. In a town this small, those two probably had a history. She dug through her purse, extracting a nail file. Not so bad to look at. Interesting enough in the sack. She'd do for a time.

He shut off the vacuum. Tomorrow would take care of itself.

* * *

They rode the highway back to Holly. After the incident with Stella, Dane had wanted to go someplace bigger, and Darlene had been up for a bit of traveling on the bike, about a half hour to Branson. To her credit, she hadn't complained about the discomfort of the ride, even though he knew she had to feel it. She'd be sore tomorrow.

Dinner had been pleasant enough. She hadn't brought up Stella, or been bitchy. She carried that perfume bottle in her purse like it was some great treasure. She pulled it out after dinner and excused herself to spritz it again. Not that she needed it. He might be regretting the purchase if she used it much more.

Summer was long gone, and while the days were warm, the chill of night cooled his cheeks as they approached town. Darlene kept her face in his back and clutched him tightly. Girls wrapping themselves around him on the bike was one of the reasons he loved motorcycles. That and the view, and the smells. A bit of oil, lots of pine, the wetness of a hidden pond in the dark. When they slowed, he could catch that perfume. Hopefully it would have faded a bit.

The sky over the tree line was a jagged field of stars. In the distance, he could make out the craggy outline of the Ozarks. He'd made a good decision, leaving Texas, his oppressive boss at the Harley shop, the dead mother. Ryker had convinced him at the funeral to come on up to Holly, start over.

He didn't have much tying him down other than his latest girlfriend. But he hadn't relaxed into her, moved in any closer than he had to. Something kept him cautious, the way you approach an overheating radiator. So he'd moved on, using his mother and brother as the excuse.

Darlene tugged on his jacket. He turned his head slightly, and she pointed to a dirt road to the right. He nodded and turned onto it, dodging the worst of the ruts.

The road narrowed, so little used that the trees encroached on them, occasionally whipping across his helmet like a slap. He slowed again, but a break in the woods revealed a ramshackle cabin. He pulled up. "This where we're headed?"

Darlene swung her leg over the bike, stiff and awkward in her steps. Not a complainer. He liked her better than he had even earlier in the day, or yesterday when he'd gone to the perfume place. Her hair was calmer now, the hair spray blown right out of it, now brown and long and flowing down the sides of her head instead of all high on top.

He killed the bike and followed her. "This yours?" he asked. No telling what sort of squatter could be living there. It looked like an old hunting cabin.

"My uncle's. He's off in Colorado."

She lifted a flowerpot, showering dead leaves across the porch, and extracted a key. Moonlight lit the face of the cabin, but barely. She seemed to know it all by feel. Dane figured she'd brought a man or two out here before.

The door opened with a squeal that set his teeth on edge. She flipped the light, but it didn't come on. "He often shuts off the power," she said. "We can find the box if you want." She turned, fumbling with something, then a beam of light crossed the room. "Or we can go by flashlight."

"Works for me." Dane stepped into the musty, dank cabin. He stifled a sneeze and closed the door behind him.

Darlene took his hand and led him to a sofa. This place was a good find, actually, as Darlene lived with her mom. Seemed like half of Holly was grown and still at home. And Dane bunked with his brother, who seemed to have a different woman there every weekend. He didn't know where he even found them all. Dane still didn't have a good sense of the town's size, or the number of available girls.

But without a car, privacy had been tough to come by. Even though he and Darlene had been together a few weeks, she hadn't brought him here before, making do with quickies while her mom was shopping or playing bridge next door. Or taking over Ryker's bedroom at their rundown duplex during lunch breaks. Maybe she hadn't trusted him before, and wisely so, to be alone in the middle of nowhere. Changing her mind about it probably had to do with Stella.

But no rush this time. This would be good, real good. Darlene set the flashlight on the floor, aiming it at the ceiling for a little light. She perched on the sofa, patting the spot beside her.

He didn't bother sitting next to her but planted his knee in the cushion and pushed her down to lie on top of her. She was better than average, plenty experienced, and he had already figured out a couple of her hot spots. He would find more.

She wriggled out of the tight skirt as he pushed her halter down. The reds of her lips and nails looked black in the dark, giving her an edgy appearance, almost evil. She unzipped his pants and pushed them down. The cool air washed across him, and then she was already leading him in, without preamble, without play.

And unprotected. He rolled off, trying to slow things, but she came right back at him, pushing him down on the other end of the sofa. She straddled, intent, but he grasped her waist and slid her forward, onto his belly. "Aren't you anxious?" he said. "Let me get something."

"I'm on the pill." She persisted, trying to move down again and ensnare him.

He sat up and shifted her back on the cushion. "That's news. You wanted a condom before." He knew all the tactics girls could use to trap a man. Pregnancy, real or faked. They just needed an incident to cast doubt. He didn't fall for none of that.

She tried to straddle him again, this time sitting up. "I didn't trust you then. That you were clean." She pushed him back against the sofa. "I know better now."

Actually, he was the one who should probably worry. He lifted her off him again and stood up. "I've never checked," he lied. "So let's assume it's not safe." He tugged his wallet out of the pocket somewhere near his knees and extracted the smooth wrapper.

He could see in the low light that her lips were pressed together. He'd pissed her off, but that didn't matter. He could coax her around. He knew the ways.

Dane slid his hand around her knee, then down to her ankle, and slipped off one high-heeled shoe, then the other. He felt her relent a little and laid his lips against her calf, working his way back up. By the time he reached her inner thigh, she'd given in again, the incident behind them.

But he wouldn't forget. His guard was up, and judging from his history, the distance that had just wedged between them would only grow.

6

STELLA'S BOOK

STELLA arrived in the shop to find Beatrice seated cross-legged, eyes closed, fingers in some weird circle position, on a mat in the back of the shop. She wore a hideous stretchy suit in lilac. Stella moved forward to ask her what the hell she was doing, then the smell hit her. Sweet. Sickly. Strong.

Stella coughed and backed away. "What is THAT?"

Beatrice opened her eyes, and Stella realized she wasn't wearing makeup. Bare eyes. Plain cheeks. Her pale mouth opened, said something, closed.

"What?" Stella asked, still hacking up a lung.

"Incense." A pale purple arm, encased like a sausage in the tight sleeve, waved at a pair of sticks in a glass vase. Thin streams of smoke curled upward from the ends.

"Like in church?" Stella had only been to Mass three times in her life, but she distinctly recalled the preacher, minister, whatever he was, swinging a smoking metal can on a chain. Pretty much the worst thing she had ever smelled.

"It's to cleanse the air," Beatrice said. "So I can find inner peace."

Stella dropped her purse on the back table. "It's going to overpower the whole shop. People are going to think we sell that crap."

"Maybe we will. Maybe we won't."

Stella slipped out of her jacket. Something was way wrong here. "What has gotten into you?"

Beatrice heaved herself up with some effort. "Yoga. Newest thing. Well, the newest old thing. I am going to become a yogi!"

"Like the bear?" Stella wanted to avert her eyes now that the full form of her boss in the lilac stretch suit was in view.

"No, no. The ancient art. Finding your center."

"So why aren't you centering at home?"

Beatrice lifted one of the sticks and stuck the smoking end into a bowl of sand. She picked up a pair of tiny cymbals and clanged them twice.

"Beatrice—"

"Shhh. You'll disturb the balance of the room." She crammed another stick in the sand, clanging the bells again.

God. Stella brushed past her and through the curtain to the shop. She unlocked the door and propped it open to let some air in. Her mother had found Jesus when Stella was sixteen and smashed all her Bee Gees albums and, most horrifically, her soundtrack to *Grease*. Hopefully Beatrice's middle-aged obsession with yoga would be less destructive.

Maybe she should hide the good stuff in the shop. Anything Beatrice might foolishly destroy to banish materialism.

The phone rang. Stella picked up the heavy receiver, wishing Beatrice would break down and get a modern push-button phone rather than the old rotary dialer. "Good Scents," she said.

"Stella? It's Joe. You forgot the car this morning."

"Right." She hadn't forgotten but wasn't up to facing postcoital Dane at dawn's early light. She glanced at the curtain. "Beatrice is a little, hmm, busy this morning. I don't think I'll be able to get over there for a few hours."

"No problem. We can hold on to it. Or I can send one of the boys over with it."

Stella's heart hammered painfully. "Dane, maybe?"

Joe cleared his throat in a half-chuckle. "Haven't seen him in yet. Late night for him, sounds like. He's usually pretty reliable."

Stella twisted the cord between her fingers, her mood dashed. "I guess it doesn't matter."

"I can wait for him to get in."

"No need, Joe. Thank you. I'll come by during lunch." She hesitated. "Or maybe I'll send Dad." If he'll get up.

Joe knew what she was thinking, both about her dad and about Dane. "Don't worry your pretty head about a thing. I can always send Ryker." He paused. "How's Angie?"

Stella leaned her head against the back wall. "Sleeping, mostly."

"All right. Well, you take care of her."

"I will. Thanks, Joe." She hung up quietly, her shoulders heavy.

Joe was a good guy. Grandma Angie had actually taken a shine to him for a bit, and the whole town had buzzed about the possible romance. Vivian had intervened, calling the whole thing "a sickness." Then Grandma had actually gotten sick. Even if she could have kept things going, Joe backed off. He'd watched one great love fade out when his first wife died slowly and painfully from cancer. He probably just couldn't do it again.

She didn't think Joe would send Dane now. She pictured Darlene straddling him and burned with disgust and misery. No doubt that girl had unloaded her entire arsenal. Stella had to let it go. Forget about him. Not worth the trouble.

She reached beneath the counter and pulled out a binder stuffed with travel brochures, newspaper clippings, and letters she'd gotten from employment agencies. She flipped through the book, pausing in the section on St. Louis. She could go to secretary school there, learn shorthand and some other skills. She typed fast. They were interested. They might even offer her a work-study to pay her way while she finished the course.

Postcards of New York spilled from the next section, so she ripped a piece of scotch tape from the spindle by the register and affixed each card to a page. She wouldn't seriously consider such a drastic move, but the pictures were beautiful and frightening. Buildings so tall you had to stretch your neck to see the top. They seemed to blot out the sky. Maybe that could be her first real vacation once she was a bona fide professional.

She wanted to skip the Texas section, knowing that that was where Dane came from. Lots of people in town called Ryker "Tex" or "Cowboy," even though his leather and tattoos didn't fit the part whatsoever. Dane was more clean-cut, but still retained that biker air. Nothing country about either one of them. Most of what Stella knew about Texas, she'd learned from *Dallas*. J. R. and Sue Ellen and Southfork.

But the brochures from there were super nice, from the oil rigs in the fields to the fancy ball of light in the big city. She liked Houston a lot, the giant supermalls and bright stores. She could make a lot more in a shop there, if she didn't want to do the secretary thing, and she was pretty sure she didn't.

Stella didn't have a whole lot of skills, but she could sell anything. At Good Scents, Beatrice made a few perfumes of her own, custom mixes for her best clients. Stella learned some of that, but she didn't think it would be useful to her out in the real world. She liked managing the business side, understanding costs of goods sold and overhead and profit and loss. She wasn't college material, so this was the best way to learn.

The door jingled and Mrs. Kramer shuffled in, her gray hair carefully spun into a cotton-candy web to make it appear she had volume, when really the entire coiffure was made of air. As usual, she wore a ball gown, this one fuchsia taffeta with giant puffed sleeves and layers of ruffles that cascaded to the floor.

"Hello, Mrs. K.," Stella said, swiftly rounding the counter before the elderly lady's walker could knock aside anything breakable. "In for another bottle of Shalimar?"

Mrs. Kramer kicked at the loose tennis ball on the base of the silver leg of her walker, revealing white sneakers. "Thought I'd shake things up a bit, Stella. What's new?" The old woman lifted her head finally, her pale eyes foggy and liquid beneath an inch of ice-blue eye shadow and fake lashes.

"Well, we have a new one in." Stella pointed inside the glass case. "Paloma Picasso."

"Like the painter?"

"It's his daughter."

Mrs. Kramer shoved the walker forward another step and almost tripped on her hem. She peered into the case. "Is it any good?"

"Let's take a sniff." Stella headed back around the counter, extracting the key from the register to open the case. She wondered if Beatrice was still doing yoga or if she'd come out in that horrid outfit.

She pulled the tester out and spritzed a card. "Here you go."

Mrs. Kramer lifted the card to her nose. "Rubbish." She tossed the card on the counter. "We'll stick with Shalimar."

This was an old routine. Stella simply smiled and lifted the royal-blue box from the row.

Mrs. Kramer heaved her purse from where it hung on a bar on the walker to the counter. Stella smiled, feigning patience as she waited for the woman to extract a worn gold wallet and peel two twenty-dollar bills from a roll inside.

"I love your gown today," Stella said.

"This old thing?" Mrs. Kramer laid the money on the counter. "I wore it in 1943 at a Mardi Gras society dinner hosted by the Krewe of Proteus."

"It's lovely." A movement in the window caught her attention. A car was pulling up. Her grandmother's car. She stuck the bills in the register and rapidly made change. Who had brought it? The glare made it impossible to see through all the layers of glass.

She dropped the change in Mrs. Kramer's outstretched hand and hurriedly slid the perfume into a bag. The door to the car opened, and Stella couldn't bear it, so she left the counter to move closer to the front.

Her chest tightened as she recognized the black waves, the sharp jaw. Dane. Joe had sent Dane.

The door jingled as he pushed through. He'd layered a flannel shirt over a T-shirt today, blue and gray plaid. A smiley face with a bullet hole in its forehead peeked out as he lifted his arm to rattle her grandmother's key chain.

Mrs. Kramer turned with painful deliberation, pushing the walker in a tight circle. "Young man, have you a date for this weekend's ball?"

Oh, boy. "Let me help you to the car," Stella said.

Mrs. Kramer lifted the walker and slammed it down again. "I'm a modern woman. I can ask a man if he's available to escort me to a dance."

Dane stepped forward and bowed deeply to her. "I must most regretfully decline your very tempting invitation. I am spoken for this Saturday eve."

"Oh, poot." Mrs. Kramer pushed the frame ahead of her and took mincing steps toward the door. "And I have the perfect dress to match your gray eyes."

"Now that would be a stunning color," Stella said, hoping he'd turn them to her. He did, and the bright mischief she saw there squeezed her heart. Damn. She was going to have to fight after all.

Dane offered his arm to Mrs. Kramer, and she gladly abandoned the walker, leaning on him as he led her out the door. Stella snatched up her perfume bag and the metal frame, holding the door as they passed through.

"I'll come back for that," Dane said, and she knew what he meant. He wanted to see her alone for a second. She tried to suppress the smile but didn't quite succeed.

Rather than watch their slow progress to Mrs. Kramer's ancient Lincoln Continental, Stella busied herself with randomly rearranging perfume bottles on the wall shelves. Where was Beatrice? Still cleansing her workspace? Vivian had forbidden Stella to do yoga. "The devil's way to steal you from Jesus," she'd said. "Call it exercise when it really brainwashes you into some ancient heathen religion."

Stella seriously wished her mother had never been saved. She liked Jesus just fine, and church was nice and the women there were great in the community, making sure the sick got checked on, and funerals had food, and little kids had Christmas presents. But Vivian's brand of Bible beating felt like a punch line in a Johnny Carson monologue.

The door jingled. Stella kept her back to it an extra moment, resisting the urge to check her hair or straighten her shirt. She didn't want to seem too eager.

"Stella?"

He'd never said her name before. She squared her shoulders and turned. Her heel caught and she lost her balance, grasping at the nearest table. Her fingers grabbed a useless tuft of tissue paper. Tugging it upset a row of Jean Naté Bath Splash bottles.

Dane leapt forward, trying to catch the breakables before they hit the floor.

"Oh, no!" Stella caught two bottles in her hand. She moved too fast, and their heads crashed together. Dane bumped the display, sending another set of bottles falling into each other like bowling pins.

Everything finally settled, and they started laughing uncontrollably. Dane set his bottles on the table and took the ones Stella was holding. "Bulls in the china shop," he said.

"Who you calling a bull?" Stella said, still laughing.

"You. I'm calling you one." A tiny set of fine lines crinkled out from his eyes.

A horn honked outside.

"Mrs. Kramer," Stella said. "She wants her things."

"What's with the ball gown?" Dane picked up the walker and hefted it onto his shoulder.

Stella handed him the bag with the Shalimar. "No one knows. She seems to be living in some other era. Always been that way."

He tugged on the door. "I'll be right back."

"I'll be waiting."

While he was loading the walker into Mrs. Kramer's car, Stella dashed to the curtain that closed off the storeroom and peeked through. Beatrice was nowhere, her yoga mat rolled up in the corner. The incense sticks poked up from their position in the sand, no longer smoking. The air was still heavy with the smell, but the curtain kept it in.

The door jingled again, and Stella thought of Pavlov's dog. She wasn't salivating, but her heart hammered painfully each time. She turned carefully. No more perfume needed to die today. She'd have to repair the display before Beatrice returned.

But no matter. Dane was here. And Darlene wouldn't be showing up to interrupt them.

7

Dane's Proposition

DANE looked over the frilly shop, wondering what the hell he was doing. Darlene would be pissed.

Stella watched him, a quizzical look on her face at his silence. Behind them, just out the front window, the old lady ran over the curb as she pulled away. "So, you're here," Stella said.

He took pride in being smooth, always saying the right thing, making the right move. But he couldn't think of a damn clever word. "You born here?" he finally managed.

"Not sure this shop was here twenty-two years ago." Her eyes crinkled in the corners with her smile. "But yeah, I grew up here in Holly."

He forced a little laugh. "Seems like a nice enough town."

"I'm not planning to hang around," she said. "I got bigger things in mind."

He understood that. "Where you think you're headed?"

She picked up a pink bottle, sort of absently, turning it in her hands. "Not sure. St. Louis, maybe. Looked at New York." She glanced up at him. "Texas."

He shuffled his boots, the chains on his hip jingling. "Big state."

"I like big." She flushed at this.

39

He cleared his throat. He wanted to be there, but he wasn't sure why. He couldn't explain it, this draw to her. She was pretty, fair and blond and tiny. He could have encircled her waist with his hands. Something about her was tough, but something else was fragile.

"I guess I should get back to Joe's."

"Do you have to?" She said it in a rush.

Joe had sent him. That meant he liked Stella, maybe wanted Dane to like her. He wouldn't meddle, not Joe, and he'd never said a mean thing about Darlene. Not about anybody. But he was here. It meant something. "I can stay."

And so Stella moved, with a bit of hesitation, behind the counter. She reached below the register and brought out a big binder. "I've been researching places to go. Cities." She opened a page pasted with pictures and cut-up brochures.

He approached the counter, watching the whir of color and text as she flipped through the book. "That's a lot of work you've done."

"I've been planning my escape for a while." She paused on Texas. "Is this stuff even right? Or all commercials?"

He turned the binder a bit to look over the pages. "Everyone thinks Texas is all oil wells and cowboy hats."

"Well, is it?"

"Nah. I mean, sure, there are cowboys. And people have oil."

"But."

"Well, most people are just, you know, normal. Def Leppard. Gimme caps. McDonald's. I don't know anyone with an oil well."

"You have a cowboy hat?" She rested her chin in her hand, her light-brown eyes on him.

She had to know how she looked, coy and flirty. But yeah, it worked.

"Hell, no." He hated the whole country scene. The look. The attitude. He'd had many a run-in with a shit-kicker.

Her bottom lip came out.

"Well, I mean. Sure. I could wear one." What the hell was he saying?

"I think it'd look good on you." She flipped the binder closed. "You know, all by itself." Her face shifted in color. She'd embarrassed herself.

He kicked the corner of the counter. "That might could be

arranged."

But they both looked away, as if simultaneously thinking of Darlene.

He exhaled in a rush. "On that, I guess I'll head on back." But he didn't move.

"Yeah, Joe will be calling." She didn't move either.

He wanted to see her again. Hear about these plans. Find out where she came from. Teach her about Texas.

"Will you be?" She didn't look at him, tracing some pattern on the glass above the rows of perfume boxes.

He didn't get it. "Will I be what?"

She bit her pink lip. "Calling."

Shit. He'd embarrassed her again. Made her ask outright. "We could just meet somewhere. I hear you like the water tower. That you've been up it a time or two."

She flushed fully red then. "Oh. I think I'm done with heights for a bit." Then she seemed stricken. "Not that I'm afraid. I just. I had a moment. On the tower."

"You don't seem like a girl afraid of much."

She straightened up suddenly. "Nope. Not afraid. So yeah. Top of the tower. No problem. Midnight?"

"Tonight?" He was supposed to see Darlene, but he could get out of that. Figure things out.

"You got other plans?" She clearly knew he did, knew his hesitation.

"Not a one." Not anymore.

"Then midnight. At the top. Like that movie."

"Which one?"

"*An Affair to Remember.*"

"Don't know it."

"They're supposed to meet on the top of the Empire State Building."

"Supposed to? So they don't?"

"She has an accident. She doesn't make it. And he thinks she doesn't love him anymore."

Dane jingled the chain on his belt. "Does she?"

Stella didn't want to look at him, he could tell, and she wiped her hand along the counter as if it were dusty. "She does. But she doesn't want him to know she's in a wheelchair now."

"Does it have a happy ending?"

"Yeah."

"Good. Then I'll see you there." He nodded at her and turned away, heading out of the shop with long steps. He'd just gotten himself tied up even more, not his intention. And all that romantic mush in her head. But something about Stella bugged him, made him not think. Just act.

8

ON THE TOWER AGAIN

STELLA approached the tower with trepidation. She peered up, curious if Dane was already up. But the night was dark, no moon, and she couldn't see anything but the gray gleam of streetlamps reflecting dimly on its surface. If the platform held any secrets, it kept them close to its metal belly.

She would not let the quivering in her gut stop her from going up. She'd done it a hundred times, well, okay, five times. Once carrying a ladder, for Christ's sake. She shut out her mother's admonishment for the foul use of the Lord and ducked through the opening in the chain-link fence. She wondered if Dane even knew how to find it.

Despite this being a date of sorts, she'd resorted to tennis shoes, unable to consider heading up the ladder barefoot, in heels, and certainly not in jellies. Even her lightweight Keds seemed slippery, so Adidas was the choice. She still did the miniskirt, though. Not much could make her wear anything else.

She set her purse behind the concrete base to one of the steel legs and jumped to grasp the first rung of the ladder. Usually she had someone with her for the initial boost. But she could do it alone. She swung back and forth, grasping the metal tightly, until she had enough momentum to bring her feet up and above her head to catch on the ladder. Her leg crept up until her knee was over the rung, then the other, and she pulled herself up to sit on the lowest bar.

Even this height made her stomach lurch. She remembered almost falling a few days before, her foot slipping off the beam. She forced herself to pull her leg through and firmly plant her shoe on the rung. She pushed up to standing and walked her hands up. Without letting her mind consider what she was doing or where she was going, she began scaling the first tier.

A low whistle below made her pause. She looked down.

"Impressive mount, good form. Definitely worth a replay."

Dane.

She turned around on the ladder, like she had that day with Janine. "And the score?"

"Nine point nine."

"Really?" She turned back around and began climbing again, faster now. "I think I just got robbed."

She finished the first tier, reaching up to cover the gap to the second ladder. A hand grasped her ankle, startling her. She gripped the bar tightly.

Dane was just below, grinning up at her, teeth bright in the dark.

"You scared the crap out of me!" Stella tried to pull her foot loose. His grip was firm, sure, then became gentler, a caress. Still, she was hopping mad. "How did you get up here so fast? You trying to kill me?"

He rose a few more feet, pulling up next to her. She shifted over, and he swung behind. "I wouldn't let anything happen to you."

He pressed her against the rungs, one arm encircling her waist.

With anyone else, she might have felt panicked, trapped. But she didn't, just a zip of danger, a thrill. "What you going to do back there?"

He pulled her to him with even more force. She felt his belt buckle against her back, the pinch of his arm wrapping securely around her middle. He moved his leg, bracing one foot on a higher rung, and fit her snugly against his pelvis.

She didn't know him at all. She shouldn't do this. But of course she would. She'd been with a man or two. Or ten. A car cruised down the street below, stopping before a house. A girl ran onto the porch, waving. She jumped into the car, and it took off again. All oblivious to the scene above.

Dane moved behind her, leaning down, his mouth on her neck. They hadn't even kissed, she realized, and now they wouldn't. She'd never had sex first, kiss later.

She shouldn't do it. He was Darlene's, really. She tried to climb up a rung, out of his embrace. He let her go up, then followed, pulling her back to him.

He ran his hand along her waist, then beneath her shirt. She leaned her forehead on a rung, concentrating on the feel of his fingers. Did he think she was just an easy roll in the hay? Was she? Her leg trembled with the effort of supporting herself. Dane felt it and increased the pressure, taking some of the weight off her, shifting her against his body.

The wind kicked up and ruffled her hair. He eased his hand up her rib cage and along the edge of her bra. Were they going to do this? Here? She didn't see how, in this precarious position. They weren't super high, but high enough. A bone-crushing fall.

He slid his fingers beneath the flimsy lace. She shuddered lightly and turned her head to him. "Dane?"

He shifted over, and now his mouth reached her, kissing her lips, a question. She flooded with relief. Somehow not kissing made her a whore, but this, this was better. She'd kissed so many boys, often sloppy, sometimes dry, but a few were absolutely right. And he was tender with it, careful and almost shy, the opposite of everything else about this moment—their position, his fingers encircling her nipple, his groin flush against her.

"This would be crazy," he whispered. "And maybe not even possible. Should I let you down now? Get to know you proper?"

But him asking changed everything. He'd given the power to her, and now she surged with the need to do it, to do this crazy, impulsive, dangerous thing. They'd never forget it, even if she ceased to know him after today. She'd remember it all her life.

She leaned into his mouth, letting go with one hand to press his palm more firmly against her breast.

He smiled against her lips. Now his hand moved down past her waist to the miniskirt, sliding it up.

She turned her face away, her neck weary, and watched another car pass below. No one could see them, she felt certain, but she'd never done anything like this before. Outdoors, sure. In fields. Backs of trucks. In barns. Once on the roof of the high school. But never this. Not even close.

His fingers slid inside the edge of her panties, tugging them down. She couldn't move, couldn't step out of them. He realized her problem and so instead, with a sharp yank, ripped them right off her.

Stella felt nothing from the tear, just the cool sensation of air where there had been fabric. She looked down just as the pale-green scrap flitted below them, caught a bit of breeze, then landed on the branch of a tree just to the right. "You owe me a pair of underwear."

He moved his hand beneath her knee, lifting her leg so that she separated her feet to rest on different rungs of the ladder. The wind cooled her even more, and she shivered. "This is crazy," she whispered.

He paused immediately, waiting, she realized, to see if she wanted to stop. She hadn't expected that from him, just the push forward, the press into the act.

"I'm game," she said. "Something to tell our grandchildren."

He chuckled. "I think that qualifies as entirely too much detail."

Stella pictured Grandma Angie on the ladder with some beau and could totally see it. "Depends on the grandmother."

Talking so casually felt strange for what they were about to do. But maybe they should be more practical than romantic. Or not do it. His hand shifted on her thigh, leaving another cool spot. She reached behind him, feeling for the belt buckle.

His belly sucked in as she missed the mark entirely and landed a little lower than she'd planned. He pushed against her, trapping her hand. Stella wanted to turn, to move into him, but that was impossible here.

Dane reached between them and unsnapped his jeans. Stella sensed more urgency in him now, and her own pulse sped up. The miniskirt moved even higher, and now she felt the scrape of his jeans against her bare skin. He shifted on the ladder, moving beneath her, then up, and she felt it, felt him, sliding right into place.

They were really doing this thing. It was going to work.

Her arms trembled, so she hugged the ladder, preparing for the additional force of him moving against her. But he stopped. Stella turned her head as much as she could. "You okay?"

"Are you? Should I?"

Ah. "I'm on the pill. And nothing catching. You?"

"Not on the pill. But nothing catching."

"But Darlene."

"Condoms, always."

He gripped her waist then and pushed hard and up. Stella sucked in a breath. Her skin felt cold in places, hot in others. Her arms were trembling again, and she didn't see how Dane could maintain this position with just one arm.

He did, in fact, let go of her waist to grip the ladder with both hands. He moved more deliberately then, and they swung lightly, locked together, into the ladder and away.

Stella watched the stars across the horizon, the lights of the town creating a haze just above the rooftops. God, she loved this. The act wasn't about anything climactic—she could see she wouldn't be near that, but about doing it, about reveling in something she hadn't done before.

"Should I wait?" His breath was hot on her ear.

She shook her head, and he pushed even harder, a strong thrust, and then the warm wetness flooded inside her and quickly trickled down. He huffed against her hair, then exhaled, slow and long, like the distant bellow of a train.

He sagged a bit, still holding on behind her, face on her shoulder. He seemed vulnerable like this, like a boy. Emotion surged through her.

Finally, he pulled away from her, tugging down her skirt before attending to himself. Stella's arms still shook, but she continued her climb, heading up the second ladder, then the third, and grasping the edge of the platform to poke through the hole.

The sensation of rising through the square brought back the helplessness of a few days before, when she'd almost fallen. She could see the pale reflection of the bent rail, and suddenly her heart hammered and her breath came in short bursts. She backed against the solid wall of the water tower, her hand pressed against her chest.

Dane's head popped through the gap. As soon as he saw her, he leapt onto the platform and drew her close. "I'm sorry, Stella. I didn't mean to upset you. I'm sorry."

She tried to shake her head against his chest. He didn't understand. But she couldn't draw a proper breath, couldn't speak.

He clutched at her hair, holding her fiercely, like an injured child. "I've wrecked things already. I should have held back. I shouldn't have pushed."

She did shake her head then, pulling back. "N-not that. N-not at all." She closed back in. Even the small glance at the town from this height set it all off again. She couldn't talk herself out of it, couldn't rationalize the panic away. She wasn't going to fall. She was fine. But no, her body reacted as though she stood on the edge, tumbling forward.

"What is it?" Dane's voice rumbled from his chest.

"The height. Too high." All she could manage.

"You're afraid of heights?"

She wasn't, or maybe she was. It was all so new. She nodded against his shirt.

He gripped her even more tightly. "Can you get back down?"

She shook her head.

He bent down, bringing her with him so they could sit. "Let's just pretend we're somewhere else," he said. "We're on a beach in Florida. The sand is hot. Kids are shrieking in every direction." At that, a child somewhere shouted, causing them both to laugh lightly.

"See?" he said. "I know what I'm talking about."

He held her in his lap, rocking. "I failed to set up the beach umbrella properly. It's just fallen over." He stroked her hair. "But I couldn't stop looking at you in a little pink Ocean Pacific bikini." He stopped. "You do have a bikini, right?"

She smiled against his shoulder and nodded.

"Good. I'm too poor for panties AND bathing suits on one paycheck."

She grinned again.

"Sand is already everywhere. It's stuck to a few beautiful places." Dane slid his hand across her shoulder, then down between her breasts.

"This hollow is like a valley of the dunes. I just want to lick it clean."

Stella felt something uncurl inside, to relax. Her breathing slowed, became manageable again.

He rested his hand against her rib cage. "I feed you grapes and fried chicken." His voice rumbled against her head, filled her with a deep, easy satisfaction. "And lick your fingers." He took one in his mouth.

She smiled against his shoulder. She'd be all right with him. They'd make it down. They'd see each other again. The whole future was laid out before her like the lights of the town, spreading out in a geometry that had logic and beauty, a natural progression from one part to the next. Whatever she was doing next, she was doing it with Dane.

9

CARBURETOR WARNING

DANE wiped his hands on a shop towel. This carburetor was gunked like nothing he'd seen before. What had the guy put in his gas tank? Molasses?

Joe came up behind him and laid a hand on his shoulder. "How's it coming?"

"Haven't gotten the floater pins off yet. Gonna have to soak 'em."

"Did the carbs come off the air box clean?"

"Yeah, just pulled them off by hand. Didn't need to ratchet it. Did he say what happened?"

"Wife caught him with a girl. Put Karo syrup in the gas tank."

Holy smokes. So he was close. "Going to have to get the floats out before I can even get to the jets."

"Yeah. Ugly work. But good for thinking things through." Joe moved farther down the workbench, sorting through a stack of wiper blades.

Dane shook his head. Damn waste of a good bike engine.

"No? You don't need to think?" Joe asked.

"What?" Dane finally worked the floater pin free and dunked it in cleaning fluid. What was Joe talking about?

"Darlene. Stella." Joe stacked and restacked the boxes of wiper blades. He was irked.

Joe must have misunderstood something. Dane ran his thumb along the next floater, trying to coax it free. "Trying not to think, actually." Damn small towns. Did Joe know about his night with Stella? He'd gotten her all calm and off the tower about 2 a.m.

"Both girls have had their troubles. Don't need any more from you."

Another floater came free. Two to go. He stole a glance at Joe, who was still messing with the blades and apparently would stay there until Dane agreed with him. "Understood."

"Pick one or the other. Don't play around."

Dane dropped another floater in the fluid. "Got it."

Joe nodded, satisfied, and headed into the office.

Dane watched him through a small, greasy window. The music kicked on suddenly, too loud, then down again. "All My Exes Live in Texas." Dane stifled a snort. Subtle, that Joe.

He worked on the third segment of the carburetor, this one not quite as bad off as the first two.

Couldn't have been too much syrup, maybe the bottle wasn't full. Dane wondered how the bike's owner had figured it out. Had the wife told him? Were they speaking still?

Maybe he had driven off on it, the wife watching smugly from the window. He might have gotten a few blocks before it started missing, goo flowing through its veins.

The last floater pin came out cleanly. He picked up a flat-head screwdriver for the jets, to see how badly they were gunked. This wasn't going to be a cheap job, for sure. Labor was killer, even if he didn't replace anything. He wiped his fingers again, black and sticky.

He imagined Darlene, shouting, face blooming red beneath wild hair, wielding a Karo bottle and chucking it after his retreating form. He had to handle this carefully. She no doubt had a mean streak a mile long. Stella wouldn't talk about her, but their verbal catfight in the bay a few days ago was probably an indication of what he could expect from either one.

He pictured Stella, vulnerable and shaking at the top of the tower. She had gone up there despite nearly falling off a few days earlier, just because of him. He'd seen the bent rail, just like she'd described it once he was able to get her talking. He exhaled in a rush. That girl had balls, going up there just because he'd told her to.

Damn it, he couldn't get that woman out of his head.

Dane began popping the jets with the screwdriver. He held one up to the light, peering through to see if it was clogged. Yup. That man had messed with the wrong woman if she was willing to fill his bike's tank with syrup. He glanced behind him. The '83 Yamaha Seca rested on its side on the floor like a dead horse. An image of Darlene loomed over it like an apparition. If some girl pulled a number like this on his Harley, well, there'd be payback.

10

BEADS

STELLA'S mother opened the door to Grandma Angie's house, her face twisted into a warning. "She's up. Made us turn down the morphine. This is probably going to be her last good day. Don't upset her."

Stella pushed past, pissed as hell. Like she would be the one to ever bring a moment's grief to Grandma. That was Vivian's job. Vivian, who had screwed half the population of Holly while Stella's father watched television. Vivian, who decided Bible beating was better than dealing with her real issues.

Grandma Angie was sitting up, surrounded by TV trays full of beads.

"Grandma! You're jeweling!" Stella set her bag on the floor, wishing she'd brought the pieces of the broken bracelet even though she didn't have all the parts.

"I am." Her hand quivered as she tugged a tray into her lap, the beads nestled in the flocked partitions. "I have all my favorites."

Stella perched on the edge of the bed and ran her fingers along the edges of the tray, the flecks of felt wearing thin. The colored rows of square boxes were filled with crystals, seed pearls, bone beads, spirals, balls, and shells.

Grandma Angie grasped Stella's wrist as if divining a secret from her bones. "A new boy." She always knew.

"Yes."

"Have you made a bracelet yet?"

Stella reached for a spool of fine wire. "I was waiting for you."

"Ahh." Grandma ran her hands across the rippling surface of the beads, as though she were reading Braille. "Usually you do them alone."

"This one's different." Stella heard the words and wondered why she'd said them. Dane couldn't be all that different. Cheated on his girlfriend already. Bad news. Totally bad news. She should stay away.

"He torments you. You are not in control of this one."

Pegged it, as usual. "I thought I could use your help this time. For this bracelet." Stella made a bracelet for each boy, just like some people compiled mix tapes. Each bead had its significance, an observation or a hope.

And when each relationship ended, she smashed them to pieces.

"Let's start with the clasp," Grandma Angie said. "Box clasp, subtle, gentle?" She held up a gold ball.

Stella shook her head.

Grandma's fingers fluttered through the largest partition, full of metals. She showed Stella a silver loop on a hinge. "Lobster claw? The most secure, more functional than beautiful?"

"Nope."

Grandma nodded knowingly. "I didn't think so. You are not like your mother."

She knew Grandma was thinking of Stella's father. They had often talked about Vivian's choice of husband, especially during the tough years, when strange men would show up at the house. Stella practically lived with Grandma Angie then.

"Toggle?" Grandma held a braided circle and a matching T-bar in antique gold.

"Too risky," Stella said. "I don't want to lose it."

Grandma tucked the toggle away and laid three ornate clasps on the flat panel of the tray, where finished pieces could be admired. "S-clasps," she said. "The most beautiful, simple, strong."

Stella ran a finger along each of them, two silver, one gold. "Possibly." One of the silvers had an edgy look, rows of tiny balls encircling the center of the "S." She touched it again. "Especially this one."

"I have one more," Grandma said, reaching to the TV tray behind Stella to tug a tiny velvet bag from another box. "I have never used one like it. Unusual. Strange. Strong."

She pulled the clasp from the bag. "I've had it a long time. I bought it on vacation, from an old woman selling bone jewelry near the Grand Canyon. An Indian woman. She had the most beautiful wampum belt."

The clasp was a slide lock, one of the more elaborate types. Intended for bracelets with multiple strands, the slide lock had two pieces that fit together perfectly, creating one slender bar.

"Most slide locks are plain silver or gold," Grandma said. "But this one was crafted by a silversmith." She rolled it out onto the blue velvet tray. "See?"

The slender clasp was still open, each rod with three small hooks. Carved on each side were four stylized swirls, like the form a woman's body might make if she curled up on a bed.

Stella picked up the pieces and fitted the slots together. They slid into place as smoothly as a caress, locking in with an almost imperceptible snap.

"I had planned to make a bracelet with it. A strand for Vivian, one for me, and one for your grandfather." Grandma paused, then said his name. "Thomas." The syllables spread out, expanding beyond the ball of lamplight and into the gloom beyond, into the spaces where he had once been. Grandma Angie ran her fingers through a bin of cool sky-blue beads. "I didn't ever make it. I let life get in the way."

"We'll make it now," Stella said quickly.

Grandma Angie shook her head. "Vivian's would be too sharp, too blood-red. It wouldn't match. It isn't the strand it would have been then." She touched the pale yellow, pine green, and peach, and Stella understood that those would have been her mother's colors, back when Vivian was a child. But she agreed with Grandma. Now they'd all be angry and dark, scarlet and jet black.

"What would Grandpa Thomas's have been?"

Grandma's face relaxed, soft and serene. "A spiral, the symbol of becoming. In blue." She lifted one from a container of cerulean glass. "And circles, for unity. Pale greens and clear."

"Which metal?" Stella asked.

"Silver, certainly. He was a calm man. Gentle. Never raised a voice to me or Vivian."

"Was he sad you didn't have more children?" Stella couldn't imagine her mother being anything but a disappointment, although if she thought hard, to when she was very small, she could remember her mother happy, smiles and kisses and cookies after lunch.

"He would never say it. Wouldn't want the grief of it to cause me any pain." Grandma lined up the beads absently, forming a pattern of blue and green, spirals and spheres.

Stella knew they had tried to have more children after Vivian, but Grandma repeatedly miscarried. One baby had been stillborn.

"I barely remember him," Stella said. "But when I picture him, I see a puffy-cloud-filled sky. Or a newly mown lawn."

"Blues and greens," Grandma said. She seemed more tired suddenly and laid her head back against the pillows. "I remember when Vivian made a bracelet for your father."

Stella pulled her fingers from where they had been buried in the beads. "Really? She has one? I never saw it."

"Oh, yes. I remember the day we made it. Your father had asked Vivian out on a third date, but he hadn't worked up the nerve to kiss her good night yet. Shy, that boy."

"So you made a kissing bracelet?"

Grandma chuckled. "Sort of. We did alternating beads for him, mostly wood, with rich bone, in all the colors."

"Love beads? Like the hippies wore?"

"Exactly. It made a beautiful piece, vibrant and yet grounded with all that texture, the lightweight and the heavy."

"Did he kiss her?" Stella couldn't believe she'd never heard this story before. It should have been basic family lore.

"He did. They were married six months later. She wore the bracelet at the wedding."

Stella walked up to a photo of her parents by the altar of a church, peering closely at her mother's wrist. Sure enough, she wore a strange bracelet, although the colors were lost in the black-and-white image. "Funny I never noticed it before."

"Sometimes the most obvious things are right before our eyes."

Stella studied her mother's young face, radiantly happy. "Then it all went to hell." Stella returned to the bed and plopped to her knees again. "When she starting boinking everything with three legs."

Grandma sighed. "That was a difficult time of all our lives."

"Not hers, apparently." Stella poked at the red beads, blisteringly bright.

Grandma picked up the small carton of red and moved it to a table on the opposite side. "Stella, my girl, you must learn to forgive and forget." She swirled her fingers in a compartment of crystal beads, clear and glittering. "So tell me about your man so that we might choose the beads."

"Dane." The word sounded beautiful to her, the forceful beginning, the soft end. "He's tall. And lean. A bit dangerous." She remembered him cradling her on the tower platform. "Kind. Very gentle. A lot of opposites."

Grandma rolled the ornate clasp. "There's your three, then."

"Three? I can see the danger strand and the gentle strand. What's in between?"

Grandma laid her fingers on the back of Stella's hand. "You."

And so they began sorting beads, bones in dark brown and crystals in fiery orange. Then earth tones in green and sand and antique gold.

And in between, for Stella, a colorful collection of bright tones, seed pearls, and, at Grandma's insistence, an eye bead, hand painted with a blue iris, for warding off evil spirits.

Like Darlene.

11

KNIFE REVENGE

DANE perched on a rickety stool, leaning against the scratched surface of the bar, waiting for his beer. Since it was mid-afternoon, the joint was mostly empty, a few old men smoking cigars in a corner, broad and silent, like a trio of Hibachi grills.

The woman tending bar was stout, mid-forties, and not too friendly. She communicated primarily in grunts, and the breadth of her upper arms suggested that she could toss any unruly boozer out on his ass.

The beer foamed over the rim as she slid it to him. "Thanks," he muttered, but she was already gone.

Two days had passed since the water tower with Stella, and he hadn't even talked to her. Darlene neither. His brother was running interference should either one of them call, but they hadn't.

He didn't blame them. He was no good at this. Stella was especially keen on getting out of this town, moving on to something bigger. He might hold her back.

Or not. He didn't have anything special to offer. Plus, there was Darlene. He shook his head. Damn.

"The loser knows his game." The voice seemed a little drunk, and more than a little belligerent.

Dane didn't turn around. Not talking to him.

Another voice. "Deaf, too, apparently."

He sipped his beer, keeping his eyes on the bottles opposite him, but he noticed the bartender's jaw tensing, the rag wiping down the counter going still.

Someone shoved him from behind, and beer spilled over the edge of his glass and onto his hand. Dane leapt up, knocking the stool backward. "What the hell?" He turned around. Some punk he'd seen around town a time or two—Allen or something—laughed into his curled-up fingers. Bobby Ray, Darlene's brother, skulked beside him, arms crossed. He turned his fist against his bicep, revealing a set of brass knuckles.

Dane had survived a fight or two. And he should have seen this one coming. "What's your problem?"

Allen cocked his head. "You need a little attitude adjustment?"

Dane laughed. "What is this? The Italian mob?" He returned to his stool, back to them, but angled just enough to catch any sudden movements in his peripheral vision. "Another Guinness?" He raised his eyebrows at the bartender, wishing she was someone he'd built a camaraderie with, so he could count on her if the punks got out of line.

Not that she couldn't tell they were no good. But he looked the same. It's as though the punk losers always found each other and fought it out, a community feeding on itself.

He sensed them moving behind him, but they passed by and sat at a table at the other end of the room. Bobby Ray must not have heard about Stella, or he wouldn't have let it go. Boys like that, even if they thought their sisters were full-blown skanks, would still use the girl's honor as an excuse to pound someone's face. Their entrance was probably just how they greeted everyone.

The barkeep brought him a fresh glass. "Watch yourself."

He couldn't tell if this was a warning about his behavior or theirs. Probably both. She seemed like an equal opportunity hardass. Didn't matter who was right or wrong, just don't come to blows in her bar.

But then he felt a breath on his neck. "Darlene tells me you came down the tower with Stella two nights ago." Bobby Ray. So he did know.

Dane lifted the beer to his lips. It was 2 a.m. when they'd descended that tower. This town was too damn small.

Bobby Ray seemed to know the direction his thoughts had gone. "Old Lady Springer lives across the street. She's friends with our mother."

"You always settle scores for your sister?"

The back of his arm pricked, like a needle, then burned with an unholy fire. He jerked it forward. "What the hell?"

"There's more where that came from." Bobby Ray headed back to sit with Allen. "If you mess with her head."

A rag landed in front of him. "You're bleeding on my bar."

Dane lifted his arm. A clean cut ran from the sleeve of his T-shirt to just above his elbow.

He jumped from the stool, upsetting it again, and raced across the room, snatching Bobby Ray from his table. Before the man could react, Dane landed a bone-crunching uppercut to his jaw, knocking him to the floor.

Bobby Ray had not even fully landed when the bartender rounded the counter and grabbed Dane by the shirt. "Out of my bar," she growled.

"Why are you throwing ME out?"

She pushed him toward the door. "You ain't the regular."

"He fucking cut me!"

"You probably had it coming." She opened the door.

Shit. Only one bar in Holly, and he'd be walking trouble from here on out. How had Ryker managed in this town?

The air cooled his flaming face and sent a roar of pain up his arm from the cut. Screw Darlene. He didn't want to have anything to do with that family.

He jumped on his Harley, aware of each throb of his arm, the wet stickiness. Damn it to hell. He roared out of the parking lot and down to Main. He'd better just get this over with. Now was as good a time as any.

He held the throttle wide open, ignoring the single stoplight. No one was sitting there anyway. Darlene worked at the car dealership on the outskirts of Holly, a questionable job where she did light office work in short skirts and low-cut tops. No doubt her manner of dress was attractive to the sales guys, all men, and she was tucked away and hidden from the disapproving public.

He parked the bike and strode into the showroom, dimly aware of the crust forming down his arm.

A poor sucker in a tie, flashing a shit-eating grin, approached him as if to expound on the qualities of a two-door sedan. Dane waved him off, darting to the back offices through the cars parked at haphazard angles.

He brushed past the manager, a fat man named Ted or Tim or something, who apparently regularly tried to make the moves on Darlene. The man stopped, so Dane shoved him hard enough that a stack of sales receipts in his arms cascaded to the floor.

"What the hell?" the manager said, then, "God, what happened to your arm?"

Darlene sat at her crappy little desk, her chair so high that she had to lean over it, cleavage hanging over a giant calendar with scribbles across its face. She glanced up from her phone pad, face registering surprise as he stalked forward and swept the entire contents of the surface onto the floor.

She rolled backward. "Dane! What's gotten into you?"

"Your brother."

Darlene bit her lip. "Yeah, he was pretty pissed."

"You got something to say to me?"

She stood up from behind the table and tugged on her short skirt, taking care with her fake nails. "Yeah. You wanna explain why you were up on the water tower with that little slut?"

"Fucking her senseless." Damn. He hadn't meant to say it. He pressed his palms into the desktop, trying to bring himself down.

Darlene dropped back into her chair, her breath rushing out. "Did I do something wrong?"

Dane stepped back to the doorway, legs spread, arms crossing over his chest. Too many bad scenes like this in his life. He forced himself calm. "I thought you were cool with whatever."

She bent down, picking up the calendar and a mug she used for pens. He noticed now the doodles, hearts and bubbles. His name, written all over it, like in high school. Damn.

But she surprised him. "You're right," she said. "Nothing big here. Move right on along." She wouldn't look at him, flipping through the loose pages.

"We had a good time."

"Yeah. Roll in the hay." She tapped the papers on the desk to straighten them. Then she noticed his arm. "Oh, Jesus." She stood for a second, then sat back down. "It was Bobby Ray."

"At the bar. Just now. Nice family."

She set the stack carefully on the desk, lining up the corners. "He's got a temper, that one."

"So do I."

She pinched her lips, staring at the bloodstained section of his shirt. "You need me to tend to that?"

"Nah."

"We done then? We through here? My job, you know." She fixed her gaze behind him.

Dane sensed someone in the hall. "Yeah. All done. See ya 'round town."

She bent down to reclaim more of the stuff on the floor, and he turned. Dickhead manager lurked in the hall.

"You all right, Darlene? Need me to throw this fucktard out on his head?"

Darlene didn't answer, and Dane pushed past the man for a second time. His arm stung like a mother, and another trickle along his elbow warned him that the wound wasn't closing up. At least Darlene hadn't been trouble. A respectable reaction. No wailing.

Once outside, he slammed his foot on the kick-starter and backed out, not sure where to go next. Clean up this arm, for sure. See what was going on. Maybe drive up to the sorry excuse of a clinic they called a hospital to see if it had to be sewn up.

Dane mentally calculated how much money he had on him, and how much was in his account. No telling what stitches would cost him. He'd tapped out quite a bit of his cash moving to Holly, losing his deposits in Texas for breaking his lease, not to mention closing out stuff on his mom. Ryker had helped out some on that, but still. She'd had to be buried, the rent house cleaned out. He hadn't even known what to do with all her stuff, so he shoved it in a storage shed.

He pulled up to a curb before he realized where he'd gone. The perfume shop was closed, but only just. He could see the figures of Stella and her boss moving inside. He shouldn't involve her. Bobby Ray was bad news. There could be a backlash. And he hadn't even talked to her since the tower. Maybe she hated him too.

But she'd seen him and rushed to the door, bells jingling as she struggled with the lock. He swung his leg over his bike, again feeling the bite of the cut. He'd been through a fight or two, banged up, teeth knocked loose, nose broken, bleeding in a hundred places. But never knifed. Dane guessed he should count himself lucky that Bobby Ray hadn't stuck it between his shoulder blades.

Stella saw the blood right away. "Oh my God, what happened?" She grabbed his good arm and dragged him inside. "Should I take you to the hospital?"

"Maybe I can wash wounds to pay for it."

Stella didn't crack a smile. "Beatrice! Come quick!"

Dane tried to stay casual, but truth be told, he was feeling a little woozy. He sat on a satin bench as Stella fussed over him, lifting his arm. He felt wetness again.

"It's still bleeding," Stella said. "But I can't see anything."

Beatrice closed in behind her, enveloping him in a dozen scents. Rose water. Vanilla. She must have been trying on every perfume in the shop.

"Let's wet it down," she said, and disappeared behind the curtain again.

"You going to tell me what happened?" Stella asked.

"Switchblade got up on the wrong side of the bed."

Stella punched his shoulder, sending a wave of pain cascading from elbow to wrist. He didn't flinch.

"I'm serious. Accident or intentional?"

Beatrice returned with dripping white hand towels. "This is going to sting."

The pressure of the cold cotton against his arm made everything go black for a second. He leaned forward, and Stella caught him. "Dane?" she asked. "You with us?" She sat him up again. "Bea, we have to take him in. I think it's bad."

"Hold on a sec," Beatrice said. "Let's take a look."

The cloth pulled away, and Dane breathed a bit easier. "Not pretty," Beatrice said, "but most of it is crusting over. Looks like the bottom of the cut is the deepest. Where someone stuck it in and went up."

"WHO?" Stella demanded. "Who did this?"

Dane shook his head. "Doesn't matter. It's over."

"Darlene? Did that bitch cut you?" She'd gone red all over, cheeks, neck, and chest bright with color. He bet if he could have seen it, she'd been the same on the tower.

"Not Darlene."

"Then her asshole brother. Bobby Ray."

"I get in lots of fights," Dane insisted.

Beatrice applied a clean cloth, causing him to suck in another breath. "This'll teach you to change your ways."

Dane shrugged. "Nah."

Stella began pacing the shop, grasping at the ends of her hair. "I knew they'd found out about the other night. I knew a fight was coming." She halted. "But this is uncalled for. He could have killed you."

"He just wanted to be an ass," Dane said. He looked back at Beatrice. "Verdict? Will I live to fight another day?"

Beatrice opened a first-aid kit and unfurled a roll of gauze. "I've got some butterfly bandages in here. I think that'll hold the wound. Just don't lift anything heavy for a couple days."

She sprayed him with something cold and acrid. He forced himself not to flinch, keeping a smile for Stella. God, she was riled. He tried not to love it.

"Tell me EXACTLY what happened," Stella insisted. "Every detail."

"It's not important."

"Dane. By God, you will say it."

He shrugged. "Bobby Ray came into the Watering Hole with a chip on his shoulder. We came to a couple blows, nothing major."

"This wasn't a blow," Beatrice said, applying the first bandage. "Nice clean cut."

"He came up behind me. I guess he had a small blade on him."

Stella clenched her fists, eyes sparking like a welder's torch. "He knifed you from BEHIND?"

"Stell, it's fine. I know to watch my back. I probably deserved it. Small towns are, well, small."

Beatrice wrapped the gauze around his arm. "Gotta keep that dick in line, mister. Everybody sees everything in Holly."

Stella bloomed scarlet yet again. He could watch that all day. She whirled around and stalked through the curtain.

"It was bad, I know," Dane said.

Beatrice tore off a bit of medical tape with her teeth. "Stella's taken a shine to you. Make sure you deserve her."

"I'll try," he said.

"More than try." She flattened the tape on his arm. "I'll go fetch Stella. Roll your bike in here for the night. You shouldn't ride until tomorrow. It'll tear open the wound. She'll drive you home."

Dane nodded. Probably not a bad idea to have his Harley hidden away somewhere anyhow. He didn't need syrup in his carburetor.

12

BROTHERS

HEADLIGHTS flashed over Stella as she and Dane sat in her grandmother's car in front of the perfume shop. She had no idea what to do, so they'd stayed there right through sunset, mostly silent. Stella occasionally asked him about his arm. She was worried. And mad. And not sure how to react to the town's newfound dislike of him, which was partly her fault.

She'd been the one to prance over to Joe's garage with her fake nails and screw-the-bitch attitude. "I'm to blame here," she said. "I knew Darlene's family history."

"She lives with her brother too?" he asked.

"He stays in a travel trailer parked in the back."

"That rotten thing? It doesn't look safe to sneeze on."

Stella drummed her fingers on the steering wheel. "Yeah." She'd been in it, once. Bobby Ray had been on her list. They'd gone out for a spell, and one night she decided to let him lead her there. But he wasn't worth the things he had in mind. He had a mean streak, and that went all the way to the bedroom. She got the hell out of there.

He'd been pretty ugly about it for weeks. As if calling her a tease and a prude and a Pollyanna had any effect. She'd known not to rile him, though, and kept her distance. That'd been two years ago. He seemed

66

cool about it now.

Dane stared out the window at the blinking "OPEN" sign reflected in the shop's window from the opposite side of the street. The diner. "You hungry?" he asked.

"Maybe we should lay low for a bit," Stella said. "Let everyone find a new topic for gossip."

He exhaled in a rush, rubbing his hands on his jeans. "Okay."

"I should probably take you home." She'd wanted to just sit there, to be with him. He hadn't asked why she never put the key in the ignition. But people were driving by, and eventually someone would notice. They had to go.

The car started with a quiet hum.

"Joe sure tuned that engine pretty," Dane said.

"He always took a shine to Grandma Angie. Everyone thought they'd get together, being so many years since my grandpa died."

"Why didn't they?"

Stella backed out of the spot. "My mother disapproved."

"And your grandmother just let it go?"

"She did."

Dane jingled the chain on his hip. "How is she?"

"We got a good visit in yesterday. Made some bracelets." She cut herself off. No need to tell him she'd made the triple-strand for him. She hadn't worn it on the job. It felt too new, too precious yet to be scrutinized by others. Lots of people knew she made them—Janine, her mother, a handful of boys who had lasted long enough to tell. A new one would be very revealing about how she felt.

"I'm sorry you're going to lose her."

"I am too."

She drove the back streets to the line of duplexes where most all the transplants lived. People rarely sold a house in Holly, only when someone died. New ones never seemed to get built. And the occupants of Renters' Row never stayed around for long either. A "For Lease" sign always seemed to hang somewhere along the road.

"Which one?" she asked. "I've never been to Ryker's place." For that she was grateful. No way to seduce a man if you've already done his brother.

"Third one down."

"You going to get your own eventually?"

"Might. See how Holly fits."

"Not great so far."

He turned to her, gray eyes just visible in the streetlight. "Depends on how you look at it."

Stella turned back to the windshield, staring at Duplex C. She'd been around a number of sweet talkers. Real slick ways. Opening doors. Acting all gracious. Compliments flowing like melted cheese. Most of them were doing it without an ounce of sincerity. And to more than one girl.

And here she was. Another one. Not quite as smooth, maybe. But obviously he'd gotten Darlene on a string. Maybe she should stay far away.

Dane unbuckled his seat belt. "You want to come in? Looks like Ryker's out."

"Yes."

Stupid. She'd meant to say no.

Dane opened his door, letting in the buzz of cicadas and the crisp night air. Someone should bottle the smell. Night Breeze. Dark-purple bottle with etched letters.

"You coming?" he asked.

Another chance to say no. But she tugged the key out of the ignition and slid it into her purse. "Lock the door," she said to Dane. "I don't normally, but tonight…"

He nodded, pressing down the button.

They crossed the dirt yard, weeds springing up like a bad-hair day. Stella tripped on an overturned pot.

Dane caught her arm. "Sorry."

He fumbled with the lock and pushed open the door. Stale pizza and the smell of old dishwater accosted her. "Sorry again," he muttered.

He kicked clothes around to make a path to the sofa. Something small might have scurried, but Stella didn't flinch. She was used to boy sloth and wasn't any sort of neat freak. Cockroaches didn't kill.

"Wanna sit?" Dane asked. "I have beer. Maybe some hard stuff."

"I think some hard stuff," she said. This day had been too much. Worse yet, the ugliness promised so much more ahead.

Dane disappeared through a doorway, and a light kicked on. He rummaged around, opening cabinets. He located a glass, then moved to the other side, out of sight.

Stella leaned back on the sofa, trying not to feel squeamish about what might have occurred on its cushions. She pictured Darlene there and grimaced. Not usually the jealous sort, this invasion of envy made her squirm.

Dane returned with two glasses filled with something clear.

"Been a busy place?" She smacked her hand on the couch.

He frowned.

So yes. She needed the drink more than ever.

"We broke it off clean," he said suddenly. "Right after the run-in with Bobby Ray."

"You and Darlene?"

"Yeah, I drove to the dealer."

"Bleeding?"

"Yeah."

She accepted the drink and clinked her glass against his. "Here's to being single."

He swallowed, an incredible gulp even to her, and she could drink most people under the table. Easier than answering, but she took that as a good thing. Maybe he didn't consider himself on the market, just out of the triangle. Suited her.

She lifted the glass, immediately overwhelmed by the medicinal smell of bad vodka. She gulped and drew it away quickly.

Dane walked off again, down a hallway this time. After a moment, music came on, a radio station. A DJ squawked something unintelligible, and heavy metal blared from speakers strung on the wall above her.

Then hissing. He was switching to something else. First country. She smiled against the cool glass. No way. More hiss. Pop hits. Not him either.

Another hiss. Let's see, what would he hit next, classical?

Sure enough, he tuned it in, popping his head around the corner.

"This okay?"

She nodded, and he took off again as a smooth ribbon of violins flowed from the walls. A cabinet opened and closed with a mouse-like squeak. At least she hoped it was the door. She slid off her shoes and pulled her feet onto the sofa.

He returned with a pale yellow sheet, more wadded than folded. "It's clean," he said, spreading it on the sofa.

Stella stood to let him tuck it against the cushions.

"I sleep here. Fabric's kind of rough on its own."

She compared the length of the sofa to his height. "You must hang off the edge."

"Close enough. And cheap." He shrugged.

She settled back down again. "So what should we do about Bobby Ray?"

"Ignore him. He'll get bored with it." Dane stretched his arm along the back of the sofa, the gauze glowing faintly in the light from the kitchen.

Stella wanted to snuggle into his side, but resisted. "You could file a report with the sheriff."

"No good. The bartender threw me out. Told me I wasn't the regular."

"Carmen threw you out?" They had closed ranks already.

"Yup." Dane picked up his glass from the overturned crate that served as a coffee table and downed the rest of his drink. "That bad?"

"It is. They've sided with Bobby Ray, and that's rare. Did she know he'd cut you?"

"She told me not to bleed on her bar."

Stella sat up on her knees, anxious and jittery. "It's ridiculous they'd default to him without knowing anything. I hate this town."

"She had no reason to believe I hadn't done something to deserve it." He ran his thumb along her arm.

She pulled away. "This is serious! You won't be able to do anything in this town. Do you know how many outsiders have been run out?" Hell, half the guys she'd slept with.

"Stell, it will be all right. It'll die down."

"It won't! I've lived here all my life!"

"And weren't you about to leave?" He reached for her arm again, and this time she relented.

"I am. I will. You too, if you know what's good for you."

"I think it's okay. Joe likes me. Beatrice likes me. And you." He slid his hand to that sensitive spot inside her elbow. "That's enough for me."

She relaxed against him. She hardly knew him. Really, she should walk right out. Let it go. But he'd split with Darlene. That was something.

He pulled her head to his shoulder. The music washed over them, simple, emotional, pretty. She didn't listen to much classical. Maybe she should. It was calming.

The door flew open, smashing against the wall. The metal doorstop snapped and sprung across the room.

Dane jumped up, leaving Stella to fall against the cushions.

Ryker barreled in and grabbed Dane by the shirt, shoving him backward. "What the HELL have you gotten yourself into?" He snatched Dane's arm, assessing the bandages. "I spend a year here trying to avoid this pissant town's bullshit, and you wreck it all in a day?"

Dane stepped back, knocking Ryker loose from his arm. "This doesn't have anything to do with you."

Ryker whirled around, noticing Stella. "And you had to bring the problem over here?"

Before Stella could say anything, Dane had already landed a punch to Ryker's jaw.

"Son of a BITCH!" Ryker rushed forward, tackling Dane. The glasses flew off the crate onto the carpet.

Stella stood on the sofa, ready to jump on Ryker. "Dane! Your arm! Stop it!"

The brothers rolled on the floor in a tumble of legs and arms, grunting, elbows landing in bellies. They knocked over a TV tray loaded with beer bottles.

Stella jumped off the sofa, kicking at the brothers with bare feet. "Stop it! Stop it! You should be on the same side!"

Ryker rolled onto his back, staring up at her. "You should have stayed out of this." He turned to Dane, both of them breathing heavily.

"You should have kept your dick in your pants."

Stella stepped over Ryker, kneeling down to assess Dane's bandage. It had come loose, and a bloody spiral rolled off as she unwound it. "You're bleeding again. We'll have to start over on this. I think you're going to have to get stitches after all."

"Screw that," Dane said, tugging the gauze tight around his arm. "Screw all of it." He sat up, forearms on his knees, head down. "This is so fucked up."

Ryker had his arm thrown over his eyes. Blood trickled from his nose. Stella nudged him with her foot. "What the hell happened? You know that Bobby Ray stuck Dane from behind, right?"

Ryker's voice was muffled from his shirt. "Yeah. At the Watering Hole. Supposedly Dane picked a fight, and Bobby Ray finished it."

"That's not exactly how it went," Dane said.

Ryker sat up. His black hair stuck up in every direction. He ended up positioned the same way as Dane, arms on his knees, and Stella was struck by how similar they looked.

"I know that," Ryker said. "Any asshole knows what Bobby Ray's like. But he's got cause. You were a dickhead." He shoved at Dane again, but good-naturedly this time.

"Not like you haven't been dipping your stick all over Holly," Dane said.

"But one at a time," Ryker said. "You can't go around like this with hometown girls."

"I'm not," Dane said. "On Tuesday I was dating Darlene." He reached for Stella. "And today it's Stella."

Stella clasped both of her hands around his arm. "If you two are done roughing each other up, we should probably look at Dane's cut." She stood and brought Dane with her, leading him into the kitchen.

The place was a wreck, boxes and beer bottles and cheap plastic dishes everywhere. "If you boys had been raised in a barn, you'd be better off," she said.

Dane dropped into a rickety metal chair by a beat-up Formica table. Ryker cleared a space, and Stella eased Dane's elbow onto it, carefully removing the gauze.

The butterfly bandages had peeled off at the edges. Most of the cut was fine still, but the bottom, the deepest part, oozed blood. "I don't suppose you guys have any sort of Band-Aids in this bachelor pad," she said.

Ryker put his hand on his heart. "I'm offended by the suggestion." He trundled off down the hallway.

Dane pulled Stella close to him. "I need to kiss you."

Finally. All that time in the car, on the sofa, and nothing. His lips were warm, a little swollen. He kept it gentle, simple.

"Break it up," Ryker said. "The man is injured."

Stella shook her head. They were joking around now. You'd never know that five minutes earlier he'd stormed into the room and struck his brother with a killer blow.

"You boys always run hot and cold like this?"

Dane grinned. "Drove our mom crazy."

Ryker handed her a rusting metal box of kiddie bandages with Smurfs on them.

"What is this?" She forced open the top, extracting one.

"Dated a chick with a kid for a while," Ryker shrugged.

Stella peeled the backing away. "This will make him look tougher."

Ryker laughed, turning to open the fridge. "Beer?"

"All around," Dane said.

"Beer after liquor, never been sicker," Stella said, wrapping the bloody gauze back around his arm. They'd have to buy a fresh roll in the morning.

"Beer BEFORE liquor," Ryker said. "Get it straight."

"I'm quite sure it's beer after liquor," Dane said.

Ryker popped the tops of the bottles. "I guess we'll find out by who pukes."

He passed the beer around as Stella used one last Smurf Band-Aid to lock down the gauze. "You'll want to wear a shirt with sleeves, I think," she said. "Unless you aim to show off your Smurfette."

"I've been meaning to get a tattoo of her," Dane said. "She's hot."

"Lots of men to service," Ryker said. "No wonder she doesn't have a job."

They clinked their beers together.

"Seriously," Dane said. "This will blow over."

Ryker shook his head. "It ought to, but I'm not sure. Apparently Bobby Ray's still got a thing for Stella here."

Stella stared into her beer. "Done a long time ago."

"Still, on top of throwing over his sister, you've got a perfect reason for him to hate Dane." Ryker stared up at the ceiling. "Gonna be trouble."

His statement was punctuated with the crash of smashing glass outside.

"What the hell?" Dane jumped up, running for the door.

"Dane, wait," Stella said. "Let them pass."

Ryker followed them into the living room, peering out the window as tires squealed away. "They got your car, Stell."

Stella flung open the door and ran outside. The car seemed fine from the front, but as she rounded the back bumper, the fractured window glittered in the light from the streetlamp.

She banged her hand on the trunk, causing chunks of shatterproof glass to sprinkle down into the backseat. "Sons of bitches," she said. "Grandma's poor Mustang."

"I'm going after those assholes," Dane said. "This is enough."

Ryker grabbed his shoulder. "This part is Stella's battle. She's the hometown girl."

"Sure," Stella said. "They'll file a report, note that there were no witnesses, and move on." She picked up a bit of glass and flung it into the street.

Stella didn't think she could take one more minute of Holly. All the incidents, the gossip, the incestuous combinations of men and women screwing around or getting married or divorced, pair after pair. Too much. She wanted somewhere else, where the outsiders and the long-timers blended, where nobody knew what everybody had for breakfast, and with whom.

She turned to Dane. "Let's leave this town." She kicked the car, sending more glass cascading from the window. "I've got money to do it. Been saving for years. Let's just get the hell out. You and me."

Ryker whistled. "Sounds like quite a proposition, bro. You find a woman with money, I say GO."

But Dane wouldn't look at her. He stared at the moon, obscured behind a cloud, strange and eerie. Stella shivered. She'd probably just embarrassed herself completely.

13

DANE CALMS STELLA

A werewolf moon, his mother used to call it.

Dane kicked at the gravel. His arm was screaming. Stella watched him, and he could feel pricks of anxiety sparking from her. He'd known this girl, what, three days? Now she wanted him to leave town with her.

"Never mind," she said. She yanked on the car door and discovered it was locked. She reached for her purse and realized it wasn't there.

Dane tried to come to her, but she walked away in mincing pained steps of bare feet on gravel.

"Stella," he said, but she ignored him, moving fast once she hit the porch.

He sped up himself. He pulled the door closed behind him and locked it to keep Ryker out, at least for a moment.

She shoved her pink shoes on, trying to snatch up her purse in the same movement. Instead, the bag tipped over, spilling lipsticks and little pouches and pens and paper all over the floor.

"Damn it," she said, dropping to her knees, and now he could see she was crying.

He knelt beside her, putting his hands over hers, stilling them, trying to make her stop. "Wait. Please."

She did, her hair hanging down to hide her face. "I hate crying," she said. "Stupidest thing to do, ever."

He wrapped his arms around her shoulders and pulled her to the sofa again. "Let's think this through."

She flung his arms away. "I don't want to think this through. It's fine. I can head out of town without you. Let you fix the mess you're in on your own. If nobody kills you."

"Nobody's going to kill me."

"This town is killing me."

She bent over, snatching up the contents of her purse like Darlene had at her desk. Two women picking up in his wake. He was like a tornado, tearing through everything.

He flung his head back on the sofa, the coolness of the sheet a relief. His arm throbbed, and his stomach grumbled. Fucked up. All of it.

Stella stood up and shoved her purse on her shoulder. He reached for her again. She couldn't walk away. He wouldn't let her just yet.

"Let's drive somewhere," he said. "Work this out."

"There's apparently nothing to work out." She swiped her hand under her nose. "It was silly and impulsive. Not a big deal."

"It is."

She tried to move forward, but he held her at the waist, his arm screaming. He flinched, and she held still. "Your arm?"

"Please, sit."

She plunked back down. "Don't make it bleed again."

He gathered her against him, smelling the perfume lingering in her hair from the shop. "Which is your favorite?" he asked.

"My favorite what?"

"Perfume."

"We can't talk about this now."

"We can. Let's do."

She relaxed a little and settled against him. "It's silly."

"Which one?"

"An old one. The cliché."

"Charlie?"

She sat up and smacked his chest. "Good God, no." She leaned back against him. "Chanel No. 5."

"A classic."

"Chanel found the number five to be intoxicating. She'd been surrounded by it since she was a girl in a convent."

She was calming down. He had to keep her talking. "So it took five chances to get it right?"

"I think she got all five at once, but legend says that she would have had none other than the fifth one."

"Good thing it didn't suck."

Stella shook her head.

"Is this what you want to do? Sell perfume?" He stroked her lightly on the arm.

"Beatrice is great. But it's not a life." She drew small circles on his thigh. "I can hardly stand it when people come in smelling cheap and buying more of it."

He nodded. His mother had never worn any scents. She'd always smelled of Pledge and Palmolive. Or, if she'd been cooking, like sweet onions and bacon, the only two things she used for flavor.

"I should go," Stella said. "Ryker will want his place back."

"Ryker can wait."

She sat up. "No, I've made a decision. I'll get Joe to put in a new windshield, and then I'm taking off. Out of here. Someplace big enough to swallow me up, let me disappear into the crowd."

"That's no picnic either." Dane knew that drill. No money for college, working menial jobs. Never getting anywhere. Spinning wheels. "At least here you have family."

Stella snorted. "Right. Dish-mop dad. Whoremonger mother turned Jesus freak. MIA sister. The only person who ever cared for me is going to die any day." Her voice broke.

Dane pulled her back down. "I understand. My dad took off when I was three. Didn't bother me none, more time with mom. But Ryker was eight. He took it real hard."

"Where is your mom now?"

"Died. A month ago. That's why I moved up here. Didn't have nobody in Texas worth staying around for."

"Ever hear from your dad?"

"Sometimes, on Father's Day. He calls up, jokes about where's his gift. Like he remembered our birthdays or Christmas. Don't think he ever sent my mom a dime."

"I hate men like that. So many of them."

"He married some other gal. She had a boy about our age. I always imagined him playing ball with him instead of us. Wasn't sure why he picked some strange kid over his own."

"So it did bother you some."

Dane squeezed her tighter. "Okay, maybe some."

"Grandma taught me all about making jewelry. Gems. Beads. Design. We made a whole world out of the character of glass and wood and crystal."

He fingered her necklace, brushing her collarbone. "This one of yours?"

"Yes. Everything I wear always is."

"You know, you can't leave right now, not with your grandmother like she is." He hated to say it, to bring her back down.

She dropped her chin to her chest. "Yes, I will wait. Of course."

He had her back. He'd work hard to fix his mistake, his hesitation that upset her too much. They needed time, and taking off right now would be a disaster. He'd buy that time, see if they had something that might work, and hopefully the town would let them be.

14

GRANDMA FALTERS

"LOOK what the cat drug in," Stella's mother yelled. She was vacuuming the rug around Grandma Angie's hospital bed.

Stella dropped her bag on a chair. "You have to do that now? It's so loud."

"She can't hear anything."

"You don't know that." Stella clasped her grandmother's limp, dry hand. She hadn't been awake at all since they'd made the bracelet. Might not again.

Vivian killed the motor on the fat canister. "Hate this old thing. She never would buy a new one."

"How is she?"

"Slow decline. Opens her eyes now and then, but I'm not sure anything registers." She rolled up the cord. "You shacking up with that boy now? You didn't come home, your dad said."

"I'm twenty-two."

"Going on sixteen. If you don't got the sense by now to stay away from trouble, I can't get it in your head at this late date."

Stella smoothed the wrinkled skin over her grandmother's brow. "I'm here, Grandma." The triple-strand bracelet slid up and down her arm.

Her mother snorted. "A bracelet already?"

Stella ignored her. Grandma's face seemed weighted down, heavy, like it was already reaching for her spot in the ground. Stella hoped she would awaken one more time. Just for a bit. She'd been so good on the beads day. Like her old self.

Vivian loomed over the head of the bed like a vulture. "Nurse'll be back by in an hour or so to check on her. There's signs, she said, that tell you about when it'll be." Vivian walked to the end of the bed and threw back the blanket. Grandma Angie's ankles and feet were purple, almost black.

Stella held back her gasp. "That's a sign?"

Vivian nodded, settling the blanket back into place. "Next she'll start breathing irregularly, so she said. Her blood pressure has already started to drop."

"But she was just awake and sitting up!"

"I told you it might be her last good day. They turned the morphine back up yesterday."

"Why are they keeping her asleep?"

"She's in pain, Stella. It hurts."

Lots of things hurt. She could use a little morphine herself right now, straight to the chest.

"We need to start thinking about closing up this house. I'll need your help cleaning things out, figuring out what you want to keep and what we should sell off." Vivian turned to a china cabinet, assessing the dishes and serving pieces.

"Not now," Stella said. "I can't now. Let her house stay in one piece until she's not in it."

"It's not going to make her any difference."

"It makes ME a difference."

Vivian's hand on the cabinet door handle stilled. "All right. We'll wait."

Stella had never felt this level of pain before without being sick. How did people manage it, the heaviness inside, the feeling that you were going to throw up at any minute? She watched her mother leave the room and suddenly wondered about her. Grandma Angie was her mother! But then, of course, Stella wasn't sure what she'd feel when Vivian's time came. Love seemed to have skipped a generation.

Stella fingered the drip going into Grandma's fragile hand. She had hidden her pain so they could jewel together one more time. "Thank you," Stella whispered. Her heart broke all over again that Dane's bracelet would be the last they'd do together. They should have fixed the one Stella had broken on the water tower. Then her last piece would be something that held no meaning with someone who might be temporary. She could never smash Dane's bracelet like the others.

It had to work out with him, it just had to. He'd been so good last night, so careful after the mess by the car. Something long-lasting with him seemed possible, like no one else ever had.

They'd slept wound together on his sofa. If Ryker returned, they didn't hear him, nor had they seen him this morning. Dane dropped her off with the promise to take the car to Joe's for a new windshield. He would meet her at the perfume shop in a couple of hours to get his motorcycle out.

She imagined what it would have been like if they had just gone off last night. Driven away without a care, heading to God-knows-where, laughing.

But there were things in the way, she realized. His bike in the perfume store. Grandma's car to fix. And, of course, Grandma herself. There'd be a funeral soon. Her breath caught in her chest, so tight it couldn't come out. She wouldn't think about it yet. Not yet. Not till she had to.

But definitely when all this was over, when Grandma was truly gone, she'd leave. With or without Dane.

* * *

Stella entered Good Scents a few hours later, still heavyhearted.

The curtains zipped open with the flourish of a theater production. Beatrice stepped through, arms high. "And presenting…" She swirled her hands through the air. "Mr. Right!"

Dane passed through the entrance with a sheepish grin, a flannel shirt loose over a black T-shirt. Hiding the Smurfs, no doubt, as it was too warm for long sleeves. "Not sure 'bout that."

"Okay, we'll go with Mr. Right Now." Beatrice repeated her gestures. "Applause!"

Stella clapped slowly. "Not sure I'm cheering-up material."

Dane kissed her with simple familiarity, as if they'd greeted each other this way a thousand times. "What's wrong, Stell?"

He didn't wait for an answer but pressed her close to him. She lifted an arm to his neck, the slide-lock bracelet sliding down from her wrist. "Grandma. She's not going to wake up again, they said."

"Awww, Stell." Dane rubbed the back of her neck.

"It's really going to happen. She's going to leave me." His shoulder smelled of detergent and dust.

Beatrice came up from behind and entered the hug. "Wasn't any Grandma any better than Angie." She patted Stella's back. "I was pleased to have known her."

But wait. Dane hadn't met her. Grandma needed to meet Dane! Why hadn't she thought of it before? She broke free of the embrace. "Dane, take me to her house."

"Is something wrong?"

She clutched his hand. "I need you to meet her, before it's too late." She began dragging him to the front door, then remembered his motorcycle. "Your bike is here, right?"

"In the back."

She changed directions. "That will be faster."

Beatrice leaned against the counter, shaking her head. "It's all right. Take the morning off."

Stella stopped. "I'm sorry. Will you be all right?"

"Of course I will. You go on. Introduce your boy to Grandma. She can still hear, even if she doesn't open her eyes." Beatrice absently rearranged the desk supplies by the register. "Be mindful what you say."

"We will." Stella tugged on Dane. His bike was parked by the back door. "I don't know why, but I feel like we have to hurry."

"I am good at speed." He rolled the bike out the door and threw his leg over the seat. "Hang on."

Stella jumped on behind him and grasped his belly tightly. She laid her head in that perfect spot between his shoulder blades, her cheek against the back of his heart. He fired up the motor, and they lurched forward, zooming down the alley to connect with the back street.

"Which way?" he shouted.

"Right on Cherry Street. Blue house on the left."

Stella's sense of urgency increased as they approached the driveway. Dane had barely come to a stop before she leapt from the bike and dashed up the walkway.

The door was locked, so she fumbled in her purse for the keys.

Dane caught up with her. "Hey, slow down." He pulled her to him. "Take a breath. One minute isn't going to change anything. This doesn't happen suddenly. Someone would have called if it was close."

"What do you mean, it doesn't happen suddenly? She was talking two days ago!"

"The time from when they stop talking to when they stop breathing is a couple days."

Stella rushed into the living room, immediately spying the form of her grandmother. A nurse sat in a rocking chair next to her, reading a book.

Seeing Stella's alarm, she closed the cover. "She's no different. No need to panic."

"Has she woke up?" Stella reached for Grandma's hand as though she hadn't seen her in months, years, even though she'd been there just an hour ago.

"I don't think she will at this point. Blood pressure is down again."

"How long?" Stella watched the gentle flicker behind Grandma's eyelids. If only she'd open them, just once!

"You never really know. But I'd guess one to three days," the nurse said.

One day! Stella stole a quick peek under the covers at her grandmother's legs as though the discoloration might be a barometer. They didn't seem to have changed. She kept having this vision of the purple creeping to her knees, her thighs, and eventually taking her over.

Dane's hands encircled her upper arms, squeezing lightly. "She's a lovely lady."

"You should see pictures of her as a girl," Stella said. "A show-stopper."

"You take after her."

Stella knelt by the bed. "I don't hold a candle to her. She was kind to everyone. You just wait. The whole town will be at her—" God, she'd almost said it. Right in front of her.

Dane got on his knees beside her. "It's a pleasure to meet you, Grandma Angie."

"This is Dane," Stella said. "The one we talked about."

Still nothing. Stella washed over with disappointment. She had hoped that maybe this would wake her up a little, sharpen her enough to cut through the morphine, just for a moment.

"We're getting along real well, Grandma, just like you said." Stella stole a glance at Dane. "Too bad you're not up for taking a look at him. You wouldn't be sorry." Her voice broke a little. Damn emotion. "He's a real looker."

"A bodacious babe," Dane chuckled. "You know, I haven't missed the Valley speak at all since I've been to Holly."

"They string you up for talking like that," Stella said.

"I can believe that."

They shouldn't talk of that either. "Isn't his voice a lovely thing, Grandma? I'm glad you at least get to hear it." She nudged Dane. "Talk some more."

"I never was much for pretty words," Dane said.

Stella nudged him again.

"But I do come from Texas. I work on motorcycles." He glanced down at Grandma and covered Stella's hand so that they both held on to Angie. "My mother passed on just a month ago. I'd be mighty appreciative if you brought along a greeting to her should you cross her path."

And Stella felt it. The tiniest twitch in Grandma's hand. She lifted it, along with Dane's, to kiss her fingers. "She moved!" She swallowed thickly, vowing not to cry. "Thank you, Grandma, for letting us know you heard him." She looked to heaven. "And thank you, too."

15

RYKER'S WARNING

DANE closed the door gently behind him. His mother had been a chronic door slammer, and he'd always hated the sound. Sometimes he imagined that was why his father had left them when Dane was little. One too many slammed doors.

Ryker sat at the kitchen table, his boot propped on one of the rickety metal chairs. He rolled a bottle of Miller Light between his palms. He'd been peeling the label, and it flapped with each movement. They hadn't seen each other all day, as Ryker had the afternoon off.

"Get through a day without anybody slicing a chunk out of you?" He tugged a fresh bottle from the six-pack and tossed it to Dane.

The throw was low, but Dane managed to snatch it before it hit the ground. Ryker normally had good aim. He must have had a few. No way to tell from the empties. The kitchen was a sea of brown bottles reclining in various positions, like whores in a Wild West brothel.

"Dick is intact." His workday had been uneventful, and for that he was damn grateful. He'd finally gotten that Yamaha running smooth again.

Ryker kicked the chair out from under the table and pushed it toward Dane.

Dane turned the seat around and straddled the back. "What's up?"

Ryker pondered the label on his beer a moment, then tore the rest of it off. "Some information has come my way." He flicked the paper on the floor. "Seems there's going to be more where that cut came from."

Dane leaned on the chair, the bottle loose in his fingers. "Why they got to keep this going? I'm clear of Darlene."

Ryker set the beer on the table. "Remember when Mom dated Mike, that asshole plumber?"

Dane grunted.

"Yeah. How many times did she try to quit him?"

Dane downed a swig. "Five, maybe."

"He just kept coming back, angrier every time."

"She should have kept it clean. I'm keeping it clean."

Ryker leaned forward on the table. "That's the thing. It's clean to Darlene, and it's clean to you, but it's not to Bobby Ray. He thinks as long as you're still seeing Stella, he's got an ax to grind."

Dane pushed the chair away to pace the kitchen, kicking pizza boxes out of his way. "We ought to bulldoze this pigsty."

Ryker jumped up, grabbing Dane by the shoulder. "You're not listening. I think they're going to fuck you up. Bad."

"I'm not going to live my life in fear of sons of bitches like Bobby Ray."

"You don't have to be afraid to see the handwriting on the wall."

"I'm not giving up Stella."

Ryker pushed Dane away and plunked back down in the chair. "She better be worth it."

Dane sat down opposite him again. "Look. He had a thing for her. That's all. He's just pissed right now. He'll get over it."

Ryker shook his head. "These people don't have anything else to do or think about. They'll keep it going just for the hell of it. So they aren't bored. Or thinking about what shit their life is."

"So what are you saying? I should get out of town? Just leave?"

"Maybe."

Dane crossed his arms over the back of the chair and laid his head down. "Stella is planning on blowing out of here."

"Well, problem solved. Leave with her."

"I've known her less than a week."

"So what? You can see if it works. If not, take off."

"Why is leaving the solution to everything for you?"

Ryker stared at him, stunned, and Dane realized what he'd said. "I didn't mean it like that."

Ryker plucked another beer out of the carton and popped the top on the edge of the table. "You always acted like I was cut from the same cloth as Dad."

"Didn't mean it like that."

Ryker took a long pull on the beer. "You going to be fucked up all your life over that?"

"Don't plan on it."

"You're doing a mighty fine imitation of it, then."

Dane lifted his head. "I hardly knew the man."

"And you always hated that I knew him longer."

Dane didn't want this. Not now, not really ever. "Dad did what he had to do. Mom was no picnic."

"You got that right."

Cars rumbled by outside. Holly began its slide into night, quieting down by degrees. Dane remembered when his mother died. "Your father" was all she'd managed. Last words on her lips were about that bastard.

Ryker rocked the chair back on two legs. "At least lay low, brother. Try to get off everybody's minds."

16

GOOD-BYE

STELLA couldn't get Dane out of her mind. Once again, two days had passed since she'd seen him. Layin' low, he'd said. But he'd called, and they made plans for the weekend. Big ones. To get on his bike and leave town for a while, be free and without worry of who might be watching or plotting.

As Grandma Angie's life clock ticked down toward inevitable silence, Beatrice sent Stella home more and more, anytime the shop was quiet. "You'll want to be there, love," she told her. "It's something everyone should do, usher a loved one out of this world and into the next."

Business had picked up that morning, though, as the first cold front blowing through Holly sent everyone into a rush of buying new scents to go with fall clothes.

"Don't get stuck with a summer perfume now that it's cold," Beatrice told some housewife whose name Stella could never remember. She spritzed Poison on a card. The look on the woman's face said she was believing the whole gambit. Stella had learned from the best.

She kept busy removing the summer displays with beach balls and sandpaper, ready to replace them with fake leaves and orange tissue. Redecorating was one of her favorite parts of the job, something she never got to do in Vivian's house. Everything had to be just so at home, the perfectly matched drapes and pillows, even though most everything was bought at Wal-Mart. Stella wasn't fond of people putting on airs in the first place, but doing it when you were barely holding on to a façade was even worse.

She'd mentioned this to Beatrice once, and immediately received a lecture on taking pride in what you had. "It isn't the price of something that makes it valuable," her boss chastised. "It's the joy it brings you in looking nice."

Of course, perfumes were an entirely different matter. Beatrice had zero patience for women who walked in wearing Givenchy but wouldn't pay more than thirty dollars for cologne.

Many of Beatrice's regulars came in looking for her. It might have made for a piss-poor commission if she hadn't been so fair about the men. Stella got to handle most of them, even Mr. Haggardy, who arrived every month or two to purchase a bottle for his "wife."

"Even I can't go through that many bottles," Beatrice said. She was so disgusted with his all-over-the-map purchases that she'd immediately handed him over to Stella, who was happy to sell him something expensive and impressive for whoever might be on the receiving end, however long she lasted.

Stella had just started spreading the brown and gold leaves in the front window when the phone rang. Beatrice was still helping the housewife, so Stella headed to the counter to get it.

"Oh, thank God," her mother said. "Stella, get here. Get here fast. It's time."

Stella hung up the phone and crashed through the curtains to grab her purse. Grandma's car was still at Joe's, as they'd had to order the glass, but she could run. She'd been wearing sneakers every day, knowing this might happen.

She barreled through the store again. Beatrice looked up, and Stella choked out, "Grandma."

Beatrice nodded and shooed her out with a sympathetic look and a wave of her hand. "Take care, love."

Lawns and shrubbery blurred past as Stella ran flat-footed through the streets of Holly to her grandmother's house. Her hair pulled loose from the banana clip, flying behind her in a tangle. The cold blistered her cheeks and nose, making her eyes water. Several cars lined the street as she pounded out the last block. Was everyone in town there before her? If Vivian had waited too long to call her, there would be hell to pay.

Anger spurred her to run even faster. She dashed up the sidewalk and burst through the front door.

She dropped her purse and scarf just inside. The house was eerily quiet. She steadied herself and walked through the foyer to the living room.

A half-dozen people stood around Grandma's bed. Vivian, of course. And Stella's father. The preacher from Vivian's church. Two neighbors. And the nurse.

Stella tried to set aside her anger that all these people had obviously been notified ahead of her, but she was furious. She wanted Grandma all to herself, to clear them all out. Nobody loved her like she had. None of them. Tears threatened, and she bit her lip painfully to keep them at bay.

She pushed past the neighbors to get to Grandma's side. Vivian was holding one of Angie's hands. The preacher had the other.

Stella stepped in front of the preacher, not caring if it was rude, to make him let go. This was HER grandmother. HER grandmother's hand. She picked it up, so fragile and limp. Was she already dead? How did you tell? She didn't want to ask.

The nurse laid a stethoscope on Grandma's chest. "She hasn't breathed in about two minutes," she whispered. "But she still has heart tones."

Stella nodded, completely unable to speak. She glanced over at her mother, who sat, lips pressed together, almost as if she were being inconvenienced. Her father hovered, shifting from foot to foot, probably anxious to get back to his television programs. None of these people cared a whit. She wished she could kick them all out, make a fuss, scream.

The room was dim, the windows shuttered. Death permeated everything, from the grayness of the light to the grim expressions. Stella wanted to fill the room with sunshine. Why would anyone want to stay in a world this gloomy? She should turn on the radio. Play a Johnny Mathis record, Grandma's favorite. In fact, screw this, she would.

"I'm going to fix this, Grandma," Stella said. "It's all wrong, and I don't blame you a bit for protesting."

She kissed her grandmother's hand and laid it back on the bed. Without a glance behind her, she strode right up to the big gray curtains and yanked them back. Sunlight flooded the room, and dust mites billowed from the fabric like bursting dandelions.

The turntable sat in the center of the wall of shelves, the records lined up neatly in a cabinet below. Stella knew exactly what to choose. She tugged out a case featuring a young Mathis in a white shirt, open at the throat, a standard 1970s-styled type spelling out his name, followed by the title of the album, *I'm Coming Home.*

She powered up the record player with a gentle hum. The album popped and hissed as she lay the needle against the edge, feeling it slip into place to start the first song.

She walked back to the bed as a triangle measured out its tinkling introduction. By the time she had resumed her place, Mathis was belting out his main theme. "I'm coming home."

Melody, the longtime neighbor across the street, patted Stella's shoulder. "She would have loved that, Stella. Johnny was her favorite."

"She likes it right now," Stella said.

"Four minutes," the nurse said.

Stella tuned that out. She let the song wash over her, the millions of times she'd heard it, Grandma Angie fluffing a pillow or dusting a table or sorting through beads. She didn't sing, but often hummed along, sometimes breathing a line or two that particularly struck her.

Stella did the same now, squeezing her hand. And then Grandma's chin jerked upward, and she inhaled a huge rushing gulp of air, almost arching. Stella held on tight. "I'm here, Grandma. Right here."

And everyone seemed to fall away as Grandma Angie relaxed into the exhale, her jaw falling, her chest settling back onto the bed, as if she were slipping into some other dimension, eternally down and away from the body lying limply on the white sheets.

The song played on, and as it ended, the nurse slid the silver disc against Grandma's chest. She sighed as she pulled it away. "She's gone."

Stella could not let go of her hand, would not let go. She knew this was it, the last trace of warmth, the last gentle curl of her fingers. In the coffin she would be waxen and cold, her hands immovable and stiff.

In science class she'd learned that energy could change forms but never went away. She hoped that somehow her grandmother's love would stay with her, travel wherever she went. Because now that the only person she really considered family was gone, Holly was already shifting into a memory.

17

WAKE

DANE straightened as the door to Stella's grandmother's house opened. The woman standing there had to be Stella's mother. Same eyes. Same chin.

Too bad she had the pinched look of a constipated bulldog.

"You must be the new boy." She stepped back to let him in. "Stella's in the kitchen."

Dane paused to see if she would point the way. She didn't. He stepped past her into the gloom.

The whole place smelled of sliced ham and piecrust. He headed down the foyer and into the darkened living room. The hospital bed was gone. People milled around or huddled in clumps. The funeral was set for the next day, so nobody was wearing black yet. Gimme caps and overalls, tacky florals and shiny overly bright dresses. But no Stella.

A couple of the women glanced his way, but no one asked who he was or why he might be there. He turned toward the doorway with the most light.

He saw her before he'd even entered the kitchen, the curve of her back as familiar as the seat of his Harley. Her hair was twisted up in some fancy concoction of clips, leaving her neck bare. He needed to press his lips right there, and he knew that it would help her too, but a gaggle of disapproving women paced the room like jackals, watching him warily.

Stella rinsed dishes in the sink, taking her time, as if she could keep the world at bay if she just concentrated on that task. Dane knew. He remembered a similar moment when he stacked plastic containers and aluminum trays after his mother's wake. No fancy dishes, just a couple neighbors bringing stuff by, not expecting two single boys to return their cake plates or Pyrex, and so using throwaway stuff.

Here, everything was perfect, silver trays and crystal bowls. A whole table full of casseroles and cakes and finger food. Dane knew Stella wouldn't turn around, so he went ahead and crossed through the firing squad, avoiding eye contact. He slid his arms right around her and rested his chin on her shoulder. He wouldn't go so far as to kiss her, not yet, but he'd be close enough to smell her.

Her chin dropped to her chest as he fitted himself to her. She sagged a little, as though a great weight had finally been lifted and she could rest. He clasped her tightly, holding her steady. "I'm here, Stell. I'm here."

They hadn't seen each other in days. Once Angie died, it was impossible to get in touch with Stella. He'd asked Joe what to do.

"Just go," the old man had said, wiping his forehead for the hundredth time in five minutes. "Nobody kicks up a fuss at a funeral. She'll be at the house, you know."

Her hands were in the dishwater, still holding a bowl. He reached around and took it from her and set it on the counter. She wore an apron, a frilly red thing that had probably been Angie's.

He backed away from the counter, pulling Stella with him, untying the apron as they moved. It fell away, and she caught it before it hit the floor. "Grandma's?" he asked.

She held it to her waist a moment.

He took it from her, folding it carefully and laying it on the counter. He leaned in close. "I met your mom. Gracious AND charming. We're running away together after this."

She leaned her forehead against his neck, and he could feel her smile. "I'm so glad you're here," she said. "I hoped you would come, even though I didn't call. I should have called."

"Shh." He wrapped her up again. "You didn't have to call."

She sagged again, and he realized how coiled she kept herself. He vowed, as much as was in his power, to keep her relaxed and able to live in this moment, this hard moment, but one best managed surrounded with people who actually cared.

"Hello, Vivian." A man's voice in the kitchen startled everyone. Dane knew it was Joe, even as strangled as it sounded.

He and Stella turned to the man, spit-shined in an aging charcoal suit, his hair slicked back.

"Well, Joe," Vivian said. "You're here." Her face seemed all lips, red, lurid, disapproving.

"You couldn't chase me away from this," Joe said, handing her a dish. "I'm done with listening to that."

Dane leaned down to Stella again. "What does that mean?"

But Stella shook her head. He didn't know if that meant she couldn't say, or if she didn't know.

Vivian's face bloomed to match her mouth. "Don't you waltz in here on this day and give me any lectures about behavior."

"I kept my peace long enough," he said. "And I'm speaking at the funeral tomorrow."

"You'll do no such thing!" Vivian shouted, then caught herself. "There will be no speeches. Just a traditional service."

"Try and stop me." Joe whirled around then and headed back out the front door.

Dane let go of Stella. "I'll be right back," he said. He dashed through the kitchen, bumping into Vivian, still holding the casserole.

She whirled around, practically tossing the foil container on the counter. He heard her say, "What has gotten into this town?" as he flew through the foyer and out the door.

* * *

Dane nearly smacked clean into Joe, who stood just outside the door, admiring a rosebush. "Bloomed without her," Joe said, snapping off a pink bud and sticking it into his lapel.

Joe straightened, tugging down on the jacket. Sweat beaded across his forehead, so he extracted a white linen handkerchief to dab across his face. "Missouri weather. You never know what it's going to bring."

Dane couldn't think of a thing to say. Joe never dressed this way, acted this way. He was pickup trucks and gimme caps, overalls and grease.

Joe took off in his jaunty walk, one leg stiff, and Dane fell in step beside him. "You okay, Joe?"

They passed lawns of every variety, trimmed and trashed, lush with green and dead with dirt. Houses were no better. The street had no rhyme or reason, poverty next to middle class, a great jumble of human conditions. You'd never see this in Houston. People stuck together by the set of circumstances that befell them.

Joe stopped by a sagging house with a brown lawn. The porch bowed in the middle, as though its load was just too heavy.

"Look at the window boxes," Joe said.

Bright white plastic boxes lined all four windows in the front of the house. Inside were geraniums in red and pink, vivid color against the weather-beaten trim and fogged windows.

"This is Stella's house," Joe said. "You haven't been here, I reckon."

Dane shook his head.

"Her dad doesn't keep things up, but Vivian—Stella's mom—does what she can."

Dane frowned. "That woman makes Stella miserable."

"She makes most everyone miserable." Joe kicked at a red ant bed burgeoning by the cracked sidewalk. "Some people get all stirred up when people mess with them." Ants poured out of the granulated mound. "Eventually you turn into that thing they poked you into becoming."

Dane backed away as the angry insects spread wide. "So she wasn't always like this."

"Vivian was one of the kindest girls imaginable, just like her mother."

"So who kicked her? Stella's dad?"

"Nah, some man in town came along. Paid real fine attention to her. Stella was small then. Vivian was feeling blue after her father died. Her husband was the quiet sort, not one to get all up and romance-like."

"So she had an affair?"

"That man riled her up. We all knew it. We all saw it. And once she had a taste for it, there was no stopping her. All the women had to keep their men locked up."

"Really?" Dane couldn't see Vivian as the harlot.

"She don't have too many friends in this town." Joe turned away and started his awkward gait again.

Dane stared at the house, wondering which window was Stella's, then rushed to catch up with Joe. "So what was all that about back at Angie's?"

"Just an old man making a spectacle of himself."

"Did Vivian say something to you?"

"She doesn't have to." Joe stopped, catching his breath. "I know I'm not welcome. I'm the one who might have stepped on her father's perfect memory." He mopped his forehead again. "As a young man of sixty, I could walk these ten blocks a hundred times a day and not notice."

"And you did, I bet."

"I took any chance to catch a glimpse of Angie. Everyone knows it." He started walking again. "Angie knew it."

"Vivian got in the way?"

"Angie knew how her daughter felt. And family came first."

They stopped at the end of another cracked walkway leading to a modest house in sound condition. Flower beds full of spindly rosebushes sprouted anemic blooms.

Joe approached the flowers and plucked one. It disintegrated into a shower of petals.

"You grow these for Angie?" Dane asked.

"I can't grow weeds," Joe said. "I planted these knowing Angie would want to come save them. And she did. Would walk down to tend them right up until she went to the nursing home. I chose yellow and orange just for her."

Joe stared at the rail of his porch, and Dane knew he could picture himself there, looking down on Angie, kneeling by his struggling roses.

A wind kicked up, sending the weak limbs to swaying. More petals fluttered to the ground. "I'm sure they'll die now. Just as well. Been a slow death for all of us."

Dane kicked at the dirt. "So what you planning on doing at the funeral?"

Joe chuckled. "Having the time of my life." He looked up at the sky. "Angelica, my girl, you're going to love it." He climbed the three short steps of his porch. "You get on back to Stella, now, boy. There's lots of Angie in her." He unlocked the door, the thud of its closing reverberating in the spindly rail.

Dane walked along the bed of flowers, looking for one that might hold up to a careful plucking. On the end, a yellow one wavered at the tip of a flimsy stem, still rolled tightly into a fresh bud. He cupped the bloom and snapped it a foot below, wincing at the bite of a tiny thorn he hadn't noticed, too small to break the skin. He kept the petals protected in his palm as he continued back to Stella's grandmother's house, and the women who surrounded her like a cage.

18

FUNERAL ESCAPADE

DANE tossed his sports jacket over his shoulder as he walked Stella to the church for the funeral. Fall had given in to one last heat wave. He was used to it. Hundred degrees in September was the norm back in Texas. Overall, Missouri had been easy going on the weather.

Stella gripped his hand like a vise. They approached the imposing entry of the Baptist church, where Vivian had insisted the funeral be held. Dane tugged on the carved wooden handle and led them into a foyer where Vivian arranged photographs and a guest book, surrounded by a gaggle of matronly women in dark dresses.

"About time you got here," Vivian snapped. "I'm guessing you decided to stay out all night again even though your grandmother was cold in a coffin."

"I'm never going to your house again." Stella's voice was a growl. "I will never see you again after today."

The church women backed away, slipping through the doors to the sanctuary.

Vivian returned to the guest book, smoothing the feather on the plumed pen. "You always were so melodramatic."

Stella tugged them forward, through the same doors as the other women. Cushioned pews spread in both directions from the main aisle.

Tall, skinny windows with colored glass showed pictures of people in robes, and what Dane assumed was Jesus, always with a circle of yellow on his head.

At the front was the coffin, gray steel with blue satin. The top part was open, but you couldn't see inside from the back. Stella moved forward, parting the church women, who whispered together in the aisle.

As they neared the front, Stella let go of his hand and rushed to the coffin. When he caught up to her, she was smoothing the gray hair off her grandmother's face.

"She looks terrible," Stella said. "I never understand how people can say they look so good."

"It's just something to say," Dane said.

"All this makeup. This frozen expression. She's so cold." Still, she grasped the fingers curled artfully atop the gray linen dress.

Dane remembered the flower, and lifted his sports coat to tug the rose from the lapel. "This is from Joe." He laid the yellow bloom in the casket by Angie's elbow.

"She'd like that," Stella said. "She always helped him with his roses."

More people entered the church, waiting patiently in the aisle for Stella to finish.

Dane squeezed her shoulders. "Where should we sit?"

Stella turned away from the coffin. "Over there, on the front row."

One of the church women approached. "Stella, darling, you can wait in the family parlor. You will walk in with your mother when the service begins."

"We'll stay right here, if you don't mind, ma'am," Dane said. Stella relaxed beside him. "Stella wants to stay close."

The woman frowned, emphasizing the red lipstick that bled into the wrinkles around her mouth. "Well, all right then."

"Mighty obliged." Dane turned back to Stella.

"Thank you," she murmured and laid her head on his shoulder. "I'd rather be here."

"I know."

Mourners filed forward, glancing at Angie, then finding a seat. This was only Dane's second funeral. Just his mother's before. He'd been too young when his grandparents died.

But really, nothing was the same. There had been no church. No funeral home. They couldn't afford any of that. Just a few words over her grave at the cemetery. Him and Ryker and a few women whose houses she cleaned before she got too sick.

Dane vowed not to die impoverished and practically alone. He looked over at Stella, whose head was bowed so he could only see the tufts of her blond hair. Not her, either.

Organ music began, and Dane turned to marvel at the machine, up high in a section in the back like a balcony. The pipes extended up to the ceiling, and a woman in a robe pumped madly away with hands and feet, her gray hair bobbing. He felt the shudder of Stella next to him, crying now. He was helpless at this point, couldn't do anything but sit there and let her hold on. He realized too late his jacket was still folded over his arm.

More people streamed in, stopped by the coffin, and moved to their seats. Dane recognized a few from the shop, but nobody he'd rather avoid appeared—the bartender, the car sales jerks, Darlene, or Bobby Ray's contingent. He relaxed against the hard back of the pew. He'd make it through this and get Stella home, wherever that might be for her now. They could sort everything else out later.

A shadow in a window caught his attention. Behind the altar, off to one side, near the back.

It flashed again, something temporarily blocking the light. Too big for a bird. Dane glanced around, but no one else seemed to notice, focused on the prayer cards, or holding Kleenex.

He sat a little straighter, focusing in on the window, which was only a few feet wide and maybe two feet tall, but set high.

The object blocked it again, and this time Dane made out the shape of a head, then a hand pressed against the glass for just a moment. Someone was jumping, trying to peer in.

He looked down at Stella. Should he tell her? Who would do such a thing? Maybe Bobby Ray was looking for another ploy. He pulled his arm from her. "I'm going to be right back," he said.

Stella's face crumpled, and he hesitated. "I'll be back before it starts.

I promise."

She leaned away, and he stood, quickly striding back to the foyer. Vivian stood talking to a sheriff by the door, and upon seeing Dane, her eyebrows flew up. He pushed past them and out into the bright morning, quickly rounding the corner of the church to the wall with the window.

Joe was bent over, hands on his knees, breathing heavily.

"What are you doing?" Dane asked, helping his boss stand erect.

Joe leaned against the wall, running a hand over his hair to try and smooth the flyaway strands. "Damn Vivian called the sheriff to keep me out. Thinks I'll make a ruckus."

"Weren't you going to?"

"Absolutely." He turned back to the window, the bottom ledge just above his head. "Should have brought a damn ladder."

"There's no other way in?"

"Locked up tight. But this window," he pointed to the latch, "is broken."

Dane reached up and pushed on the bottom of the pane. It shifted a little. "It'll open all right. You sure that's what you want to do? You'll land right in front."

"Splendid. Now give me a boost."

Oh, man. "This is crazy, even for me."

"These are the things in life worth being crazy for."

"You know what you're going to say when you get in there?"

"I've known what I was going to say longer than you've been pissing in a toilet."

Dane spread his legs for stability and linked his fingers. "All right, then. Foot here, count of three. I'll lift you, you get the window open, second count, I'll push you through." He inhaled deeply, rushing out a breath. This was going to hurt like a mother.

Joe set his mud-caked dress shoe in Dane's hands. "I'm ready." He looked up to the window.

"One, two, THREE!" Dane shoved the old man in the air. "Get your elbows on the ledge."

Joe braced himself against the window, taking the pressure off Dane to hold him up. He pushed up the pane with one hand and wriggled partway through.

"Here you go the rest of the way!" Dane said, and lifted him again. Joe tumbled through, his feet flailing, then disappeared through the window.

He hoped the old man survived the fall.

19

JOE SAYS HIS PIECE

THE whole room gasped as Joe flung himself through a window by the altar, slithering headfirst down the wall and crashing into the acolyte's bench.

Stella stood up, clutching her Kleenex, which disintegrated in her fingers. "Joe!"

Nathan, one of the older members of the congregation, rushed to the front to help Joe stand. "You all right?"

"I am," Joe said, straightening his jacket, though he winced when he tried to take a step. "All things considered."

Nathan backed away as Vivian and the sheriff hurried up the aisle.

"Oh, no, you DON'T!" Vivian cried. "Arrest him, Terry."

Stella plopped back down on her pew, holding on to the back so she could see behind her. She hated that sheriff. He'd been one of the many men to lounge around the house in Vivian's glory days.

The sheriff shook his head slowly. "Viv, now, I can ask him to leave. But I can't arrest him without the church people pressing charges."

Vivian's face bloomed purple. "Where is the preacher? Or a deacon?"

"I won't be pushed aside," Joe said. He laid his hand on Angie's casket and looked down at her, losing his composure for a moment.

Stella sagged against the seat, wishing for Dane. Why wasn't he back?

Vivian rushed back up the aisle, the sheriff trailing. "At least keep HIM out!"

Stella turned to see the sheriff clutching Dane by the arm, leading him back toward the door.

She jumped from the pew. "Mother, stop it!" She raced up the aisle and grabbed the sheriff's arm to stop him.

"Hello, everyone," Joe said from the front.

The sheriff turned, as did Vivian. Stella took the moment to dash to Dane, wrapping her arms around his belly to prevent anyone from separating them. He pulled her in close, shifting to one side so they could see the front.

Joe tugged a handkerchief from his breast pocket and turned it over in his hands. "I loved Angelica Sutton," he said. "It wasn't any secret. She'd been alone a long time. Her husband had been a good man. One of Holly's finest. I had a lot of respect for him, and back then I had my own Maybelle. We both lost our loves the same year."

He looked down at Angie again. "Some people in this town thought it wasn't right for me to court Angie, even though we both waited for a proper mourning. There wasn't nothing wrong with how we felt. How I felt."

He looked out at Vivian. "I know Angie would want all this settled. For her family to stop living like they do, so mean-hearted."

"Well, I never!" Vivian rasped and moved on out the door.

Stella shifted aside to let her pass. Good riddance.

"Stella." Joe was talking to her now, so she turned back to the front. "Don't let her meanness cause you any more grief. Don't let her hate soil another love." He pointed toward Dane. "There's no reason why she shouldn't like that feller, or anyone else you take a shine to. Don't listen to her. I did, and now…" He pressed the handkerchief to his chest. "I'm going to do something I always meant to do."

And old Joe started singing, his voice high and wavering, "You are so beautiful."

The sheriff backed away, heading in the direction of Vivian, and so Stella let go of Dane. She walked back up to the front of the church and stood on the other side of Grandma's coffin while he finished his song.

When he was done, she took his elbow and led him down to the front pew. "You sit with the family," she said. They waited together for the pastor to come out, to deliver his standard speech about everlasting life and not weeping for the dead.

Dane sat on the other side of her. Vivian stayed away, and Stella closed her eyes, holding on to this moment, the last time she'd be in the same room as Grandma, and possibly, the last day she'd be in her hometown of Holly, Missouri.

20

PACKING

JANINE tumbled through the door of Dane's duplex, loaded down with collapsed cardboard boxes and duffel bags. "Okay, I scrounged up everything I could find. You ready for this?"

Stella pushed herself off the sofa. "Was the house empty?" They had waited for dark, assuming it would be easier to get around town unnoticed.

"Yes, I checked. Your mom and dad are at your grandmother's. Half the town is."

Dane returned from the kitchen, pressing a glass into Stella's hand. "Drink this up, and we'll go get you packed."

Stella downed the alcohol. "You stay here, Dane. Janine and I can handle my room."

"You sure?" Dane took the glass back and handed Stella his.

"Yes. In case Vivian comes back. No telling what she might have the sheriff do if you're there." She drained the second drink and set it on the crate. "That's better."

She took part of Janine's load from her. "We'll be back here in two hours."

Dane moved past them to open the door wide. "That's not much time to put a lifetime in boxes."

108

Stella lurched forward, dragging a duffel bag behind her. "I'll manage. Not that much I need to take."

Dane set the glasses on the floor and picked up the trailing bags. "You going in your grandmother's car? The Mustang doesn't have a lot of trunk space."

Stella shrugged. "No choice. Another reason to pack light." The night had cooled considerably, a fierce wind kicking up her hair. She unlatched the trunk and popped it wide. Everything inside was immaculate. Joe had taken good care of the car after replacing the back window.

She shoved the boxes and bags inside and moved over to let Janine dump hers in. Dane stood off to the side, looking at the moon. She remembered the night she'd asked him to come with her. She still wasn't clear if he was going along or not. She couldn't bring herself to ask him directly.

He stepped forward and laid the last things in the trunk. "We'll sort this out." He closed the lid and moved into her, kissing her lightly.

What did that mean, *sort this out?* Still, Stella couldn't bear to ask. "See you in a couple hours." She jumped in the driver's seat and cranked up the car, now humming as evenly as if it were new.

She backed out, watching him stand there in the dirt, barefoot, his white bandage glowing in the moonlight, his face dark. She wondered if she'd ever see him again. For some reason, she had doubts.

They avoided Angie's street but could see the cars lined along the curb leading to it. "They'll be tied up for a while yet," Janine said.

"Not sure I'll get a chance to say good-bye to the place," Stella said. Surely her mom would go home eventually, and Stella could sneak back in Grandma's house super late.

"You going to leave tonight?" Janine asked.

"Probably." Stella slowed as they turned onto her street, squinting at the house. "I want as many miles as possible between me and this godforsaken town before dawn."

"What about Dane?"

Stella slammed the car into park. "I don't know. I'm afraid to ask."

"He wasn't packing anything."

Stella opened the door. "I noticed."

The living room sat empty and dark, so rare. Stella couldn't imagine a time when her father wasn't propped in his recliner, TV flickering, even when she stumbled in at all hours. She didn't think he'd gone to his own bed in years. He definitely hadn't worked in a decade, after an oil-rig injury left him with a permanent limp.

They dragged the bags and boxes to Stella's room and dumped them on the floor. "There's some packing tape in the drawer by the kitchen sink," Stella said. "We can get these boxes back in shape."

Janine headed out, and Stella surveyed her room. She'd never see it again, of that she was sure. Bon Jovi posters hung at odd angles, remnants of her teen years. Dried flowers hung upside-down from a corkboard. Pictures, love notes, a calendar from 1982 still sitting on December, a gift from Grandma.

Stella sat on the pink bedspread, not sure where to start, heavy with emotion, and angry at the sentimental notion that she might miss the place. She shot back up, heading to the closet, jerking the clothes she wanted off the hangers and tossing them on the bed.

Janine returned with the tape and began assembling the boxes. "You'll need something to cushion anything breakable."

"We can layer the clothes in with the fragile stuff," Stella said. She wrapped each bottle of perfume in a shirt and placed them gently in a box. A drawer full of socks covered those, and she nestled her favorite lamp, pink with white crystals, into the socks and panties. She topped that box with her pillow, squished it down, and Janine sealed the box with tape.

"One down," Stella said, shoving it near the door.

"What about yearbooks?" Janine held up a shiny red one, from their senior year.

"Not interested," Stella said.

"This?" Janine held up a family picture from when Stella was three. "You've kept it out all this time."

Stella took it, looking at herself, tiny, sprigs of white ponytails sticking straight out, happy as a lamb. And her sister Marjorie, gangly and shy, a hand on Stella's shoulder. Even Vivian seemed softer, grinning, no scowl, her arm tucked around her husband's, who didn't smile, but still, amusement crinkled around his eyes, before the accident, and the rehab, and Vivian's indiscretions.

Stella tossed it on the bed. "Vivian can have it." She reached onto the shelf, a picture of her and Janine. "But I'll take this one." Then one of Grandma Angie with Stella and Marjorie. "And this one." Stella wrapped them in nightgowns and tucked them inside a red duffel bag.

They worked silently and quickly, Stella making a pile on the floor of things to take, and Janine dutifully filling the bags and cartons. Stella realized how little of her old life she wanted with her. "I think we're done," she said an hour later. Her room didn't look all that different, just more bare spaces on the flat surfaces.

"You ought to take some sheets," Janine said. "And dishes. You don't want to have to rebuy everything when you get where you're going."

"I don't want anything from here." Stella pushed one of the bigger boxes down the hall. "Maybe some things from Grandma's."

Janine dragged a suitcase behind her. "Might could have used some boys."

"We can do it." Stella kicked the door open, and the two of them together lifted the heaviest box, containing her stereo, into the trunk.

Headlights turned down their street, and they froze, waiting to see who it might be. The car slowed as it approached. "Your parents?" Janine asked.

The blinkers signaled a turn, but the car passed their driveway and pulled in next door. "The Grubers," Stella said. "Let's go in."

They hustled back inside, shutting the door. "Will she call your mother?" Janine asked.

"Probably," Stella said. "Let's hurry."

They ran to Stella's room, frantic now, and snatched up duffel bags and smaller boxes. As they darted back outside, car lights moved down the streets, turning corners, passing other blocks. "They have to be leaving Angie's," Janine said. "Nothing else is going on tonight."

"Crap, crap, crap," Stella said. "Move faster."

Back in her room, Stella assessed what was left. The Mustang wouldn't hold much more, plus Dane might have something. She hoped.

"One more trip, I think." Stella hefted one last large box and stumbled into the hall. "See if you can manage that suitcase."

Stella couldn't see in front of her, but the sound of crickets let her know the front door was wide open.

"Stella?"

She set down the box, grateful for a male voice. Her father.

"Yeah, Dad?"

He blocked the doorway, slightly stooped, looking every one of his fifty years and then some. "So soon?"

"Yeah. I gotta go."

Janine came up behind her and stopped abruptly.

Her father turned his felt hat in endless circles, gnarled fingers pinched and red. "I wish you wouldn't go."

Stella picked the box back up. "I'm all grown up. Time to leave the nest."

He moved aside as she barreled toward him with the box. By the time she had shoved the carton in the backseat and returned, he'd moved back to his recliner.

But when she passed the living room with her last load of bags, the TV remained dark. The dim reflection of her father in the screen didn't move or look her way. Stella paused, trying to think of something else to say, a good memory maybe, a trite farewell, but eventually gave up and just walked on by.

* * *

"That was close," Janine said when they were closed up in the car. "I guess your mother is still at Angie's."

"No doubt talking to her church biddies about how I wrecked the funeral." Stella backed out of the driveway. She refused to look out at the yard where she'd once jumped rope with her sister. It was done.

"So what now?" Janine reached down to flip on the radio. When Air Supply's "I'm All Out of Love" came on, she immediately shut it off again.

"I guess find Dane." Stella turned onto Main to head toward

Renters' Row. "Kill time until I can stop by Grandma's to pick up a few things."

"So this is really it?" Janine wouldn't look at her, fixed on the darkened windows of the shuttered businesses.

Stella slowed in front of Good Scents. She hoped Beatrice understood that she had to leave now. God, she should say good-bye. But she couldn't bring herself to watch even one more sunrise over Holly.

She reached in front of Janine and fished a set of keys out of the glove compartment. "Give these to Beatrice tomorrow, will you? The shop keys."

Janine took them. "Okay."

Stella sped up and turned onto Dane's street. "This part sucks."

They pulled up to the duplex, but everything was dark.

"I don't think he's here," Janine said.

"Figures." Stella killed the motor. "I guess I'll make sure."

Her tennis shoes sunk into the mushy dirt as she walked up to the door. What was he doing? Why hadn't he at least waited to say something to her? Good luck, maybe? Or thanks for nothing?

She knocked, waited, and knocked again. The wind kicked up. Fall was reestablishing its presence after the warm day. She shivered in her cropped shirt and tried to cover the one bare shoulder of her pink halter as she headed back to the car.

"We're early, you know," Janine said. "He might be here when we said, in another hour."

Stella plunked into the seat and rested her forehead on the steering wheel. "I can't just sit here."

"Let's see if they've left Angie's," Janine said. "We could hang out there and pick up the things you wanted."

"Yeah. I want the Mathis records. An address book. Some little things."

She started the car again and headed back to the center of town. Cars were pulling into the Watering Hole.

"Hey," Janine said. "Isn't that Ryker?"

Stella slowed and peered at the parking lot. Sure enough, Ryker was heading into the bar. She jerked on the wheel and pulled into a spot.

"Don't park by the road," Janine said. "Your mother."

"Right." Stella backed up again and cruised through the lot, hiding the Mustang behind a jacked-up truck.

Janine blew a rush of air out. "I don't think we should go in there."

Stella tugged the keys from the ignition. "I know. Nothing but trouble here before."

"Maybe we could wait out here?"

"We don't even know if Dane is in there." Stella opened her door.

They picked their way across the rough lot, asphalt kicked up in places, toward the noise and light. Janine suddenly halted.

"What is it?" Stella asked.

"That motorcycle," Janine said. "Is it Dane's?"

They approached it, partly hidden behind a shrub at the back corner of the bar. "Yeah," Stella said. "That's it."

"Now I really think we shouldn't go in." Janine didn't look like she was going to take another step.

Stella tugged on her arm. "I need to know what this is about. What Dane's planning to do."

Janine stepped forward hesitantly. "This could be a bad scene." She pointed across the lot.

Stella turned around. Bobby Ray's battered pickup was unmistakable in canary yellow. She let go of Janine and raced to the door.

21

MACHISMO

"WHAT the hell are you doing in here?" Ryker slid into a chair opposite him. "You got a death wish?"

Dane shoved the empty beer bottle away. "Not much into skulking out of town in the night." He'd figured Ryker would show even if he hid the bike.

"So you not going?"

"Yes, I'm going. Just not interested in looking like a coward."

A waitress appeared, and Ryker pointed at Dane's bottle. "Times two." When she left, he said, "I know that bullshit look in your eye." He jerked his head toward the bar. "And nobody misses that yellow piece of shit that Bobby Ray drives."

"I'm not looking for a fight."

"You're going to get one." Ryker waved across the bar. "Damn it all if Darlene isn't here too. What is it, a reunion?"

"I'm popular," Dane muttered. He'd positioned himself with his back to the corner for a reason. Couldn't have any of Bobby Ray's weasels sticking him from behind again. He knew it was stupid to come, but he wasn't up for looking chickenshit. Not if he was taking off. Ryker should appreciate that. He'd still be here. "I'm only thinking of you, brother," he said.

115

The girl came back with the beers, and Ryker tossed some bills on her tray. He handed one to Dane. "Here's to a clean getaway," he said and clicked his bottle against Dane's. "Not that I expect it."

Dane tugged at the corner of the label. The burly woman bartender was gone, and in her place was a skinny old man, more than happy to hover beneath the girls who took turns gyrating on the broad counter.

"So if we finish this round, I can get you out of here, right?" Ryker asked.

Dane kicked back his chair, rocking on two legs. "Brother, you are entirely too uptight." He checked his watch. "It's a good half hour until Stella will be back."

"Maybe I'm sentimental with good-byes."

Dane remembered the last time they'd parted, right after their mother's funeral. Ryker had taken it harder than Dane'd figured. Seemed to feel like he'd deserted her. Dane hadn't done much better, even though he'd lived in the same town. He rarely saw her, just picked up a few groceries occasionally and took them over. She hadn't wanted any fuss.

His eye caught a bit of peacock blue going in the air, and he shifted just enough to see Darlene stepping up on the bar to dance beside the other girl. She turned his direction and lifted a piece of her denim skirt to show him a long length of thigh.

Bobby Ray turned around to see who his sister was strutting for and glared hard at Dane.

Ryker groaned. "And here we go."

22

STELLA'S ARRIVAL

STELLA opened the door to a blast of sound. Bottles clinked, and the smell of stale beer made her think instantly of home and the endless TV trays of empties her father built up before Vivian could clear them out.

Damn, you'd think she was homesick. She clutched tight to Janine, taking a step toward the long counter, trying to ignore the girls dancing on it—someone was always up there shaking their hips. It was a town tradition, Holly's lowbrow debutante dance. She'd done it more than once. She scanned the tables. She saw Ryker first, and when he shifted his head, Dane. She was about to lunge forward when Janine held her firm. She followed his line of sight back to the bar, and then she noticed.

Darlene. Pulling up the hem of her skirt to show off for Dane.

Stella wasn't sure who to be pissed at. Him or her. But she couldn't keep the rage going, all the energy draining down into despair. She wouldn't even see Dane again. Not ever. She'd have to leave town without him.

Stella's legs wouldn't work. Dane was worth more than this. She couldn't just walk away without a good-bye. If it didn't go well, she would leave him to Darlene. She wouldn't let the end of their love affair stop her from leaving. Just another kick in the butt on the way out the door.

She straightened up, covertly sliding the triple-strand bracelet off her wrist and dropping it into her bag. He'd never known about it, and now she was glad. Nobody should know what a fool she had been.

Stella stared up at the girls, then back down at Dane, trying to figure out how to get him alone for a second, see what he was thinking. He picked up a bottle, scanned the bar, and saw her. He froze, his beer in the air.

23

DANE STEPS IN

DANE felt like a two-ton gorilla lumbering across the bar. Damn it all if Stella wouldn't show up right then. "I thought you were packing."

"I finished. What are you doing here?"

Janine jumped between them. "We got done early. We went looking for you."

He could tell Stella was pissed. Her friend was trying to run interference. Damn it all.

Stella pushed away from the counter. "Looks like you're already entertained. I'll be on my way."

Dane yanked her toward him. "I had nothing to do with her dancing on this bar. I couldn't care less."

"Didn't look that way to me."

"Woman, you have bad timing."

"And you have bad judgment."

He did. He knew it. But he couldn't say it, not with the whole bar watching. So he kissed her instead, hoping he could calm her down, convince her that Darlene's dancing was her doing, not his. He'd begun to think the whole thing was planned, waiting on some opportunity like tonight to play out.

The jukebox fired up Eddie Rabbitt's "The Best Year of My Life."

Stella cocked her head at him, and Dane knew he had to make this right, show her that Darlene meant nothing. He grasped her slender waist and hoisted her up to sit on the bar. "I'd much rather look at you," he said. "Will you dance for me?"

She sat there a moment, unsure. He pulled her knees apart and squeezed in tight against her. "You'll be the one everyone remembers."

Stella pushed him back, half smiling. "We are the couple everyone likes to talk about." She whipped her feet around and planted her sneakers on the bar to stand.

Dane could see the other girls in his peripheral vision, but still never turned his head. Stella watched him, shuffling her feet to the driving rhythm of the song. Janine sat on a barstool, looking worried. Bobby Ray must still be close, hovering, as she couldn't break her gaze from something just over his shoulder. He remembered the prick of the knife and wondered if he shouldn't avoid having his back to the man, but surely in a bar this crowded, Bobby Ray wouldn't try anything stupid.

The song rolled to its conclusion, and Stella stopped dancing. He could see she was done and raised his hands to help her down. Her eyes widened, but before Dane could determine why, he was abruptly shoved aside and knocked to the floor. Bobby Ray grinned down at him and snatched at Stella, grasping her around the knees and bringing her down.

Stella screamed just as Dane bounced right back up and jerked on Bobby Ray's arm to let her go. The moment Stella was free, he landed a beefy uppercut to Bobby Ray's jaw. Bobby Ray stumbled back for a moment, then grinned like this was what he had wanted all along. Everyone in the bar backed away, and Dane stood his ground, waiting for Bobby Ray's next move.

The man lurched forward, trying to knock a blow into Dane's belly, but Dane darted aside, grasping Bobby Ray's arm and twisting it under. Bobby Ray pulled loose and whipped around to knock a lucky shot straight into Dane's nose. Blood dripped from his face, but he simply wiped it on the back of his hand, sidestepping in a circle around Bobby Ray, deciding where to land the next punch.

Bobby Ray laughed. "You got a little something—on your face." When he turned to see if his cohorts were noticing his success, Dane rushed forward, plowing into Bobby Ray and taking him to the ground. A chair fell aside, splintering, and Dane knocked three hard shots into Bobby Ray's face before rolling off him. Surely the boy would be done after that. Dane was ready to walk away, and he didn't give a flying fuck what any of them might say.

He turned to Stella, who was white-faced, fear in her eyes. "Let's go," he said. She pointed behind him, and he turned to see Bobby Ray charging at him again. This boy was no match. Why couldn't he see that? Dane stepped aside once more, but Bobby Ray managed to adjust and attempt a light blow to his side.

Dane grabbed his arm and, while he had it, clipped Bobby Ray in the side of the head, then wrapped his arm around his neck, bending him over so he could shove a knee in his belly and knock him to the ground again.

"Dane! This has to stop!" Stella shouted.

He took in the room, the drunk girls and their boyfriends standing around, looking horrified or amused. The bartender, phone to his ear, no doubt calling the cops. Shit. They had to get out of town. He reached his hand out for Stella. "Time, Stella, now or never."

In the corner of his eye, he saw Bobby Ray get up, pulling on the legs of a barstool, then lifting the heavy wood base over his head. Good grief. The man hurtled forward, his aim as bad as the other two charges, and Dane snagged the leg of the barstool and yanked it toward him. They wrangled over it for a moment, then Dane switched tactics and, instead of pulling at it, shoved it hard back at Bobby Ray, smacking the edge of the seat into Bobby Ray's nose.

He hadn't realized how sharp the blow had been until he heard, seconds after it happened, the gasp of the bystanders, and the world went in slow motion, Bobby Ray's eyes rolling up into his head. They both let go of the stool, and Bobby Ray fell back. Dane knocked the stool aside and tried to catch him as he went down, breaking his fall so his head wouldn't crash against the floor.

"I've called the po-lice," the bartender said. "Y'all best chill it out now."

Stella dashed up to Dane, hands around his arm, pulling him back. "Let's go now," she said. "They can sort this out." She dragged him through the crowd toward the door. Dane glanced back. Darlene had her brother's head in her lap. Blood streamed from his nose, and now, out his ears. It looked bad. He'd lost it. Really fucked that boy up. And over what? A bar dance. A chickenshit show of two rutting bucks.

The whine of an ambulance grew louder as they headed to Dane's bike. "They'll take care of him," Stella said. "He'll be all right."

Janine showed up with Stella's purse. She was crying.

"Hush, Janine," Stella said. "Bobby Ray was asking for a fight."

Dane had nothing to say. He swung his leg over the Harley and jumped on the kick-starter. Stella took the purse from Janine. "Take my car," she told her. She got on behind Dane, and he relaxed a little, feeling her tucked close behind him. They were getting away, out of this town, far from the damn scene inside the bar.

The ambulance pulled in as they roared out, paramedics hopping from the back to drop a stretcher from the doors. Dane figured the police would come for him eventually, disorderly conduct for sure, probably assault. God damn it.

He headed straight out of town. The Harley would lead them somewhere, at least for that night.

24

MOTORCYCLE RIDE

STELLA tried to let the wind blow the memory of the last half hour from her mind. Her arms encircled Dane, the leather jacket scrunching inside the crook of her elbows. She inhaled. Oil and aftershave. Hint of the leather. It calmed her.

The bike raced forward, out of the parking lot and into the street. They passed the courthouse, the convenience store where the creepy guy once plotted to flash her, the grocery where Janine sacked and worried about getting sacked, the perfume shop, and then out, beyond the town, along the highway heading to nowhere, everywhere that wasn't here.

The wind tore at her hair, ripping through the perfect bangs and tangling the ends. Stella laid her cheek on Dane's shoulder blade, watching the trees whiz by, tall and majestic, the smell of pine overwhelming everything. She felt reckless, drunk, totally out of control.

Dane turned off the highway and onto a dirt road, slowing down as they bounced hard in the ruts. Stella knew the way. Ahead was a bridge, but you could take a side path and come right up on the river itself. The fork approached, and she tapped Dane's shoulder, pointing toward it. He turned, and the cone of light cut through the dark as they left the open road and moved into dense forest.

The motorcycle clipped the brush as they roared down the little-used path. Dane slowed, but Stella tapped him again, yelling, "Creek just ahead."

"Should we stop?"

She nodded against his back.

He pulled up just short of the drop-off and killed the motor. The creek gurgled below. Moonlight crossed the trees and glittered on the whitecaps below, rocks jutting through the stream.

"What now?" Dane asked. "Turn around?"

Her head buzzed. She answered without thinking. "Jump it."

Dane turned back to the creek, squinting. He could see the other side. "Two to a bike. Not sure we'd make it."

"We'll make it."

"You jumped it before?"

"Nope."

He hesitated, looking out. She knew they were both thinking of Bobby Ray, bleeding on the bar floor. Cheating death. He circled the bike around, going back as far as he could before the fork forced a turn.

The rush of it overwhelmed her. It felt good. Grandma Angie seemed suddenly close. She wondered if they would die after all, if fates were pushing them to risk themselves after what they'd just done.

The engine revved, a wild sound in the near-dark. The bike rumbled between her thighs, powerful and almost painful.

She clutched him, setting her feet firmly on the footrests. His body was tense, his arms stiff. She wondered why he did it, just because she asked. She wanted to ask for more, push him past every limit.

The bike took off, and she nearly lost her grip, but clamped down, her jaw tight. They raced along the path, limbs whipping at their knees, and the creek approached, closer, dim in the low light.

Dane kicked up the front end, and they were airborne, sailing through the night, over the creek. They descended too fast, and Stella knew they were lost. They'd go down into the rocky creek, bleeding into the current.

But one wheel touched down, then the other. They landed cleanly, and Dane eased back the power. The road curved suddenly, and he had to bank hard. Stella didn't move with him, and he overcorrected, and now they were in a skid, the ground sawing into her leg and everything a rush as they halted in a bruising collision with dirt and brush.

Dane flung the bike away to avoid getting crushed and was no more on the ground then back up, tugging at her. "Are you hurt? How bad is it?" He had no concern for himself, although she could see skin through his jeans, jagged tears filled with dirt.

Her thigh screamed with agony, but she'd landed in pine needles, so the damage was minimal. The skin was abraded, but nothing that needed medical help. He carried her nearer the creek, where the moonlight was better without the canopy of trees. "We'll live," he said grimly, and she laughed, louder and harder than she'd ever before. He set her on the ground, and she pulled him down, heart pounding, thrilled that they had done it, crashed and survived.

He didn't seem to get it, didn't understand what she was after, so she dragged him to the ground and rolled on top. Her knee howled, but she ignored it, bending down, pressing her lips into his mouth. Then he did understand, and they rolled, tumbling into the brush, coated in pine needles, bleeding and messy but alive, so alive.

The situation didn't call for romance, so she unbuckled him, exposed him just enough, and tugged off her panties beneath the short skirt, already near her waist. The forest stayed silent around them, the tree dwellers keeping their distance, until they rose again, stumbling back to the bike. "We can't go back now," Stella said.

Dane nodded. "Need to check the bike in daylight anyway." He knelt to spread his jacket in the pine needles. "Might be a rough night."

Stella shrugged and lay down, her head on the jacket. She was with Dane, and they were almost free. It would be enough.

* * *

Stella sat up and shook pine needles from her hair. Pretty much everything hurt. Her leg disgusted her, covered in bruises and scraped-up skin, blood encrusted in a few places. Her bangs hung in her eyes, and a quick swipe under her eyes yielded a finger covered in smudged mascara.

Dane nudged her with his knee. "Hey. You look beautiful."

Stella slid back down onto his shoulder. "Thank God we broke all the mirrors."

He pulled her in close, but she couldn't relax, aching and itchy and aware of the heat of the day rising around them. She sat up again. "Do you think the motorcycle will work?"

Dane propped himself up on his elbows. "I guess it's time to take a look."

They shuffled through the leaves and needles and crossed the road to where the Harley still lay on its side. Dane circled it a moment, then grasped the handlebar and the seat and heaved it upright.

Stella rubbed her arms and stared into the canopy of trees. Pale light filtered through, low and weak. Had to be early. Birds flitted among the trees, sitting on limbs and cocking their heads at her. She felt like she was in church, not that stuffy old building with all the biddies like Vivian, but pure, close to God Almighty himself. She wondered if she should pray, and for whom. Herself, or Dane. Or Bobby Ray.

She wondered if they'd taken him to a bigger hospital or if he was in town. They should probably stay clear of Holly for a bit. She could go to Grandma Angie's that night, after dark, when the town wouldn't be watching.

Her car. She'd have to find a pay phone and call Janine.

Dane sat astride the Harley and jumped on the starter. It roared and went out a couple of times, then finally fired up steady. He lurched forward, and stopped, then backed up to make a tight circle.

Stella wanted to cover her ears. The motor seemed so loud and painful at this hour, in such a quiet place.

"You okay, Stell?" Dane had to yell over the engine.

She nodded. "Is it okay?"

"Seems to be."

Stella looked around for her purse. It lay at the base of a tree, its contents scattered. She tried to kneel, but when pain shot through her, she plunked down on her butt and began tossing everything into the bag. Dane killed the bike to help her.

She spotted the bracelet a foot away the same time as Dane. He reached over and plucked it from the leaves. "It survived." He passed it to her.

Stella laid the triple strands on her wrist and slid the slide lock into place. She wouldn't take it off again. "I think I have everything," she said. "Where should we go?"

"Not to your grandmother's?" he asked.

"I don't think we should go to Holly today."

He brushed caked mud from his jeans. "Why not?"

"I'm pretty sure some people are going to have sore feelings over Bobby Ray."

"They should. He's hurt pretty bad." Dane stood and stared up into the trees, dots of light crossing his face. "I should have stopped it sooner."

Stella knew this was coming. "He started it."

"I shouldn't have let it go anywhere."

She heaved herself up from the ground. "It happened. We can't change it. All we can do is decide where we go and what we do from here."

"So where do we go from here?"

"Let's drive into Branson. I'll take out some money, and we can pick up something to wear." She looked down at their tattered outfits. "If any place will let us in."

"Sure you don't want to go home and clean up?" He picked a pine needle from her hair.

"I don't have a home, remember?" Stella shook her head, sending dirt and leaves flying.

"We can go to the duplex."

"No. Not Holly. I can't go there. Branson isn't far."

Dane straddled the bike. "Branson it is."

"And I'll call Janine."

"Sounds like we have a plan."

He fired up the motor again, and Stella climbed on behind him. They took the long way around the creek on the road. By the time they hit the highway, Stella felt better. The wind tore the trash from her hair, and she held on to Dane. As long as she was putting miles between herself and Holly, she'd be all right.

Dane pulled up to a truck stop a few miles south of Branson. "We can clean up here," he said after cutting the motor.

Stella watched a burly bush-bearded man in a gimme cap limp out of the diner and climb up into his eighteen-wheeler. "We definitely won't scare the regulars."

Dane laughed. "Nope. And they have showers plus a little shop in the back. We can pick up something to wear, as long as you like your overalls loose." He wrapped an arm around her. "We could get a matching set."

She punched his shoulder as they crossed the parking lot. The place was immense. The glass doors opened to a diner on the right and a big open shop on the left. Dane led her to the back corner, where pay-phone booths lined one wall. "You can call Janine here." He tried to fix the torn sleeve to her shirt. "I'll grab you a T-shirt or something."

Stella opened the door to a booth and flipped on the light. The air was stale and muggy, smelling faintly of beer. She dug a quarter out of her purse. She was asking a lot from Janine, who was no doubt still upset about the bar. "Please be my friend still," she whispered and dialed her home number.

Janine's mother answered. Not a good thing. She already borderline hated Stella.

"Is Janine around?"

"Stella? Where are you? And that boy?"

"I really need to talk to Janine."

"I don't want her mixed up in all this."

"It was just a fight."

"Then you haven't heard."

Stella stomach lurched. "Heard what?"

"That boyfriend of yours really hurt Bobby Ray bad. They had to fly him to County in a helicopter."

Stella almost fainted with relief. She'd just known Bobby Ray was dead. "How is he?"

"Bad. Getting surgery. More than one, from what I hear."

"Mrs. Thomas—Bobby Ray started that fight."

Silence.

Stella twisted the cord around her fingers. "And most people don't seem to realize Bobby Ray cut Dane up with a knife a few days ago."

"You were always into trouble, Stella. I need you to stay away from my daughter."

The line went dead.

Stella held the receiver in her hands. What would she do now? Janine had her car and everything in it.

Dane pressed his face against the window, smashing his nose. Stella wanted to laugh at him, her beautiful Dane. He had no idea how bad things were. Stella couldn't get her car. They couldn't go home. What would they do?

He noticed her distress and popped open the door.

"Stell? You okay?"

She could see on his face the same worry, that something worse had happened.

"Oh, Janine's mother wouldn't let me talk to her."

He exhaled slowly, and Stella knew he'd been worried she'd tell him Bobby Ray was dead.

"You got any other way to get in touch with her? Her boyfriend?"

"Yeah, I can call Nick." She smiled up at him. "You're the brains of this getaway."

He held up a bright green "Show-Me State" T-shirt. "Still feel the same?"

She snatched the shirt from his hands. "I never said you had good taste."

"It said 'show me,' and I thought of you." He scooted her over on the booth and closed the door. "I knew the words would give me an excuse to look exactly where I wanted to all the time."

She dropped the shirt and wrapped her arms around his neck.

He pulled her close. "It's a rough day. We'll get through this."

"You make me want to slow things down."

"Well, today, we will do that."

Stella looked down at the shirt. She didn't want to tell him about Bobby Ray. Maybe she just wouldn't. He'd probably be fine. Just some recovery before going back to his ugly self. It was an unfortunate thing, but not something that ruined their lives. Today, they'd play. They'd have each other.

She whipped off her pink halter. "That perked you up, now, didn't it?"

Dane glanced at the window to the booth. He hung the shirt from a little hook made for coats, then stretched it over the window, opening the door and closing it to catch the sleeve so it stayed in place. "I'm feeling quite perky now."

And despite the tight quarters and a bevy of bruises, she found they could escape no matter where they were or what might wait for them in the next hour. Even so, Stella worried. Something this good had to have a downside. Just how far it might slide, she didn't know.

25

NIGHT AT ANGIE'S

DANE throttled the bike down as they entered Holly from a back street around midnight. He didn't know all the alleyways and cut-throughs as well as Stella, but she'd shown him the way. Once they arrived at the end of her grandmother's street, he killed the Harley and they walked it along the sidewalk.

"House looks dark," Dane said.

"Yeah. I think we'll be all right," Stella said. "Let's go in from the back. Bring the bike around."

They cut across the yard and pushed through a broken-down gate. Stella dug through her purse and pulled out her keys. Dane leaned the bike against the house. The moon slid behind a cloud, pitching them into near-blackness. Stella dropped the keys and cursed. He felt his way along the house, tripping over a coil of garden hose.

The landscape brightened again, and Stella fumbled with the door. "I don't get it," she said.

He came up behind her on the stoop. "Get what?"

"The key. It isn't working."

"Here." He fished his own keys from his pocket and squeezed a tiny light hanging on the chain. He took the key from her. It wouldn't go in the lock.

"Sure it's the right one?"

"I've been going in this door all my life."

He shone the light on the lock. "It's new."

"What?"

Stella crowded in. "Holy shit. She changed the locks. My mother changed the locks."

Dane squeezed her arm. "She's upset, Stell, that's all."

Stella turned and leaned her back on the door. "She locked me out of the only place I ever called home."

Dane could feel the trembling in her legs. "I'll get you in. Not like a little lock can stop someone like me."

He shone the light on the lock again. He could break it, but he'd rather try another way first. Something quicker and easier. "What are the windows on the back side?"

They stepped off the porch just as the moon faded out again. They waited, and Dane pulled Stella against him, nice and tight, so she wouldn't get any worse off. They'd had a pretty good day, riding through the Ozarks and eating fried fish in paper trays near Table Rock. Stella looked different after showering at the truck stop, all fresh and shiny, no hair spray or makeup. He liked her just fine that way. Better, even, though she kept fussing over it.

She'd wanted to toss the pink halter, but he'd torn a strip from it, a swath of hot pink he'd tied in a knot on the metal chain he kept on his hip. Something about the shirt was important to him, like it marked a big moment. He couldn't explain it, just went with it.

"When is Nick bringing the car?" he whispered. Stella had arranged for Janine's boyfriend to leave the Mustang with her stuff in it in front of Angie's house.

"Anytime now. I had planned to hide it in the garage."

The moon appeared, and Dane surveyed the back. A high bathroom window was no good, but all the other rooms had nice low sashes. He quickly pushed up on them all. Locked.

"You okay with me breaking one?" he asked her. "I can do it quiet-like."

"Yes. I'd do the living-room one. It has a sofa beneath it."

They walked along the house. Dane bent and snatched one of the big stones that bordered the flower garden, now overgrown and beset with weeds. He thought of Joe and the roses. He wouldn't get a chance to say good-bye to him. The old man might not even want to see him again, after all that happened. Stella had finally told him about Bobby Ray after dinner. He hoped for all their sakes that the boy would pull it out.

Dane pulled his shirt over his head and wrapped the stone in it. He checked the panes and tapped the corner of the rock against it. The window didn't yield at first, so he finally reared back and smashed it through. The noise wasn't as tremendous as they thought it might be, but still, they waited.

A few dogs barked. A neighbor somewhere along the line shouted at one to be quiet. After a few minutes, all settled down again.

Dane picked carefully at the glass, pulling out shards rather than letting them fall through. He used the shirt not just to protect his hands, but to avoid obvious fingerprints. He was quite sure Vivian and the sheriff would be glad to implicate him on as many crimes as possible.

"Let me go in," Stella said. "I can find my way around more easily."

He reached in and unlatched the window, shoving it wide. He grasped Stella's waist and lifted, flashing back to the same moment in the bar. He couldn't change things, no sense thinking about it. She clutched the window and wiggled through.

She popped her head back out. "I'll let you in the back door."

Crazy mission they were on. Glass tinkled from his shirt as he shook it. He crossed the yard, pulling it over his head. He looked forward to when they could leave. He still had all his stuff over at Ryker's. They'd go for that once he had the car. At this point, he was sure he wanted to leave Holly, and he knew that going with Stella was the right thing.

Stella opened the back door and stepped aside. They came into the kitchen, where he'd seen her with all the women and their food. It seemed a lifetime ago.

"Let's just sit a minute." Stella collapsed on the sofa. "I have to think about what I want to get."

"Everything looks in place still," Dane said.

"Yeah, I half expected the house to be empty."

"Not even your mother could accomplish that in a day."

"Don't be sure. She got the locks changed." Stella jumped back up and headed to the entryway.

Dane followed, arriving just as she bent before the front door to examine the lock. "Yep. Every last one. Why would she want to keep me out?"

"You left her."

"Did she think I'd steal everything? It's more mine than hers anyway." Stella leaned wearily against the wall. "I guess we don't have time to sleep."

He pulled her to him. "We have time to do anything we want."

Stella turned to the kitchen. "She'll be here tomorrow. She's already moving things around. Look." The kitchen floor was covered in collapsed boxes.

"We should probably leave before dawn, then," Dane said. "Might as well take one of those and get the things you were wanting."

Stella retrieved an already-assembled box from the counter. "Can you find all the Johnny Mathis records? They are on the bookshelf in the living room."

"Will do." He took the box and returned to the darkened room, shining his key light around until he found a small lamp. He brought it to the floor and covered the top with a book to keep the light low.

The records were easy to locate and pack. He sat back on the floor, wondering where Stella was, and if she wanted to be alone or if he should find her. A clock ticked in the silence. Finally, he got up to see where she might be.

He almost didn't notice her, sitting on the floor on the far side of a great flowery bed in what had to be Angie's room. She'd tied the drapes closed and turned on the bedside lamp. Her head was down, so he could only see her blond hair cascading to her shoulders over the green shirt.

"Stella?"

She looked up at him. "I found something."

He lay across the bed, immediately feeling better, the relief of resting. "What?"

She laid a bracelet in front of him, beads strung on two wires.

"It's pretty."

"I've never seen it, and I saw everything of Grandma's."

"What do you think it's for?"

She pointed to several colored bits. "These are love beads."

"Okay."

"But these aren't the colors she used for Grandpa."

"So some other love."

"Exactly. But why these bright ones? Yellow and orange? They weren't colors she ever wore."

The roses. He remembered the flowers in front of Joe's house. "They were for Joe."

"What?"

"He planted roses for her. Yellow and orange. He told me, the day I came to see you before the funeral."

Stella ran her finger along the beads. "I see it now. A strand of yellow and orange. For him. And the love beads. For her." She looked up at him. "Oh, Dane. They never got to be together."

She came up and onto the bed then, shivering. They lay together, the bracelet between them. He clasped it around her wrist, beside the other one, with three strings. "You make bracelets too?"

"It's yours," she said. "I made this one for you." She fingered the triple strand.

"You did?"

"It was—" She touched the beads. "It was the last one Grandma and I did together. The day after the night on the tower."

Dane lifted her arm and kissed the bracelets. "You knew already."

"I was delusional." She tried to laugh.

"You were right. What do our colors mean?"

She pointed to the wood beads. "Calmness. Gentleness." Then to the brighter ones. "Danger. Recklessness."

He chuckled. "What about the middle?"

"Those are for me."

He fitted her even closer against him.

"I'm so tired," Stella said. "Tired of everything."

"We can sleep for a bit." Dane also felt himself shifting down. It had been a long time since they had rested, really rested. "We have to wait on your car anyway."

"We can't sleep all night. I still have to gather some things."

"We won't. I'll listen for the car."

"Vivian will be here in the morning."

"We'll be gone."

She settled back down against him. "Just for a little while, then."

"Shhhh."

He knew he shouldn't fall asleep, that Vivian discovering them would make Stella even more upset.

He awoke to a loud insistent banging on the front door, and the shouts of "Police! Open up!"

26

ARREST

STELLA startled awake. "What was that?" She jumped out of bed and yanked at the curtains. Still dark outside, but the first signs of dawn were beginning to show in the grayness over the rooftops.

The banging came again. "You have thirty seconds to open this door, or we'll break it in!"

Stella peered harder at the backyard. One of the deputies stood beside Dane's motorcycle. The stone they'd used to break the window was at his feet.

She closed the drapes. "Shit. Vivian's called her ex. She'll probably try to get you arrested for breaking and entering."

Dane jumped off the bed. "I'll go talk to them."

"No," Stella said. "I'll handle it. This is my house too. Vivian's not going to get anywhere. Please stay back here."

Stella rushed to the entryway. "Stop it!" she shouted. "I'm here. I'm opening the door."

But when it swung open, the man on the porch wasn't the sheriff she knew, the one Vivian liked to cart around. "Who are you?"

"I'm Sheriff Dunning. I'm looking for Dane Scoffield."

She knew it. "You realize I'm the one who broke into my own house."

"Ma'am, this is a felony charge."

"What? Since when is breaking your own window a felony?"

"Is Dane Scoffield here?"

Dane turned the corner and came into the entryway. "I am."

"Dane! I asked you not to come up!"

"I think there's more to it than us being here, Stell."

The sheriff stepped inside, followed by another officer holding handcuffs.

Stella felt faint and explosive simultaneously. "What are you arresting him for?"

"The charges will be announced by the judge at his arraignment within 48 hours of his arrest," the sheriff said. "Please turn around."

Dane turned his back to them to be cuffed.

Stella walked around to his front. "I'll be there, baby. I'll make Vivian call it off."

He kept his eyes on the floor, shaking his head.

She bent down to look him in the face. "You think this is about Bobby Ray?"

"The boy is dead." The voice came from the kitchen. Stella moved to the doorway and saw her mother examining the lock. "Figures I couldn't keep that delinquent out." Vivian shut the door. "Bobby Ray died last night at County from swelling in his brain." She grasped Stella's arm. "You're coming with me. I've had cops swarming my house since 5 a.m., looking for you two."

"I'm sure you didn't mind that, with your taste for the badge."

Vivian slapped her flat across the cheek. The sound echoed in Stella's ears, reverberating. "Mother, I already left you. You can stop acting like a parent."

"You will come home with me. And you will stay away from that man." She tried to grab Stella, but Stella fought hard and got free.

"Don't touch me, Mother. If I have it my way, I will never see you again."

The sheriff was reading off something to Dane. Stella ran back to him. "I'll see you very soon. Okay?"

But Dane stared at the ground, resigned, it seemed, to whatever happened.

"Dane! Look at me!"

He lifted his head, so defeated that Stella couldn't stand it. "I will stand by you on this. You hear?" The sheriff stopped his droning, and the deputy tugged on the cuffs, pulling Dane back.

Dane swallowed and turned toward the porch. The sheriff led them to a squad car, opening the back door and pushing down on Dane's head to force him in.

Stella ran into the yard, grateful to see the Mustang out front. Nick had brought it, and they hadn't even noticed.

Several neighbors were standing on their porches in robes, holding their papers. The sun was just cresting the horizon to the east. Stella watched the car as it pulled away from the curb and into the street. She looked down at her T-shirt. She had to change, dress in something more suitable, get down to the jail. She had money. She would get Dane out on bail. And she'd never speak to her mother again.

PART TWO: *Separation*

27

BAIL BONDS

STELLA examined her reflection in Beatrice's bathroom mirror. Long black skirt, silky white blouse, pearlized twister beads. All respectable. She teased her hair a little less than usual and kept the eye shadow to shades of gray.

Beatrice's voice still droned in the hall, where she kept her telephone on a little combination table and chair, talking to bail bondsmen. It was all so complicated, cashier's checks and not knowing how much bail would even be.

She stepped through the door, watching Beatrice's head bob as she listened. "Yes, he was arrested this morning. No, I'm not sure when the arraignment will be."

She nodded at Stella and covered the mouthpiece. "I've got one. He's going to check when Dane is most likely to go before the judge for bail. Dane's the only one in there as far as he can tell, so it will either be at eleven or at three."

One good thing about Holly, Stella guessed. It held its own courthouse, a tiny jail with two cells, and Dane wouldn't have to sit around waiting his turn to be released. "Does he know the judge?"

She shook her head. "Didn't ask. But Betty Wainsfield works up there as a clerk. We can call her next."

Stella's stomach iced over. "But Betty is Bobby Ray's aunt."

"Used to be," Beatrice corrected. "She was married to Bobby Ray's no-good uncle. But she left him a couple years ago. Bad blood there. She's nice enough. Don't worry."

But Stella did worry. Surely Dane's lawyer would move the trial. No way could they be fair in Holly.

Beatrice uncovered the mouthpiece. "Yes? This afternoon? Okay. We'll be there." She hung up. "It'll be at three."

"Do we need to find him a lawyer?"

"Mooner said Dane was already holed up with the public defender."

"Mooner?"

"The bondsman."

Stella didn't know anyone who went by Mooner. "Is that going to be good enough? Shouldn't we get him his own lawyer?"

Beatrice flipped through the tiny Holly phone directory, the size of an Avon catalog. "There's Rick Pierce we could call local. I'm sure there's tons in Branson who'd take the case."

Stella braced herself against a wall, still feeling achy and sore from the motorcycle crash. "How do we know what to do?"

Beatrice shoved herself to standing and enveloped Stella in a Chanel-drenched hug. "Let's see how the arraignment goes. Besides, Dane or Ryker might have already called someone in. We don't know anything."

"I don't think I can stand around all day," Stella said. "I'll go crazy. Can we just hang out at the courthouse, see what news we can get?"

"Okay, Stella. Let me finish getting myself together. Bring a book or something. You'll really go crazy if you just sit up there with nothing to do."

* * *

Beatrice had been right. After an hour sitting on a hard bench outside the lone courtroom door, Stella was going crazy, pacing the hall, pausing constantly to listen and see if anything was happening inside. Only a hungover drunk had been dragged in for the 11 a.m. session, and he'd been sent home. Otherwise, people with parking fines or speeding tickets came and went, going up to the window to pay or arrange for defensive driving. The deputies had been busy earning their paychecks. Without a car, Stella had almost never run into them, although Janine had been stopped a time or two.

"I'm going to walk over to the shop," Beatrice said. "It'll stay closed, but I just want to check to see if I missed any deliveries."

Stella plunked back down on the bench. "You don't have to be stuck here with me."

"I'm glad to." Beatrice pushed herself up, rubbing her rump. "Everyone knows where to find me if they need me. Not like there is ever a perfume emergency."

"I know I should go, get away from here. But I just can't." Stella leaned her head back against the wall, staring up at the dusty false ceiling above, its dirty rectangles no longer white.

"I understand that, sweetpea. Don't think twice about it. Your whole life is on the line here. I get that." Beatrice swept her purse up from the bench. "I'll be right back. Should I bring you something to eat?"

"No. I couldn't. I'm in knots." The very thought of food made her stomach lurch.

"Maybe some juice, then. I'll be back. Maybe I'll try to get in touch with Joe. See if Ryker came to work. He should be here." Beatrice waddled toward the massive front doors, surrounded by stone. The grand entry fell quiet, the marble floor gleaming, a bird perched in the windowed arch above the doors. Typewriter keys clacked from some distant desk behind the glassed-in counter, now empty.

Dane. She closed her eyes and tried to conjure him. On the tower, behind her. Kneeling beside Grandma's bed. Curling her into him on his sheet-covered sofa. In the woods. The phone booth. Breaking the window. But the other scene kept coming forward, his hands, holding that barstool, shoving it hard forward, into Bobby Ray's face. The way Bobby Ray fell, straight back, blood streaming everywhere.

If only she'd never taken Grandma's car to the garage, never tried to get herself between Dane and Darlene. She was a part of this, the whole turn of horrible events. And now Bobby Ray was dead. She remembered suddenly his fifth-grade picture in the yearbook. Before he'd gotten all weird and nasty, bullying kids and popping girls' bras, cornering them and trying to make them kiss him. She'd actually drawn a heart around his picture, his cute smiling face, like he was somebody she might love.

What had changed him after that year, led him into the man he had become, the one who would stick a knife in a stranger over a woman who didn't want him? She ought to know. Everybody in Holly knew what warped everybody else. But the town must still hold some secrets.

Her stomach burned so hot and sick that she felt sure she'd throw up in the potted plant by the bench. She gulped air, trying to figure out if she could make it to the restroom or should just sit tight.

The door opened, and Darlene came in, clutching her mother. Stella wanted to hide somewhere, but they saw her. "You little whore," the mother said. "You little bitch."

A man in a suit followed close behind. "In here, ladies," he said, holding open the door to the courtroom. "We can wait inside."

Stella stood. They could go in now? But the man closed the door behind them, so she plunked back down. She didn't want to go in there alone, with them and their sobs and their taunts. But they were right. She was the whore and the bitch. And even though Bobby Ray was an asshole and had something coming, he didn't deserve to die.

Maybe she should go in and apologize or something. She smoothed her skirt but knew she couldn't do it. They didn't want to see her. They wanted to hate her, and she'd have to let them.

Beatrice pushed through the doors again, this time with her own man. He wore a rumpled suit that didn't fit, gray with prominent white pinstripes, something her father might have worn decades ago. His blue socks were electric in white shoes.

"This is Mooner," Beatrice said, clearly displeased. "Found him in the parking lot. He'll be ready to post the bond."

"My fee is ten percent," Mooner said. "I've never seen the judge do more than $100,000 bail, but if he does, that's ten grand you'll need. You got that?"

"I got that," Stella said. It would wipe her out, years and years of saving to leave Holly, but she had it.

"It won't be that bad," Beatrice said. "They might even let him out on his own recognizance."

"Don't bet on that," Mooner said, hitching up the back of his pants, revealing more blue sock. "They had quite a search for him, and they'll want to make sure he don't run."

"Will you being here make the judge feel better?" Stella asked.

Mooner rocked back on his heels. "You bet. Never lost a man. Nobody jumps on my bonds."

Stella wondered why a man who could command that kind of money dressed so poorly.

A deputy came out the door of the courtroom. "You may come in. Mooner, you carrying?"

Mooner lifted a pants leg to reveal a pale calf encircled with a black strap and a Colt revolver. He tugged the gun out and handed it to the deputy. "Right-e-o," he said. "Don't lose it!"

The deputy dropped the gun in a bag and stepped back to let them inside.

The courtroom only had three small rows of benches, then the two tables for the lawyers, and a couple rows of chairs to one side for a jury. It was empty except for Darlene, her mother, and the man in the suit. The women were boohooing into linen handkerchiefs. Despite living all her life in Holly, this was one place Stella had never been. She would have been perfectly happy to leave without ever seeing it.

Beatrice held tight to Stella. "You'll be fine," she said. "Let's sit over here."

They chose a spot farthest from the others. The cushion was a great relief after the hard seat outside. Air conditioning blasted them from the ducts set in another false ceiling. Stella kept watch on a side door, where she guessed they'd bring Dane in.

A large clock above the judge's bench ticked loudly. The other women quieted down, and they waited. Three o'clock came and went, and Beatrice shifted uncomfortably on the bench. Finally, the same deputy entered the room from the side door, taking a position near the front to stand guard. "Will he be the bailiff?" Stella asked.

"Probably," Beatrice whispered. "Everyone pulls double duty around here."

The door popped open again, and this time, Dane came through first, followed by one of the deputies from that morning, pushing him forward. Stella's heart clenched. He wore slate-blue scrubs and had clearly been washed down. His hair lay flat against his head, and without his jeans and black shirts and chain, he looked more all-American boy than edgy biker. She didn't care. He was still beautiful, even more so in his vulnerability.

"Murderer." Bobby Ray's mother only muttered it, but in the quiet of the room, it had reach. Dane looked across the benches, noting Darlene and her mother, then settled on Stella. She saw his shoulders sag, but she had no idea if it might be relief or unhappiness. She gave him the tiniest wave, and he nodded grimly.

The deputy pushed him onto a chair behind one of the tables. The door opened again, and a disheveled twenty-something entered, holding a stack of papers that he plunked down on the table next to Dane.

"The public defender," Beatrice whispered. "Looks a bit wet behind the ears."

Stella didn't know him. He must not live in Holly proper. Another man entered, and this one she did know. Arthur Mendell had been a big-shot lawyer in Springfield until he decided to move to Holly to be near his daughter after his wife died of cancer. Stella had sold him perfume a time or two. She knew he did something at the courthouse, but hadn't paid much attention to what. Must have been a step down for him, but she felt better seeing him there. Surely someone like him wouldn't do anything untoward to Dane.

Arthur nodded politely at all of them and rested his briefcase on the other table. The first deputy left the room for a moment, and a harried-looking Carmen, a woman who regularly came into the shop, hustled in from the side door. She sat at a small table off on one side and uncovered a little machine. The secretary, or whatever they were called, Stella guessed. She had no idea Carmen worked here.

The deputy returned and announced, "All rise."

They stood, Stella wincing when she saw Dane struggle to get up in his cuffs, no doubt still hurting from the crash. She wished she had sat closer to that side. She hadn't known where he'd be. She'd never felt so far away from someone, despite being so near.

The judge entered in his black robes, certainly pushing seventy, a little stooped with barely a hair on his head. He sat down, and everyone else followed suit except Arthur and the young guy. Stella's heart hammered painfully.

"Tell me what we have here," the judge said, shuffling through some papers.

Arthur began. "We have the defendant, Daniel Scoffield, arrested this morning at 976 Cherry Drive."

"What are the charges?"

"Murder one."

Stella couldn't breathe, and Beatrice gripped her hand. What were they doing?

The younger man sorted through his stack. "No history of violence, sir. Gainfully employed locally at Joe's Garage. Family in town."

The judge pointed to Mooner. "You here to post bond for this fellow?"

Mooner rocked on his heels. "I am."

"Is he a flight risk?"

"No, sir."

Arthur stepped forward. "If I may, your honor. The defendant has had altercations not only with the victim, but also with another young man from this town, Allen Worth. And the victim's sister and mother also feel threatened by the defendant. He made a spectacle at the sister's place of work. We have two witnesses willing to testify to his angry state and his potential for violence."

The judge looked up. "Which one is the sister?"

Darlene rose shakily. "I am, sir."

The bailiff stepped forward. "You want me to swear her in?"

The judge waved him away. "Come up here, child."

Darlene walked to the end of the bench and approached the judge with obvious nerves.

"Why are you afraid of this man?" the judge asked.

"He—he attacked Bobby Ray," she said. "And we used to go together."

"And now you don't."

"No, sir."

He looked out at Dane, assessing him. "And what happened at work?"

"He came in, really mad."

"What about?"

"My brother. Got him mad."

The young man in the suit stood up. "Objection? She isn't even sworn in, and she's giving testimony that may be pertinent to the case."

The judge waved him away. "I'm just trying to decide on bail. Sit down, Mr. Flemming." He turned back to Darlene. "So what happens when this particular young man gets angry?"

"He—blows up. Gets really mad. It's scary."

The judge rubbed his chin. "Okay. Thank you, my dear. You may sit."

The door opened and closed behind them. Stella could see Joe come in and sit in the back. She felt better, as though Dane had people on his side. But still no Ryker.

The judge turned back to Arthur. "First-degree murder? We don't get much of that around here."

"No, sir. Thank goodness."

The judge looked back at Dane. "I think this is going to require a preliminary hearing. I'll set it quickly, so we can get to the bottom of what happened here. Until then, I am remanding the defendant back to jail for the safety of the victim's family."

Stella stood up, but Beatrice pulled her back down instantly. "You can only do harm here. Sit."

Joe stood up. "Mike? Your honor? Can I speak on behalf of Dane?"

The judge waved him up, looking crossly at Flemming. "This was your job."

Stella looked back and forth between the lawyer, the judge, and Joe. Dane's lawyer could have brought people here to help him? And didn't?

"Hello, Joe," the judge said. "You got my wife's old rambler running yet?"

"Still waiting on parts, Mike. Those foreign jobs."

"Damn Japanese cars. I tried to tell her." The judge laughed. "Tell me about this boy here."

"He's a fine employee and knows his stuff. I really can't spare him."

"You don't think he's a danger?"

"Not a bit, sir."

The judge rubbed his chin again. Darlene and her mother started sobbing, howling, really. Stella wanted to throw something at them.

"Well, Joe, ordinarily your word's good with me, but we got a dead boy, and a couple distraught women."

"I can call witnesses to his violent behavior," Arthur said. "I can have them here."

"I'll set the hearing for Monday," the judge said. "That'll cool his jets." He looked at Dane. "If you do well, and the charges get downgraded, we'll see about bail then."

He slammed his gavel and stood.

"All rise," the deputy called out.

Stella stood, but her knees felt like water. Dane had to go back to jail for a whole week! All because Darlene made a show. A lying show. Dane would never have hurt her.

But when the women turned around, she saw no smugness or vindication. Just grief. They were doing what they felt they had to do.

Stella didn't think she could walk. Nothing seemed to work right. Still, she waited for Dane to be taken out, to stay until the last glimpse. He didn't turn back to her and disappeared out the door.

Stella nudged Beatrice. "We have to get him a lawyer. Arthur is good, and the defender is going to blow this."

Beatrice led her out the back. "I agree, Stella. But lawyers don't come cheap."

"I didn't have to pay Mooner."

Beatrice held the door open. "You might need the money next week."

"I don't think we can wait."

Beatrice glanced back into the courtroom where Darlene and her mother still held each other, crying. "You may be right."

28

LAWYER HIRE

DANE looked up as Deputy Barnes poked his face in the barred window of his cell. "Lawyer's here to talk to you."

Lot of good that would do. The boy was younger than him and didn't seem too interested in his job. Fumbling around like a fifteen-year-old unhooking his first bra.

The door clanged as the deputy slid back the locks. "I don't have to cuff you for this, but no funny business. Walk the straight and narrow."

They followed a corridor through another set of locked doors and into a conference room. Barnes kicked a chair away from the table. "Sit there. They'll be here in a minute."

They. More than one this time. Good. Maybe the boy would have some help.

The laminate table was chilly. The walls were bare, just white plaster, except for a large gray mirror in one. He could have stood up to put his finger against it, the gap telling him that it was actually a one-way window, but he knew it was. No telling who was watching.

He'd been in jail two days now, and the night wasn't too bad. The cot was about the same as the sofa. Ryker had tried to see him, his lawyer had told him, but he couldn't have visitors other than counsel with the murder charge standing. Supposedly at the hearing it would get downgraded to manslaughter and he could go home if he made bail. Depended on how much the judge set it for. Or if Darlene or the others convinced the judge he was dangerous.

Maybe he was. Cold air blew on him, but he could still barely clamp down on his rage. He wanted to hit something, no doubt about it, but that was what got him here in the first place. Fucked up his life at 27. Killed a man. Thank God his mother wasn't around to see it.

The door opened, and a strange man entered, slicked up in a suit and fancy haircut.

"I'm Justin Spears," he said, offering a hand.

Dane took it. "Dane Scoffield."

"Stella hired me to represent you."

His face bloomed hot. "What did she do that for?"

"She was concerned about the public defender's handling of your case so far. She was right."

"But this is expensive."

Justin sat back. "It is. It's what she wants. And honestly, you're going to need some help here."

Dane stood up, saw the man tense, then sat back down. "I don't want her spending her savings. She wants to get out of Holly."

"I can't convince her of that."

"Can I talk to her?"

"I tried to bring her back. They wouldn't let her in."

"Can my brother come?"

"I might can get him in. Maybe. They aren't too kindly when first-degree murder is on the table."

"I thought it was getting changed to manslaughter."

"I'm pretty sure we can get that. Murder isn't the usual charge in cases like this. I'm not sure what the prosecutor is after here."

Dane couldn't stop himself, but stood and paced the room. Someone knocked at the door, but Justin waved his hand and no one came in. So they were watching.

"Why can't the public defender handle this?"

Justin shifted in his chair. "He can. You can refuse me."

"What's Stella out if I do?"

"Just the consult."

"How much is that?"

"Dane, your life is on the line here. If they succeed with murder, you're looking at life over a barroom fight that really shouldn't be giving you time at all."

"I have a temper. People will say that."

"Yes, I heard about the statements in the arraignment. We'll get this trial moved. Get the local folks out of the works. Then we can start with a clean slate. The knife incident in the bar is plenty to show a need for self-defense, although I sure wish you'd gone to the hospital with it, get it documented."

"How much will this cost Stella?"

"Hard to say. We'll have the preliminary hearing, discovery, serving witnesses, then the trial itself, which could go on several days."

"How much?"

"Ballpark? Twenty grand."

Dane punched the wall, and this time there was no knock, but Barnes stepped right in. "Want me to cuff him?"

Justin shook his head. "No. We're fine."

Barnes stepped back out.

"Let's not make matters worse here. The town's on edge. I need to get you through this hearing, down to manslaughter, and taken to a new trial location."

Stella didn't have that much money. He was stealing her future. "No. I want to plead guilty. Just go to jail."

"Dane. You cannot plead guilty to murder. A trial will go in your favor on this. Honestly, I don't think the prosecutor will push for murder. He has to know he can't win that."

"But I hit him first."

"But you had cause to believe he could knife you again. We can make this work. We'll get this down to manslaughter."

Nobody could guarantee shit. Dane knew that. "How can I avoid a trial?"

Justin opened his briefcase. "Well, you can plea out. We can take the lesser charge, try to lowball the sentence."

"And no trial then?"

"No. We'd make an agreement, as long as the prosecutor will do it. I'd try for six, but if they think their case is strong, you'd be looking at fifteen years, probably." He pulled a chart. "Possibility of parole after 85 percent served. There was no weapon involved, right?"

"No. Just the barstool."

"No weapon on you when you were arrested?"

"No."

"Okay. So yeah, you're looking at about twelve years if you plea out. I will work for less, but coming off murder, that's probably where we're at. Really, though, a trial is your best bet. A jury will be sympathetic. You won't get more time than that, and it's possible you'll get off, or only get probation."

"No. I won't trade my life for Stella's."

"Money can be earned. Freedom cannot."

"I want her to be free to go."

"All right, then." He closed the briefcase and stood up. "I'll call the prosecutor, work out the terms."

"What will that run her?"

"A couple grand, tops."

"Your word on that?"

He held out his hand. "My word."

Dane accepted his hand and shook it. "Can you not tell her? I don't think she'll like it."

"You want her to hear the plea at the hearing?"

"Yes."

"Okay. Your call." He pushed the chair back under the table. "See you Monday. I'll come by if I have a question. But you won't be testifying. We'll have already worked out the deal. Just sit tight and stay cool." He rapped on the door, and Barnes let him out.

Dane followed the deputy back down the corridor. After Monday, this would be over, and Stella would be free. It'd cost her a bit, but he'd pay her back eventually, maybe send the money to Beatrice. And Stella could go on with her life. She wouldn't have any choice. None of them did, not anymore.

29

STELLA'S PLAN

STELLA rearranged a shelf of Jean Naté Bath Splash for the tenth time, crinkling the blue paper along the edges, trying to keep her hands and mind busy.

Beatrice wiped down the glass counter despite it sparkling from the last cleaning five minutes before. Neither of them had much to say.

"Been a long week," Beatrice finally said. "Just the weekend to get through now."

Stella flattened the tissue out to make another attempt at a wave. The paper was almost beyond use now, she'd done it so many times. "I wonder what he's doing. Just sitting on a chair? Watching TV? Going crazy?"

"Yeah, I don't think they've got much going on back there. Not that I've been. No call to." She dropped the cloth back in a cabinet. "Maybe they are all playing cards or something."

"I doubt that." Stella gave up on the bath display, collecting the extra paper and glitter to take to the back. "I'm sure they've closed ranks back there. He's the stranger."

"Not everybody thinks like that," Beatrice said. "Some of us like people for being people without considering where they were born."

Stella pushed through the curtains to put away the supplies. She hadn't expected to still be there, working. She needed the paycheck now, she knew, but she'd given up this life, that job. Her car remained in Beatrice's driveway, still mostly packed. She'd only taken her clothes out.

She began sorting the various packages of tissue paper by color, just to have something to do. Even if Dane got out on bail Monday, they'd probably have to stay close until the trial. Her getaway was permanently suspended.

The front door jingled, but Stella stayed back. Some of the town's women had taken to stopping by the shop just to eyeball her. They'd sold all that cheap perfume, as Beatrice had foisted it on them, making them purchase something if they were going to darken her door. All the commissions went to Stella, even though she often fled to the back. The storeroom had never been more dusted or organized.

Beatrice popped her head through the curtains. "It's Janine."

Stella barreled into the shop and straight into the arms of her friend. "You got away from your mom!"

Janine hugged her fiercely. "She's been a total bear. I have to get out of there." She stepped back. "But the whole thing seemed to get Nick's butt in gear. She waved her hand in front of Stella, showing off a tiny diamond on a thin band.

"Janine!" Stella clutched at her again. "You're finally going to do it!"

Beatrice picked up Janine's hand. "Aww, how lovely. Congratulations."

They sat on the red cushioned bench. "When are you going to have the wedding?" Stella asked. She was genuinely happy for Janine, but still, an unsettledness uncurled within her. She might not get this day with Dane. It was the first time she'd ever wanted it.

"In the spring, I think. I don't know. Maybe sooner. It won't be anything fancy." Janine admired her ring. "I can't believe it!"

Beatrice headed to the back. "I'm going to fetch some lunch. I'll let you girls chitchat."

Stella clenched her hands in her lap. "I'm glad for you. Really." She could feel them separating already. Janine's life moving forward, while hers was still stuck.

"Oh, Stella. I've been so worried. How is Dane? Have you seen him?"

Stella picked at her nail polish. "No. They wouldn't let me back. Only his lawyer."

"I heard Darlene made a fuss at court."

"Yeah, she really put it on. That's why he didn't get bail."

"That girl."

Flecks of pink floated to the floor as Stella pulled off more polish. "Well, it was her brother."

"If only he'd just…"

Stella understood. If only Bobby Ray hadn't been a jerk. If only Dane hadn't taken the stool. If only Stella hadn't danced on the bar. Too many things to count.

"So what are you going to do?" Janine asked. "Just keep working here? Did you go home?"

"Hell, no. I'm living with Beatrice."

"I'm sorry my mom was so awful."

Stella kicked at the bits of polish on the floor. "Not your fault."

"What can I do?"

Stella walked over to the counter and pulled her binder from the shelf. "Help me decide where Dane and I should go once he gets out." She plunked the book on the glass and flipped through the pages. "New York? Bound to be lots of troublemakers there. Dane would seem downright upstanding."

Janine fingered the book. "I think New Orleans is the murder capital of the world."

Stella's hand froze over the page.

"God, I'm sorry. Stella. I'm sorry." Janine's face crumpled. "I didn't mean it like that."

Stella closed the book. "No, it's fine. I started it. And we probably can't go anywhere anyway. Not until after the trial."

"They can't find him guilty, can they? I mean, Bobby Ray was looking for that fight."

"The lawyer said that they wouldn't be able to go for murder in the end. They wouldn't win."

"Oh, good. Will they just drop the whole thing?"

Stella shoved the binder back under the counter. "No. But hopefully the jury will see the situation for what it was, and give him probation."

"Surely they will. Dane's a nice guy."

Stella braced her elbows on the counter, looking out the window. She could just catch the corner of the courthouse from here. Somewhere inside was Dane, awaiting his fate. As bad as it was for them out here, it had to be so much worse for him in there.

30

HEARING

"YOU ready for this?"

Dane glanced up at the barred window. Justin, the new lawyer, grinned at him through the small rectangle. The silver lines in front of his face made him look like he was the one in a cage.

But he was familiar with the view. For a week he'd mostly just sat there. The jail wasn't equipped for long-term inmates. He'd had to shower in the officers' quarters, and meals were brought to him three times a day from the diner down the street, except Sunday morning, when a deputy had arrived with donuts. A sympathetic woman who came to give him a clean set of scrubs brought a newspaper and a crossword-puzzle book.

Dane stood up, smoothing the jacket and shirt he'd last worn at the funeral. Ryker had brought it by yesterday, although they'd only allowed the brothers the briefest of "Hey" and "You look like shit" before sending him off again. Ryker had managed to say that he was splitting town. The scene was no good, and he felt Joe's business might suffer if he stayed. Said he'd leave a number with Joe when he got settled again.

For an hour after Ryker had left, Dane had held the jacket to his face, smelling the traces of perfume still lingering there from when Stella had held on to him at the service. He wanted to smash something after learning Ryker had to leave town, but the smell of her calmed him. He'd only known her two weeks. And barely that. It's all they'd ever have.

The door screeched open, and the deputy ushered him into the corridor. Justin strode confidently, animated, and Dane could see that this was the sort of thing he lived for—the thrill of someone else's life hanging in the balance.

The deputy stepped behind Dane, cuffing his wrists.

"What's that for?" Justin asked.

"He's got a history," the deputy said. "Smith said to bring him in cuffed."

"Who is Smith?"

"The sheriff."

Dane tightened his fists. That man from the funeral. Vivian's stooge.

"Put him back in the cell," Justin said. "I'm going to file a continuance instead. I'm not having him go out in cuffs."

"Awww, don't do that," the deputy said. "Smith will get his panties all in a wad."

"Then remove the cuffs."

"Hold on just a minute." The deputy trotted down the short hall and through the locked doors.

"What was that about?" Dane asked.

"Not sure. But damned if I'm going to let them make you look like you can't handle yourself right before we issue a plea."

The door swung open again, and the deputy returned, followed by the sheriff from the funeral.

"That one's got an ax to grind," Dane said.

"Not today." Justin held out his hand, but the sheriff ignored it.

The sheriff's voice was a growl. "He got violent in the interview room. He's got a history with multiple witnesses. He's cuffed."

"Fine," Justin said. "Then put him back in the cell. I'll file a continuance and a request for a change of venue due to prejudice. You guys are poster children for an unfair trial."

The sheriff rocked forward, one hand on his belt, the other on his holster. "You city lawyers are all alike. Thinking you can come in here and showboat."

"We can indeed," Justin said. "It's called balance of justice. Dane, let's get you settled back in the cell. I'll see you again in Springfield, or maybe we'll have to go as far as Columbia or St. Louis. You ever been to St. Louis?"

The sheriff grumbled low under his breath. "Uncuff him."

Justin stepped back so the deputy could release Dane. "Good choice," he said. "It would have been mighty inconvenient when I had to subpoena you about that funeral. Were you there in an official capacity? Or do you just wear your uniform for fun and intimidation?"

The sheriff growled again, but Justin took Dane's arm and led him away. They passed through two more doors, then stood outside the hall that led to the courtroom. "Just be cool," Justin said. "If you show any emotion on your face, make it be remorse. Otherwise, keep your head down and your hands on the table."

Dane would do anything this boy said. He was downright grateful to have the man now. He'd pay Stella back every dime, but this guy was worth it.

Justin pushed through the door and led them to their table. Dane kept his head down, but still saw Stella, who had positioned herself just behind his chair. His body went on alert, and he didn't feel in control anymore. He wanted to sweep her up and escape, get out of this hellhole and back onto the open road, knocking aside anyone who got in his way. Even crashing on the banks of a creek had felt better than this.

He sensed her lean forward, and his back burned with the anticipation that she might reach out and touch him. She was that close. But the bailiff came out and called, "All rise," so they stood.

Dane forced himself to think of other things, his mother's funeral, Joe's roses, his motorcycle locked up at the impound lot. The old judge entered, his hair flying in wisps around his bare head, and they all sat again.

The movement sent a waft of perfume his way. Stella. He could barely contain himself, only just able to avoid turning around.

Suddenly the plea bargain seemed a mistake. Maybe he could get off, avoid doing time.

But when the sheriff took a staunch position by the witness stand, sneering at Dane in front of the whole courtroom, Dane realized the odds were stacked against him here. His fate had already been decided in some back room. And no Justin or slick city ways were going to change what happened here today. Justin had already made the call. The prosecutor had agreed to the terms. They just had to state the plan and make sure the judge approved the plea.

The old man shuffled his papers. "I understand you two have come to an agreement."

The prosecutor, a large man in a fancy suit, approached the judge and laid a paper before him. "Daniel Scoffield has agreed to plead guilty to a lesser charge of manslaughter."

Dane heard the gasp behind him but could not afford to turn around. This was it.

The judge looked sternly just behind Dane, then back at the prosecutor. "Was a term agreed upon?"

"Twelve years, your honor."

Dane sensed Stella stand up. "You can't do that!"

The judge banged his gavel. "Young lady, take your seat."

"But that asshole knifed Dane from behind! You can't send him to jail for twelve years! It isn't right!"

"Take your seat, or you will be removed from this courtroom!"

Dane could hear shuffling behind him, probably someone trying to calm Stella down. He caught another strong draft of perfume. Bound to be Beatrice. She must have come in after he did.

He could hear muffled crying, then he caught sight of Stella moving to the center aisle. "I won't be quiet! This is wrong! You are railroading him because he's not from here!"

She was wrong, and Dane wanted to tell her this was his choice. But he sat numbly, staring at his chewed-up hands, scabs from the motorcycle crash flaking off his fingers. Still, in his peripheral vision, he could see her, all dressed up in a black skirt and shiny top.

Justin stood up then, putting an arm around her. "Stella, calm yourself. Dane arranged this deal. It was his choice."

She turned to him then. "What? Why would he do that?"

"Please sit down," Justin said. "Let us finish this."

But Stella wouldn't sit down. Her face was bright red. "I hate you! I hate you, you son of a bitch! Stand up for yourself! Do something! Don't let these people walk all over you!"

The judge banged the gavel again. "Smith. Get her out of here, and make sure she stays out." He pointed at Stella. "You're about to get yourself fined, missy."

Smith took Stella firmly by the elbow and led her down the aisle. She turned around, staring at Dane. He tried not to watch, but still moved tightly on his chair so he could see her until they pushed through the doors at the back.

So she hated him now. That was probably for the best. Now all of them could go on, and hopefully she could find that new city she wanted so bad, and a better life, like they'd never met at all.

* * *

Stella's feet looked warped and pale against the bottom of the kiddie pool. She'd been soaking them for an hour in Beatrice's backyard, trying to get the ache out from wearing those tight pumps.

So much for her whole attempt at reinventing herself, dressing respectably in long skirts and nice clothes, no more *Flashdance* or micro-minis or jelly flats. She'd still blown up in a courtroom, and now her feet were raw and sore, her shirt untucked as she sat among grass and weeds and dirt like the common girl she had always been.

The back door slammed, and Beatrice settled in a splintering lawn chair.

Stella wiggled her toes, bright with pink polish. "What are you doing with a kiddie pool anyway?"

The chair groaned with the weight of her boss, and Stella hoped it would hold together.

Beatrice kicked off her own shoes. "I got a cute little niece."

"In Holly?"

"Nah. Up in Jefferson City. She came down over the summer, though."

"Oh, yeah. I remember that now." Before Dane. Before Grandma Angie. Her life was like the calendar. BC and AD. Before chaos. After

Dane.

Beatrice scooted the chair forward. "So you want to know what happened after your little show?"

"Do I want to know?"

Beatrice dunked her feet in the pool. Stella hoped hers never looked like that, bloated white hunks of flesh, lined from the pinch of the shoes.

"He got the twelve. Fifteen, actually, but eligible for parole in twelve."

Stella bent over her knees, the air knocked out of her.

"I know, honey. It's a long stint."

"Did the lawyer not do him any good?"

"He did. I talked with him. They tried to pull some shenanigans at the end, but Justin kept them in line."

"Did you get to talk to…" She couldn't say his name.

"Dane? No, honey. They took him right out."

Stella stared into the pool, leaves dropping from the trees overhead onto the surface of the water. The wind blew a chill through her. They were probably at the last of the decent weather. Fall would be sliding into winter soon. "What happens now?"

"Justin said most likely he'll go straight to the Missouri State Pen."

"Can I see him there?"

"Not for at least thirty days. He has to go through some orientation."

Stella lay back in the grass. Fat clouds floated carefree across the blue expanse of sky. She wanted to take a shotgun and blow a smoking hole right through the big white puffs.

"He won't want to see me."

"I wouldn't assume that."

"I called him a son of a bitch."

"He knows you. Knows you were upset."

Stella covered her face with her arm. "How will I even know where he's gone?"

"You can write him. He'll tell you."

"I don't think he will want to hear from me."

"I think he will. Write him."

Stella listened to birds cawing, and some little kids screeching a few yards over. A car chugged down a nearby street, missing on one cylinder. Life was going right on. Everybody else's life. Hers had come to a halt.

"Stella, I know he was important to you. But maybe you need some perspective. You only knew him a couple weeks. Maybe it's best you keep on with that plan you had to move out of Holly and start a new life."

Stella swallowed hard. She ought to do exactly that. Even after she paid the lawyer, she still had some cash. She could go. Forget everything that happened. She was totally free now.

"I don't feel free," she said. "Suddenly I'm more attached to this damn place than ever."

"Well, don't think I'm pushing you away. I'm happy to keep you around." Beatrice pulled her feet from the pool with a splash. "You can stay here as long as you like, and I won't allow any tomfoolery in my shop. I don't need the business that bad."

Stella sat up. "You think my being in your shop is a bad thing?"

"Not in the least."

She pulled her feet from the pool. "Where is Ryker? He wasn't there today."

Beatrice wouldn't look at her, messing with her shoes.

"Bea! Where is Ryker?"

"He was catching some flak. Left town."

Stella jumped to her feet. "Why didn't anyone tell me? Where did he go?"

"Just told Joe he'd get in touch."

"How will Dane find him? What about Dane's stuff?" She stuffed her wet feet back into the pumps.

"I don't rightly know."

Stella dashed across the lawn and into the house. She snatched up her purse and the keys to Grandma's Mustang.

Beatrice caught up with her. "Where are you off to?"

"I don't know. Dane's place? Joe's?" Hysteria rose in her. Things were changing too fast now. If Ryker was gone, how would she know anything about Dane?

"Be careful, darling."

Stella hurtled through the front door and into the car. The engine roared as she backed out of the driveway and onto the street. He couldn't be gone. Not yet. She needed him.

Kids riding bikes turned to stare as she careened through Holly toward Renters' Row. Other cars simply stopped, letting her pass by, as if they knew and understood not to get in her way.

The duplex stood empty, the dirt yard looking more forlorn than ever. A "For Lease" sign stood in front of it, shiny and new.

Stella killed the car and rushed to the door, almost tripping once again on the overturned pot, still blocking the path.

She banged on the door, but no one answered.

She moved to the front, trying to peer in the window to the living room. The blinds were down. She tried the pane, to see if it was locked, but it was shut tight.

She walked around to the back door leading to the kitchen. Also locked.

The kitchen window didn't have blinds, so she dragged a weathered water hose under it, making a tight coil that got her an extra two feet to stand on. She could just peer over the sash, somehow hoping to still see the wobbly table stacked high with beer bottles and pizza cartons.

The table remained, cleared off, and all the counters were empty. The fridge hung open, all its contents gone. Stella sagged against the siding. Ryker was gone.

Her pumps sank into the soft ground as she trudged back to her car. She opened the door and just sat there, staring at the front of the duplex, remembering the three of them in that spot the night the assholes broke her window. How did they get away with that? And the knifing? And now her Dane was doing time.

And this was it, a moment she'd dreaded but was a long time in coming. She laid her head on the steering wheel and bawled her eyes out.

* * *

"State your name."

Dane held his state-issued towel, white shirt, and gray pants in front

165

of him, naked except for a pair of rubbery shoes. His wet hair dripped down his back. His face felt raw from the shaving. "Dane Scoffield."

The attendant ran a finger down the list on his clipboard. "Daniel Scoffield?"

"Yes."

"In here you are Daniel Scoffield. You got that?"

"Yes, sir."

The guy liked the deference Dane gave him, squaring his shoulders. "All right. Get dressed. You'll see your caseworker next. And I wouldn't go barefoot in here." He gestured to the perpetually damp floor outside the showers.

When the man didn't move, Dane realized he would have an audience. He laid the stack on a bench and knocked off one shoe, awkwardly sticking a leg into a pair of gray boxers, putting one shoe back on, then repeating with the other leg.

"You're gettin' it," the attendant said. "You'll have a second set of everything checked out to you later today."

Dane nodded, pulling the top over his head.

"All right." The attendant unlocked and opened the metal door. "Let's get you to Miz Penders. She'll get you situated."

They walked down a long corridor with large wooden doors. The attendant led Dane into a room, austere with peeling walls. A woman sat at a large desk behind stacks of folders.

She watched him behind giant coke-bottle glasses. Her hair was a helmet of Aqua Net, and a blue suit with huge shoulder pads made her look like a linebacker. Her voice was tinny and high. "All right, Mr. Scoffield. I'm here to determine which of our housing units will be best suited for your situation and to answer any questions you have. Go ahead and sit down."

He perched on the edge of the gray chair, leaning forward on the table, hands splayed in front of him.

"No need to be nervous now. I'm just here to talk to you."

Dane tried to relax his shoulders, but they drifted back up, tense and tight. "Is this where I'll stay?" The Missouri State Penitentiary had a terrible rep. "The Walls," one of the deputies had called it. The riots had been famous, even in Texas. Suddenly he longed for Huntsville. Its history was no better, but at least it was the devil he knew. Two high school buddies had ended up working stints there, though he'd never heard from them after.

She shuffled through some papers. "Yes. You're a pretty standard case. No history of mental illness. No medical problems. No special dispensations by the judge or contingencies on your sentence." She flipped through the papers. "Medium sentence. No special risks."

So his wall-slamming incident hadn't followed him. Maybe Justin had helped. Dane breathed a little easier. He'd feared solitary confinement or something worse. He'd never known anyone on the inside, so movies and television were his only clue. The head-bashing-with-a-pipe scene from *On the Yard* had popped into his head more than once. He wondered about cigarettes and contraband and prison hierarchy and, grimly, if he'd have to fight off people trying to poke him. He wondered how far he'd go for his own protection, if he'd end up fighting and getting even more time. His shoulders tensed again.

"Hey." The caseworker tapped on the table to get his attention. "You're going to be fine."

He tried to really look at her now. She wore a soft pink lipstick, something a child might choose, and this made her gentler somehow.

"Let's try this again. I'm Maggie. I'm going to get you assigned to a hall and your inmate paperwork complete."

"I didn't mean to kill that guy."

Maggie lifted a stack of papers and tapped them lightly to straighten the edges. "I don't judge on that. I just look at your needs, what skills you have, and where you'll fit best. You're a mechanic?"

"Yes."

"We can't get you in the shop right off. But maybe a transfer if you have good behavior."

Dane nodded.

She pulled an oversized manila envelope forward. "These are the effects you had on you during your arrest that you will be allowed to keep with you if you want them." She pulled out a list. "You also had some things that will be kept in storage for your release, or we can destroy them—boots, spiked belt, jeans, a watch chain, keys, cash." She made a note on the form. "I'll get the cash put in your inmate account." She dumped the contents of the envelope on the table. "These you may take to your housing unit. Inmates are allowed approved personal items."

His T-shirt came out first, one he'd bought at the truck stop along with the Show Me one for Stella. It was black with a small emblem on the chest in the shape of Missouri. He resisted the urge to grab it and see if it smelled of her like his jacket had.

Second was his wallet. "Your IDs are in your case file," Maggie said. "But there were some inconsequential scraps of paper, receipts, and whatnot in there."

She peered into the bag. "One last thing." She reached in and pulled out a bit of pink fabric, the one he'd torn from Stella's shirt. "It was short enough to meet regulation. Is it important?"

He swallowed. He had no idea if he'd ever see Stella again. "I'll keep it."

She laid it on the T-shirt and wallet, and pushed them toward him. "Next we have some forms." She pulled a sheet of paper from a folder. "This is where you'll list the visitors you'll be allowing to see you."

Visitors. Ryker, maybe? He didn't have any other family. Stella's image drifted forward, but he shoved her back. She wouldn't want to come. "I have a brother."

"Good. Put him down. Any others?"

He hesitated. "There was a girl."

"A girlfriend? That's fine." She tugged another page from a blue folder. "We have very strict rules of decorum on visits. She can only wear certain things. She can't bring anything in on the visits."

"Will I get to really see her? Or just through glass?"

"If you have good behavior, you'll be allowed to sit with her in a visitors' room."

"I don't know if she'll want to come."

Maggie rolled a pen toward him. "You can write her first. You are only allowed twenty names on the list. But I wouldn't wait too long. We have to mail her a form for her to return. Then we do a criminal check. Once all that is done, then you can have her visit. Same with your brother."

"So I'll know if she's willing based on whether she returns the form."

"It's better to write her first before the form arrives, if you're not sure."

"I don't even have my brother's address right now. He just moved." Hell, even Stella could have blown out of town.

"You can always add him when you get it."

Dane stared at the form for names and addresses and numbers. He didn't know anything.

He pushed the empty paper back at her. "I'll do this later."

Maggie slipped the form back in the folder. "I'll arrange for some paper and envelopes to be sent to you. You should write your girl. It's important to have visitors, to keep some link to your old life."

He didn't want any links to that.

Maggie pulled out another paper. "You'll want to contact your bank to have some money moved into your prison account, so you have money for stamps and incidentals you might want to buy from the store." She pushed another form at him.

This, at least, he could fill out. Nothing personal. Just lines on a page, black and white questions with simple answers. Completely unlike a letter to Stella.

If he even sent one.

31

STELLA'S DETERMINATION

"LOOKS like you got something interesting." Bobby, the seventy-year-old postal carrier, still as spry as the WWII soldier he once was, handed the stack of mail to Stella.

She pushed aside the spindle of kiddie perfume necklaces she'd been assembling and set the pile of catalogs and bills on the glass counter. Faceup, right on top, was a rough gray envelope clearly marked "INMATE, Missouri State Penitentiary."

Stella's heart skittered. "Who all have you already told?" she asked. He loved gossip more than any old biddy in town.

He lifted his hands in innocence. "Just pulled it out of the bag!"

"But you sorted it this morning." Stella considered his path. There were three carriers in Holly. Bobby had this side of town, including Grandma Angie's house and Vivian.

"I might have mentioned it to a few folks. Not too often a hardened criminal writes one of our own."

Stella snatched the envelope and hid it under the register. "You tell my mother?"

"Now, I just dropped the mail in her box by the door like the proper carrier I am." Bobby rocked back on his heels, the rough canvas bag pinched to his side. It was hard to be mad at a man with such a merry twinkle in his eyes, but she was pretty furious.

"Well, keep this to yourself. I can't have Vivian storming in here. She's managed to stay away this long." In fact, hardly anyone had seen Stella's mother at all since the funeral. Beatrice had driven the block a time or two and reported that Vivian must be holed up at Grandma Angie's house.

"Ain't right for a mother and daughter to be at odds." Bobby leaned an elbow on the counter like he planned to sit and chat a spell.

Stella returned to the spindle of necklaces, knowing full well how to get rid of Bobby. She opened one of the caps on the miniature hearts, revealing the spray nozzle. Bobby had hard-core allergies. "How about you do a little test of this, see if maybe one of your granddaughters would like it?"

Bobby backed away swiftly. "No, no, thanks. I must get back to my route." He saluted her and spun away, striding toward the door in long lanky steps.

Stella waited until the door clanged shut to pull the envelope back out.

She didn't have cause to know his handwriting. He'd never given her anything. The address was neat and perfectly aligned, as if he'd used a ruler. "Stella Ashton. Good Scents. 432 Main. Holly, Missouri 65624."

Beatrice pushed through the curtain to the main shop. "Mail call?"

Stella slid the stack of bills along the glass without looking up.

Beatrice came up behind her and squeezed her shoulders. "You look like you've seen a ghost." She leaned over to peer at Stella's envelope. "So you have. You going to open it?"

Stella laid the letter back on the glass. Dane had been gone three weeks. She hadn't known what to do, where to go, and Beatrice didn't seem to mind having a houseguest. With Vivian leaving her alone, it seemed well enough to hang around and help Janine plan her wedding, a welcome distraction. The bracelet on her wrist tinkled against the counter, the orange and yellow one Grandma Angie had made for Joe. It comforted her to wear it, to know that someone so close to her had suffered an impossible love as well.

Beatrice collected the other mail. "You afraid of what it says?"

Stella shook her head. "I'm sure he wants to see me." Loneliness had to be kicking in.

"You want to see him?"

Stella ran a finger across the address. He had held this envelope, sealing it in some forlorn cell. She didn't know what he hoped for, and she didn't know what he could say to make her come. She didn't know herself.

Beatrice patted Stella's shoulder and moved out from behind the counter. "Why don't you take the day off? Read your letter. Think about things."

The door jingled, and a cluster of giggly teen girls arrived. One of them held a tiny case that held a band instrument—Stella never could remember which was which. A flute, maybe. Or a clarinet. She thought of the band rehearsal when she was stuck up on the tower, and knew exactly where she needed to go.

"I'll do that," Stella said.

When she spoke, the girls silenced, looking at her with alarm. One elbowed the other. The youngest one looked absolutely petrified, as if Stella might attack.

Stella wanted to tell them to stop staring but instead picked up her envelope and exited through the back curtain. She was beyond tired of trying to fit in.

The air outside had cooled considerably. Stella walked the block to the Mustang, the water tower just visible among the trees. Instead of getting in, she opened the door and pulled out a sweater. It would be even colder up top. She was about to walk away when she turned back to the car and opened the console, tugging out the triple-strand bracelet she had made for Dane. Instead of wearing it, though, she tucked it into her front pocket.

Stella jogged lightly for a couple blocks, pulling a hood over her hair. A few cars passed, but she didn't recognize the drivers. Funny how she'd been so cocky just a month or so ago, climbing the tower in the middle of the day, not really caring if she got caught. This time she had to be more careful.

She looked around. The school maintenance man was backing a lawn mower into the shed at the tower's base. She slowed her step. He came back out, dusting off his hands, and lowered the overhead door. Stella turned at the next block, taking the long way around, hoping he'd be gone when she made it back. She passed a green house where an elementary school friend had lived. They used to jump off the front porch wearing capes and playing Wonder Woman. The girl had moved away years ago.

Around the corner, a charred foundation was all that remained of the Muellers' house, burned down a decade before from a kitchen fire. The Muellers were still around, living a block over, but had never rebuilt.

She turned up the last street back toward the school and the tower. The maintenance man was loading a coil of rope into the back of his truck. Stella slowed down again, but he quickly jumped into the front seat and took off down the road. A straggler teacher walked out the front of the school and hurried to her car. The front lot was mostly deserted. Unless she was unlucky, Stella should make it up without incident.

She stayed on the opposite side of the street for as long as possible, then quickly crossed behind the line of bushes that grew alongside the chain-link fence. She ducked through the cut section that never seemed to get repaired and waited near the base of a tree, checking if anyone had seen her move inside.

So far, so good. She jumped up and grasped the bottom rung of the ladder, swinging her legs and catching the bar with the backs of her knees. As she pulled herself up, her head went woozy. She sat a moment, holding on to the ladder, legs dangling, waiting to see if she would still be frightened by the height. She wouldn't have Dane this time.

The world righted itself, so she stood up, taking a few quick steps to get past the trees and check if she could spot any twitching in Old Lady Springer's curtains.

All good. She climbed swiftly upward, pausing only a moment at the first break in the ladder to remember Dane behind her, that first time they were together. The wind picked up and blew her hair all around her face. She'd stopped using so much hair spray, preferring the looser flowing look now. She just wasn't the same girl as that night at the Watering Hole. She wouldn't be again.

She checked that the envelope in her back pocket was still secure and then moved upward again, not stopping until she was at the base of the platform. The sight of the town brought on another wave of lightheadedness, but she pushed it aside, bracing her elbows on the metal so she could wriggle through the opening.

Then she was up, unable to stand without feeling sick, so she crawled to the silver dome to sit with her back against it.

Only when her heart slowed and her breathing seemed back to normal did she tug the triple-strand bracelet from her front jean pocket and fasten it to her wrist. Then she pulled the envelope out and clutched it tightly in the whipping wind.

She considered for a moment just letting it go, tumbling through the air over Holly, landing on someone's lawn or a windshield or maybe the creek they'd jumped. But then, it could make its way to Darlene or even the parking lot of the bar. Maybe the sheriff would pick it up and use it against Dane somehow.

She tore open the flap. Inside was a single sheet of the same rough gray paper, the writing neat and aligned.

My dearest beautiful Stella,

She had to stop already, her heart beating so hard she could barely breathe. She leaned against the wall, the cold of the metal biting into her back through her sweater. She'd only known Dane two weeks. This was so crazy. She'd let boys come and go by the dozen. Why did this one stick?

She turned back to the letter.

I shouldn't write you. I should let you go, make the escape you're wanting. But seeing you so upset in the courtroom that day was so hard. One of the things they tell you here is to make amends. And I want to make amends with you.

I should have held my temper. I should have walked away. And you were right, if I'd done the right thing, I wouldn't have been in that bar at all. I would've waited for you like you asked.

Stella had to break away from the letter again. So hard. So many things to go back and change. How did anybody live with this much regret?

A bird landed on the rail of the tower, cocked its head at Stella, then flitted down to sit by her. She was yellow, so bright, like a canary, but that would mean she was a lost pet, as that sort of bird didn't live around here naturally.

"Hello, birdie," Stella said, grateful for the distraction. "Are you lost?"

She lifted her hand, and Grandma's yellow bracelet flashed in the afternoon light. Stella understood then, and looked into the sky. She wasn't alone. Somebody was looking after her, God, or Grandma Angie, or maybe just the universe. The canary flew in a tight circle, then landed on the rail again.

The paper fluttered in the wind, and Stella gripped it tight. "Let's finish this," she said to the bird. "And then I'll figure out what to do."

I won't ask for you to visit me, even though I want to see you so much. I understand that I've done a lot to screw everything up, and very little to earn any piece of you. But if you are willing, I can't think of anything that matters more to me than you. I don't want you to wait for me. And I don't expect to see you at the end of all this. But if you'd come see me just one more time, I will make that enough to last me. Because it is you, it will be enough.

The cold bit into her eyes, and she knew she was crying again, blasted stupid emotion, such weakness. Stella looked out over Holly, the streets laid out between the trees, and beyond, in the deeply forested land that led to the Ozarks, some of the most beautiful country on earth.

How far did she have to go to get away? Jefferson City was almost 200 miles away and like another universe from this small town. She'd been there once, and remembered vaguely the massive Missouri State Penitentiary, huge stone walls right on the river, like a castle. She remembered being frightened by it, and astonished that normal houses sat just across the street from the imposing watchtowers. She knew there had been riots there, and that it was a very bad place to be. She couldn't imagine the things Dane might be seeing or enduring. She looked down at the paper. But he'd asked her to visit, just once. And she would do that.

She folded the letter back into its envelope. The bird still waited on the rail, hopping side to side and occasionally spreading its wings. "I'm going to go," Stella said. "At least once." The canary flew in a little circle, then took off across the sky, a tiny yellow dot on the horizon.

Time to go down. Pack a few things. A weekend in the city. Sounded like fun. Maybe Janine would come along, look for her wedding dress.

She remembered the last time she went down wearing bracelets, so she unfastened both Dane's and Grandma Angie's strands and stuffed them deep in her pocket. She looked through the hole that led to the ladder, then scrambled back against the dome. Her mother! And who else?

She lay on her belly, peeking down. That damn sheriff! And one of the lackey deputies. Shit. Shit. Shit.

She crawled over to the edge of the platform on the other side. Sure enough, Old Lady Springer was standing on her porch, watching everything. Stella banged the metal. She was stuck.

She shifted back to the hole. Someone else was walking up—Joe! Hell, was the whole town going to show? A car pulled up with a screech, the door flying open. Beatrice.

This had to be some comical version of This Is Your Life. Stella figured she might as well not bother waiting. This crew would be there no matter when she came down. She'd just lowered her foot onto the first rung when a booming voice almost made her lose her grip.

"Stella Ashton, we are sending the firemen up to get you." The sheriff was talking through a huge white megaphone.

She shook her head. No firemen. That was ridiculous. She began descending the ladder.

"I order you to halt!"

Whatever. She had already made it to the second ladder. She now noticed the whirling lights of the fire truck and looked down. Two of the volunteer men were staring up at her. She couldn't quite make out who they were in their hats. Probably Janine's dad was one. He'd been doing the volunteer gig for a while.

Sure enough, Janine herself came running up the sidewalk. He must have called her. At least she had some allies down there.

Stella descended the second ladder until her mother's voice came through the megaphone. "Stella Louise! Stop right now."

She looked down. Vivian was wrestling the megaphone from the sheriff. Good grief. She rapidly went down to the final ladder.

The wind was less powerful this low, so now she could hear them talking. "Why aren't you going up after her?" Vivian asked.

"Ma'am, she's probably got more experience on this here tower than we do." Definitely Janine's father.

Stella slowed down as she approached the bottom of the ladder, just a few feet above everyone's head. This was going to get interesting. She laughed.

Vivian's face was bordering on purple. "This is not funny, young lady! You are wasting the time of all these good people!"

"So send them home," Stella said. "I can get down fine on my own."

"Let's get her," the sheriff said. "Can one of you men bring her down?"

Janine's dad came forward and grasped the bottom rung near Stella's feet. He couldn't quite haul himself up, so the other fireman gave him a boost. He wrapped his arms around the rung, but still couldn't get his foot high enough to catch.

Stella wrapped her knees around the ladder and hung just above his face. "Need some help, Mr. Parker?" She held out a hand.

He shook his head and dropped back down to the ground. "You coming now?" he asked.

Stella guessed she might as well. "Sure. It's easier if you give me some room."

The firemen backed away, and Stella sat on the bottom rung, glad today for no miniskirt. She ducked her head through the rungs and rolled backward. She pulled her feet through and hung, now only a few feet from the ground, and dropped in front of her mother.

Vivian snatched her arm and dragged her forward. "I'll handle her," she said to the sheriff. "It's high time she got herself back home."

Stella yanked away. "I'm twenty-two, mother. I'm never going home again."

Beatrice rushed forward. "She's living with me now and doing just fine. No trouble at all."

Vivian waved a hand at the tower. "This looks like trouble to me."

Beatrice stepped between Vivian and Stella. "I think it's best you leave her alone now."

Stella backed away, running smack into Joe, who steadied her with hands on both shoulders. "You're all right, Stella."

"Not until she leaves," Stella said. "I will never be all right until she's out of my life."

"She's your mother."

"Not anymore. I don't need a mother like that." Stella remembered the bracelet. "Joe, there's something I want you to have." She pulled the tangle of beads from her pocket and separated Grandma Angie's from Dane's. "Grandma Angie made this for you. For your roses." She showed him the yellow and orange beads. "I think you should have it."

Joe held the strands against his palm, pain crossing his face. "She made me a bracelet?"

Stella swallowed. She had done the right thing, giving it up. "Yes. She kept it by her bed, no telling how long."

He looked past his hand and back at her. "Thank you, Stella." He pulled her into an embrace. "I sure have missed her."

"I got a letter from Dane," she said. "I'm going to see him. Have you heard from him?"

He shook his head. "Not yet. I'm sure you were first."

"Do you know where Ryker went?"

"No. I expect to hear, though."

"Must be quiet at that garage without them."

His eyes went back to the bracelet. "It is indeed."

Beatrice turned around. "So you've decided to go?"

"To see him, yes." Stella waved Janine over, who was standing near her dad. "You want to come to Jefferson City?"

"She most certainly will not!" Vivian tried to push back through to her. "Her parents will never allow it."

Stella ignored her mother. "We could shop for gowns."

Janine's face lit into a smile. "Well, I AM getting married, and I don't think my parents really have much say anymore."

"You girls have a good time," Beatrice said. "Be careful up there."

"The State Pen is pretty intimidating," Joe said. "I've never been inside."

Stella looked around at the group. "So am I getting a ticket or what? I have plans to make! So write me up or I'm out of here."

The sheriff stepped forward, but Vivian held him back. "It's no use, Terry. I can't be responsible for her anymore."

Stella turned away, threading her arms through Janine's and Beatrice's. This was it, she realized. Definitely time to move on.

32

ON THE INSIDE

THE prison movies got it right. Except for the parts they got wrong.

The worst stuff was pretty accurate. On his first day on the main cell block, he'd seen no fewer than ten shivs and shanks, all made of the most unimaginable things. Metal spoons, sharpened on the floor and made longer by binding twigs to them with twine. A broken handle of a paint roller, filed down so it could slide between someone's ribs with ease. Even plastic tableware could be fashioned into weapons. Anyone who wanted to demonstrate power to the new inmate had flashed him theirs.

Dane hadn't wanted the fear, hated the terror that crept over him, making him anxious and unable to handle himself like he knew was necessary—laid back and cocksure. His anger had gotten him here. Only a total lockdown from the inside out would get him through it. So when someone lifted a pants leg to reveal a toothbrush whittled to a point, Dane just nodded in acknowledgment and turned away.

The stuff the films got wrong was the tedium. Long boring hours in the housing units or out in the yard filled much of the day. Work duty was the best part, as he had something to actually do.

Dane walked the yard, a large dusty hole littered with inmates. Some of the men lounged on the lowest of the crumbling steps up a rolling hillside. He preferred to climb to the top of it, generally out of the main fray of men doing push-ups or talking in clumps, jostling and laughing, often plotting some scheme or another.

A month in, he had assumed his position in the inmate hierarchy. Mostly he flew beneath the radar of the big shots, the ones with cigarettes behind their ears, shafts strapped to their calves, and flaunting their power even before the guards. A few small-timers, hoping to ply him with their contraband, tried to mess with him, but he'd shown enough instability to make them wary, but not enough to incite counteraction.

He kept to himself. The caseworker had said he might earn a spot in the mechanic shop if he had good behavior, but he realized already he didn't want it. Access to the metal and tools meant thugs wanted you to steal for them, and you had little choice in the matter. The shoe factory was better, well watched and fewer items of interest. But for now he was just fine in the laundry room, where the soaps and bleaches were on lockdown and all he ever handled was the endless white shirts and gray pants. He didn't even get to the sheets, as they could be stolen and made into rope. He tried to be just competent enough to keep his position, but not so noteworthy as to get promoted anywhere with more responsibility and risk.

He kicked at a pebble, watching it tumble through the dirt and down the fragmented steps. He liked to walk the grounds, ascending and descending the crumbling stone, listening for the passage of a train just beyond the back wall. The sound reminded him of his childhood in Houston, living in a cheap house near the railroad tracks, the vague whistle and rumble so familiar that it lulled him to sleep.

He avoided the Supermax building, where the hard-timers lived. He knew that fighting or contraband could land him there, since he already had a man's death on his rap sheet. He was established in Unit 4, one of the oldest, spare, just a sink and toilet and desk, two rickety beds, and no cellmate yet. He'd made it four weeks, he could do 620 more.

He sat for a moment, toeing the dirt, and realized he was spelling Stella's name. He finished the letters, realizing this was only the second time he'd written them. The first was on the letter he'd mailed only a week ago. Still, she had not replied. It was probably better this way. He looked up into the sky. The clouds were the sort that as a kid, you would stare at and decide what animal they might be. One of them, almost right above his head, looked precisely like a circus elephant, fat body, squat legs, and an uplifted trunk that trailed out like smoke. The sight of it cheered him just a notch, an ever-so-slight loosening in his chest.

Unit 4 was lining up below, so he stood, brushed off his pants, and descended into the dust. He was settled, and right now all he could hope for was more of the same, that he'd be left alone, washing laundry, eating sparely, lying on the hard shelf with its thin mattress, listening for the train. It would have to be enough. He would make it be enough. If he was careful, he'd only be thirty-nine when he got out. Still time for some living.

But already, his life was changing. As they walked down the block of his unit, his cell door was open, two guards outside. And Dane knew what this meant. His cellmate had arrived.

33

FAILED VISIT

STELLA eased off the gas as the Mustang rolled slowly down Capitol Ave. The high stone walls of the Missouri State Penitentiary were unrelenting, stretching for blocks, punctuated by angled watchtowers topped by glass. Stella stared up at one of them, trying to spot the guard. The severity of the scene was lightened considerably by the most oddly shaped cloud, like an elephant with its trunk in the air. She almost laughed.

"Sure you don't want me to go in with you?" Janine asked, but the quiver in her voice let Stella know she didn't want to.

"No, that's okay. There's probably a list or something. I don't think just anyone can visit anyone."

"How do you know what to do?"

"I don't." Stella passed the main gate. "I don't even know where to go in."

"Seems like he should have sent instructions, or something. Didn't you call?"

"I didn't think about it. I guess I should have." Stella pulled up to a stop sign. "But we're here now. Might as well learn."

Stella drove away from the prison and back toward the heart of town. "So I'll drop you off at that dreamy little shop. There's a cafe next door. If you're done looking before I get back, I'll meet you there."

"Okay." Janine's face had returned to full color. "I won't buy anything until you see it."

"I don't think I'll be long," Stella said. "I don't know if I'll even get in." She pulled up before a row of stores. "Have fun looking—I'll be right back!"

Janine opened the door. "I hope you get to see him. I really do." She gave Stella a quick hug.

The slamming of Janine's door sent Stella to shaking. She'd never done anything like this. She had no idea what to expect, although in movies she had seen people talking on telephones through glass. Was that the way it would be?

She approached the prison again. This time she noticed a small sign that said "Staff and Visitor Parking." Okay, so one hurdle crossed.

She pulled up before a gate, and a thin guard in a gray uniform walked up. "Visiting?" he asked. His mouth seemed to have a permanent sneer. Occupational hazard, probably.

"Yes."

He checked his watch. "Only half an hour left. You might want to come back in the afternoon."

"Can I just pop in for a second?"

The man rolled his eyes. "Must be your first time. Nothing here happens in a second. ID?"

She dug the license from her purse. He wrote down something on a clipboard. "Park over there. Main door's in the middle. Mind you don't bring in anything but your ID and your keys. No purses, no bags, nothing." He leaned into the car. "I don't think they'll let you in with that skirt. Too short. You got something else?"

Stella squeezed her knees tightly together. "Some jeans."

"Change in the car. And read the instructions you got after your approval letter. They don't like people ignoring their rules. They can prevent you from coming in."

Stella didn't tell him she didn't have an approval letter. Surely she could find out what she needed inside. "Thank you."

He pushed a button to open the gate. Another guard just inside waved her through.

She parked in a far corner and reached in the back for her bag. People were coming out the door of the red-and-white-striped building the guard had shown her. She tugged on the jeans, pushing the seat back to make it easier to maneuver. She had no idea about any of the rules. What did it matter what she wore?

Once Stella had changed, she jumped out of the car and locked the door, holding only her keys and ID as they had instructed.

A crying woman dashed out the entrance, trailed by a child, maybe five years old, who was sucking his thumb. She pushed past Stella. Another older man held the door open for her, shaking his head. "Tough times, tough times," he muttered as she passed.

Just inside the entrance a large woman sat behind a table. "ID," she barked.

Stella handed her the driver's license, taking in the large room, a line of windows in the wall, like bank tellers, and two steel doors on either end. Two rows of benches housed people who seemed to be waiting expectantly, mostly women, all older than her. Stella suddenly flashed ahead ten years. Is that what she would look like then? Had they been young when they first came?

"Name of prisoner?"

"Dane Scoffield. Daniel. Daniel Scoffield."

The woman flipped some pages in a large black binder. "No approved visitors for Daniel Scoffield." She handed the ID back.

"I can't see him?"

"Only approved visitors can see inmates."

"But he wrote me a letter asking me to come." Stella reached for her purse and realized it wasn't there. "It's in the car."

The women didn't look up, shutting her binder. "Only approved visitors can see inmates."

"How do I get approved?"

The woman stared up at her as though she'd just asked to take Dane home. "Go talk to Mrs. Murchison. She'll tell you the procedure." She gestured vaguely toward the wall of windows.

Stella didn't want to ask which one, but only two of them were occupied. One was a man, so that left the other. "Mrs. Murchison?" she asked tentatively. The robust woman perched on a stool, her hair tied severely back in a bun. She also wore the gray uniform, buttons straining across her bosom.

She had apparently already taken in the conversation, and she shoved a paper at Stella. "These are the rules of decorum and dress. No short skirts. No slit skirts. No cleavage. No jewelry. No purses or bags. No food. You can bring change for the vending machine. Your keys and ID will go over there." She pointed at another window, where a bored young man leaned on his elbows.

"How do I get approved?"

"The inmate will send you a form to fill out. Once we have it, we will do a criminal background check. If you get cleared, you will receive another letter letting you know your approval status."

"I don't have the form."

"Well, then, maybe he hasn't listed you. He only gets twenty for his list."

"I—I think he would. He wrote me asking me to come." Stella was so confused. Maybe Dane didn't know the procedure either?

Mrs. Murchison opened another binder. "Inmate?"

"Daniel Scoffield."

She flipped through. "He's new. Not even eligible for visitors yet, although"—she glanced at the calendar—"if he's had good behavior, he can start seeing them tomorrow." She flipped another page. "But that's irrelevant. His list is blank. Did you turn in your form?"

Stella tried not to get impatient. "I didn't get a form."

"Well, he either hasn't sent any out or he sent them out late." She closed the book. "You can write him. Tell him you are willing to come."

"Can I send the message here?"

"No, it has to go through the mail. We have a process."

"So another several days before I can get a form?"

"If he sends one. Then a couple weeks on the criminal history."

So another month she'd have to wait. If Dane even sent her the paperwork. She felt tears coming and got more angry with herself. When had she become such a sniveling wreck? She took the paper. "I see.

Okay."

"I can make a registry of your visit," Mrs. Murchison said. "The caseworker might notice. She might tell him you were here. No promises. ID?"

Stella passed her the license and watched as her name and number were scribbled in the blank space near Dane's name.

"Here ya go." The woman attempted a mildly sympathetic look as she passed back the ID. "You got a phone number?"

Stella wasn't sure which one to give her, Beatrice's or the perfume shop's. But the shop had an answering machine. She gave her that one.

One of the big steel doors opened, and she peered through, hoping to see anything inside. Just a corridor. An elderly woman came out, ushered by yet another guard. She was bent over, her gray hair pale against her dark forehead, which was all Stella could see as she was so stooped.

The woman lifted her chin, revealing tired eyes behind tiny silver spectacles on a chain. "I remember my first time here," she said, and Stella wondered how they could tell who was new. "I looked a lot like you, young and fresh." Her hand trembled on a black cane.

Stella whirled around and barreled toward the door.

She gulped in sunshine and air. Two guards stood near each other, smoking cigarettes by the stone wall. They saw her and laughed. "Bad visit?" one jeered.

Stella ran to her car in a full-on sprint. The Mustang roared to life, and she hightailed it back toward the guard station. The inside guard held up his hands. She rolled down her window. "Whoa, Nelly," he said. "You can't be rushing out like this. People will get antsy."

"I have to go," she said. "Please let me out."

He chortled. "First-timers." Still, he inspected the backseat before signaling the other guard, who opened the gate. The moment it had swung wide enough, she pushed the gas, aiming to put as much distance between her car and the prison as she could. Maybe forever.

34

DANE GETS THE NUMBER

DANE startled awake when the guard rapped on the bars. "You have a message."

"Who, me?" Dane asked. His cellmate Alex still lay on his bed, a towel over his face.

"Yes, you. From the office." The guard pushed the paper through the bars.

Dane shuffled forward. He hated midday naps, but even after a month, he could not get used to the 5 a.m. starts, the dark making his eyelids want to droop even as they were herded down to the showers. Each night he tried to sleep, but restlessness coupled with the misery coming from other members of the cellblock kept him up. He needed to stay sharp, and during the midday inmate count, they were stuck in their cells for over an hour. So he slept then.

The guard was the just-doing-my-job sort, not one of the blowhards who enjoyed authority. So the paper was simply passed over to him rather than crumpled or tossed or laid just out of reach on the ground. You learned to not give a shit about small stuff like that, and to never be too eager for anything.

He returned to his bed, unfolding the paper. At the top were his name and prisoner number. Then one line, "Prisoner has earned telephone privileges." Then instructions on placing collect calls.

He glanced out the window, the sun lighting up the dome of his cell, carved from stone quarried by the very prisoners the rooms once housed. The walls had been painted so many times that they peeled in colors, white, brown—someone at some point had coated them in dusty blue.

He didn't know Stella's number. Or even where she was. He'd mailed her at the shop hoping Beatrice would know. He knew addresses. Just not numbers. They didn't give them phone books. Information was a big thing, powerful, and in short supply on the inside.

He flipped the page over. On the back was a handwritten note.

Stella Ashton visited 10-20-84. Visitor services explained her lack of visitation status. Left phone number. 555-490-2309.

Call her. We can start the forms. Maggie

Dane's hand gripped the paper so hard, it crumpled. He panicked, realizing how easily this number could be lost. He glanced at Alex. A difficult cellmate, hyper, overanimated, always making jokes Dane didn't get. Alex came from Brooklyn originally and had failed to get extradited after a botched armed robbery. Dane had never explained his own crime, but obviously the inmates talked, as Alex came in on the second day saying, "I ain't gonna get you mad. I ain't ever gonna make you mad."

But there could be worse. Alex might be emaciated and jacked up, already working the system for contraband and hoping for drugs, but fortunately he didn't have any street cred or cash. Dane expected, though, that as much as the boy asked around, their cell would be subject to more searches than usual. Didn't matter. He had nothing but his blank envelopes and paper. Having nothing to lose made life easier, although he did keep the scrap of pink fabric that was Stella's hidden in a crumpled piece of paper in the back corner of the desk.

But now there was this. He opened the drawer and took out the pen. He wrote the number on another piece of blank stationery. Then he waited for the guards to pass again, and quickly scribbled the number both on the side of the desk, and on the wall by his pillow. He lay back on his bed, and for the first time in a long time, just to be sure he could not lose it, committed a phone number to memory.

* * *

The three phone booths in the rec area were all taken, so Dane sat on a rickety chair nearby to wait. He refused to let his anxiety show, something that could be used against him. If he didn't get to call today, tomorrow was just another day.

But it did matter. Stella had come by yesterday, a Saturday. She'd left her number, so she wouldn't know why he didn't call. She had no idea how limited their time was, how hard it could be for someone new on the block to get to a phone. He tried to look like he wasn't waiting, and didn't care, but stayed close, to be the first in if someone left a booth. He kept the paper folded tightly in his palm, hidden, a dead giveaway that he was a first-timer. Didn't matter, he'd memorized everything. The dial-out number, the prisoner code. But he had no idea where Stella's number would lead. A hotel, or the shop, or one of Stella's friends. He doubted she'd moved back home. She'd come to see him. Hopefully that didn't mean something was wrong. God, what if she were pregnant? Or getting arrested for being there too? What if Darlene had gone after her?

His anxiety rose until his face felt like it would pop from the pressure. Another inmate, Carter, one of the real jackasses and seriously dangerous, strolled up to the phone booths and rapped on the door. "Out, motherfucker," he said to the guy inside. The man shook his head, and Carter yanked open the door and jerked him out.

Dane glanced over at the guard who watched not fifteen feet away. Another plain Jane, nobody who would get all puffed up and overreact. Carter had already known this, which was why he'd risk it.

The door slid shut, and Dane continued to wait. The ejected inmate cursed to himself and wandered off. None of the others seemed to be ready to go anytime soon. He had to stay cool. The numbers were easy, straightforward, and comforting to simply recite in his mind. He laid them out backward, then rolled them out from the outside in, rearranged them numerically, categorized them by odd and even, added them up. And finally, the man on the end left his booth.

Dane didn't even let the glass close but rushed inside. The small room was rank, airless, and hot. Nothing like the one with Stella at the truck stop, a lifetime ago. He picked up the black receiver, strung on a metal coil too short to wrap around someone's neck, and thus not long enough to allow you to stand up straight, or sit on the floor. Dane leaned in as he punched the numbers on the worn gray keypad.

"Your name?" an operator with a whiny voice asked.

"Dane Scoffield."

After a couple of clicks, he could hear the phone ringing, distantly, like it was in another booth. Once. Twice. Three times. Could be no one home.

Then another click. "You've got the good sense to call Good Scents. Please leave a message at the tone."

"Sowwwy," the operator said. "Can't do collect on an answering machine."

But then, they heard a series of beeps, and a muffled "Crap!" Then "Hello? Hello?"

"I have a collect call from the Missouri State Penitentiary. A Dane Scuffield. Do you accept the charges?"

Scoffield! She'd gotten it wrong.

"Yes! Yes!"

Dane recognized Beatrice's voice. With another click, the sounds all got louder, and Dane realized the operator was gone.

"Dane, is that you?"

"Yes. Hello, Beatrice."

"Are you all right? How are you? Are you okay?"

Dane felt himself smiling into the mouthpiece. "As good as can be expected. How is Stella?"

"She's fine. She's, crap, let me get her. Just hold on!"

The receiver thunked in his ear. He pictured the phone resting on the glass cabinet, and the register, hiding Stella's dream book, and the cushioned seats, the rows of bottles, the heavy air laden with mingling perfumes.

The receiver moved, something rubbed on it, then she was there,

Stella. "Dane? Dane? Is that you?"

"It's me, Stell."

He thought she might have sobbed, or something. Maybe she was having a hard time thinking what to say. "They told me you came to visit."

"I didn't have the forms!"

"I know. I didn't know." He should have done it different.

"You didn't know I needed them? Don't they tell you anything?" Her voice was high, strident.

"No, I mean, I didn't know if you'd want to come. I wanted to write you first."

"Oh. But, yes. Of course. And I came."

"Thank you."

He could hear her breathing and squeezed his eyes closed, trying to blot out the marked-up wall of the booth, the stench, the noise outside, and the fear that he'd be ripped from the conversation. "Listen, these calls end suddenly sometimes. But I wanted to talk to you. To hear you."

"Dane, I've been so worried."

"I'm fine in here. It's not that bad. Really. Sort of boring."

She forced a laugh. "Boring?"

"Sure, not much to do. Bunch of angry boys all trying to get the best corner of the sandbox."

"You be careful. I've heard such terrible stories."

He sensed a movement by the door but refused to look. "Don't believe them. It's dull as dishwater, and I'm going to get fat."

She laughed again. "More of you to love."

He swallowed. "I don't deserve any of that."

The silence was long and hard, but finally she said, "So you going to send me that damn form?"

"I'll send you all twenty."

"But you only get twenty."

"Then you get them all."

She laughed again. "I don't know what to do without you."

He had no idea how to answer that. "I'll get the form to you." The air changed as the door came open. Still, he didn't look. "Rec time is over.

I'll call again. Okay? You can write me, make sure I have your numbers. This is the time of day I can call." A hand gripped his shoulder. He still wouldn't look.

"Bye, Dane," she said.

"Bye." He pushed down on the hook to disconnect and set the receiver into place. Then, and only then, did he turn.

It was the guard. "Time's up. To the yard."

Dane exhaled slowly. He kept a grip on the paper he hadn't needed and whistled lightly as he lined up with the other gray pants and white shirts. This had been the best day in over a month.

35

FAREWELL, HOLLY

STELLA set the phone back down slowly even though the dial tone had buzzed in her ear for several seconds. He'd sounded so normal. He could have been calling from anywhere. Joe's. Or his duplex.

Beatrice stepped back through the curtain. "How is he?"

"He sounds fine. Totally normal."

"That's good, isn't it?" Beatrice set a box on the counter. "We want him to be fine."

"I'm not fine!"

Beatrice went around the cash register to envelop Stella in a hug. "What would make you fine?"

Stella felt swallowed by the cushy embrace and the overpowering smell of Chanel No. 19. "I need to see him. It's like he isn't real."

"Is that what you want? To be near him?"

Stella paced the shop, stopping to straighten a bottle or tuck a bit of tissue paper back into a basket. "Yes, I do. I'm too far." She'd been too far from Grandma. She wouldn't make the same mistake twice. Who else in this world did she love?

Crap. Love. She'd thought it. She aligned a bottle of bath splash with the row. Hell of a time to figure that out.

Beatrice was following her. "It'll be hard, not being around anybody

194

who cares for you, starting over with your man in prison."

Stella plunked down onto the cushioned bench. "I understand that. And maybe I'll hate it and leave again. But I have to do something."

"Well, I'd agree with that. You're going stir-crazy."

Stella dropped her forehead into her hands. "And as much as I love Janine, her wedding...it's awful. I can't...do anything more. I'll be her maid of honor, I will. And I'll be there. But day in and day out. Colors and flowers and picking out doilies."

"I know. It seems so silly to you with what you have to deal with."

"It's important to her, I know. But I can't do it. It's so far from what I get."

"She'll understand."

But Janine wouldn't. She'd be upset, just like in Jefferson, when Stella had shown up at the dress shop and not been completely focused on the twenty gowns that all looked the same. They were all beautiful. Why did anyone have to spend so much energy deciding between necklines?

Stella walked back to Beatrice. "I know it seems like I've left a dozen times already and didn't get out the door. But I think this one is really it. I'm moving to Jefferson. Get a job. A little apartment. I'll be all right for a while, with the savings."

"I'll help in any way I can."

"I know you will. You've been great." Like the mom she never had.

Stella tugged the book of brochures and flyers out from under the cash register. "Time for a new dream." She chucked the binder into the trash.

"Not what you expected."

"Nothing ever is." Stella looked around the shop. "I think I'm leaving you in pretty good shape."

Beatrice sniffed, her eyes red. "You aren't, and you know it."

Stella hugged her this time. "I do know. You would have been a great mom, Bea. You should have had kids."

"Tell that to the men who never married me," Beatrice sniffed. "But I got you to carry on about. You better call me. And invite me up when you get all settled so I can see your place."

"I will." Stella pulled away. "It won't take me a couple hours to get everything back in the car. Most of it is still in boxes."

"I'll write you a letter of recommendation. I'll go type it right now."

Beatrice hurried to the back room again, and Stella circled the shop slowly. She'd seen Dane for the first time right there. And this was where they'd agreed to meet on the tower. No place would ever mean more to her. It wasn't going to work out with Dane, she could see that. Twelve years was just too much. But for now, she might as well go. Play it out for a bit longer. She did love him, though she'd never said it. And that would carry her through, until it couldn't anymore.

* * *

Stella roared out of Holly early the next morning, Beatrice waving from the porch, instructed to tell Dane how to find Stella if he called Good Scents again. She'd already written him a letter and left it in the mailbox, saying the same thing. She felt confident now that they'd be in contact more often, even if the paperwork meant it would be a while before she could visit him.

The three hours passed slowly, though she did take time to walk through the truck stop outside Branson where they'd cleaned up that last day together. She bought another one of the green "Show-Me State" shirts and kept it in her lap the rest of the drive. She only had one set of pictures of them together, taken that same day in a photo booth at a restaurant, a strip of four shots in black and white. Now she clipped it to the rear-view mirror. She looked frightful in them, hair loose and down, no makeup, but happy. Her head rested against Dane's shoulder as he stared straight into the camera in one. In another, they kissed. One was blurry as he pretended to attack her. In the last, you could only see his head and back as he grabbed her.

Stella pulled off at a dime store on the outskirts of Jefferson City around lunchtime, hoping to pick up a newspaper for help-wanted ads and maybe a place to rent. The city wasn't huge like normal state capitals, not that she'd been to many, but it was large enough to get lost in. She didn't know what areas to look in, what might be expensive or unsafe.

Inside she spotted a simple black frame, long and skinny like her strip of pictures, so she took it to the counter. A teenager just out of high school, or a dropout maybe, sat on a stool blowing big pink bubbles. Her hair was teased, held in place by a lace headband. Stella had never seen anything like it. "Your hair," she said. "Wow."

The girl grasped a chunk of it and crunched it with her hand. "Madonna style. Didn't you see her on MTV? The Music Awards?"

At Stella's confused stare, she pulled out a magazine. "Last month. 'Like a Virgin.'" On the cover was a woman in white underwear, a big poofy skirt, and her hair was just like this girl's—full of stiff waves.

"Huh." She'd been dealing with Dane's arrest and waiting for the hearing. Holly didn't have MTV anyway. They didn't even have cable yet.

"That'll be three dollars," she said, sticking the frame in the bag. "Iff'n you want the magazine too, it'll be five."

"That's okay." She passed over the bills, taking one more glance at the cover. She didn't have time for music or scrunched-up hair. She needed a place to live, and a job. "So where are there apartments? Or some place to rent?"

The girl cracked her gum. "I dunno. All over. Cheap near the university, but kind of ratty. Southside is nice."

Stella picked up the bag. "Okay, thanks." Not much, but it was something.

She drove to the center of town, slowing as she passed the walls of the prison. A different guard was at the visitor gate. Hopefully no one would remember her by the time she went back. She paused at the stop sign, staring up at the guard tower. That man could see her Dane, but she couldn't. He took for granted, maybe even hated, the very view she longed for.

36

SINNERS' CAFE

STELLA plopped down on the hotel bed, the newspaper spread in front of her. She'd passed a couple of Help Wanted signs on the drive through town but still wasn't sure how to find a place. That probably needed to come first, as it wasn't safe to leave her life's possessions in her car. She'd chosen a fancier hotel in hopes the parking garage would be safer than some motel lot, even though the sixty dollars a night would cut through her fund in a hurry.

Maybe the job was a priority. She rolled onto her back. Beatrice hadn't heard from Dane that day. Stella left the number of her hotel and told her to ask how often he got a chance to call. It might only be once a week.

She was anxious to get somewhere permanent and to get into some routine where she could predictably be home when he could call, and that she would be off during visiting hours.

Stella turned back to the newspaper. Not many duplexes in her price range. She'd just have to call and go looking. She flipped back to the jobs. Not much she was qualified for. She'd hoped for another small shop. One small classified ad caught her attention. "Sinners' Cafe. Need waitress. Will train. Night hours. Flexible weekends."

Stella had waited tables a time or two. Not her favorite thing, but she could manage until something else came up. Plus, she was starving. Might as well go check out the place.

She asked the front desk for directions and took off again through town, driving slowly to learn the names of streets and to spot any signs for rentals. She almost missed the cafe, a sprawling glass building with a cracked unpainted parking lot.

A giant wooden sign, painted garishly red, formed a heart. A neon arrow flashed in alternating colors to cross the surface. "Sinners' Cafe" crackled in bright white on a rectangle below. Stella parked the car and glanced back at the boxes stuffed in her backseat. This place made her nervous. Maybe she should just drive away.

But her stomach rumbled, and a pair of men walking out the door didn't seem too scary, just blue-collar types like she'd seen every day in Holly. So she carefully locked all the doors and crossed the lot to the door.

As soon as she stepped inside, she knew she was overdressed. Her black skirt and heels did not fit in whatsoever. The diners all wore work shirts and jeans, or overalls. Even the women were dressed way down, sweats and T-shirts. The waitresses were mostly older, in navy-blue skirts with white aprons and silly caps. A sixty-something woman with a puff of white hair and a badge that proclaimed her name as "Rennie" gestured to an empty booth along the windows. "Take that one, lovey," she said, her accent clearly not Missouri, almost Irish.

Stella slid onto the cold red vinyl, shiny and cracked. The tables were all bright blue with embedded sparkles. The place looked like it coughed glitter, although seriously worn around the edges. She half expected girls to come out in roller skates, but whoever owned the Sinners' Cafe seemed to want the help to be matronly. Stella didn't stand much of a chance.

She spread the paper on the table, ready to cross out the circled classified. Rennie approached with her pad, spotting the marks before Stella could close it. "You here about the job?" She whirled around. "Corgie! You got an applicant!"

"Wait, I'm not sure," Stella sputtered. "I might be wrong." She acutely felt her ill-chosen outfit, and she flooded hot with anxiety.

Another waitress stopped to stare, a pitcher in each hand. This one was younger, late twenties, her eyebrows shaved and penciled back in for a dramatic arch that made her look angry. "What is it, then? You applying or not?"

Stella wanted to sink into the red vinyl. Were the waitresses always all up in everything?

"Corgie!" Rennie called again. "You comin'?"

A man in a white cook's hat stuck his head through the opening between the bar and the kitchen. "Woman, I'm about to burn some burgers." He disappeared again.

"He'll be out shortly. You want a drink while you wait?"

Stella shook her head. "I'm fine." Her stomach rumbled again. She wouldn't be eating now, it seemed.

"I'll bring you some water. You look like you're about to faint clean away." She stuck her pad into a pocket of her apron. "Don't worry about Corgie. He don't bite, despite the name." She burst out laughing, and Stella wondered what sort of freak show she had just entered. Maybe she should run for it.

A man in the booth in front of her turned around in his seat. "Whooeee, I hope he hires this one!" he said.

The younger waitress strolled back by and acted like she might dump the pitcher on his head from behind. "Say that around Corgie, and he'll throw your sorry ass out."

"Touchy, touchy," the man said.

Obviously the place had a core of regulars. Stella hadn't expected such familiarity, something you'd see in Holly, in a big city. Maybe things really were the same everywhere.

Corgie himself finally pushed through a pair of swinging red doors and sat down opposite her.

"Name?" he asked.

So much for small-town manners. "Stella Ashton."

"Experience?" His small black eyes bore straight into her.

She stared at his grease-smeared apron instead. "Two gigs waitressing."

"You get fired?"

"No."

"You quit?"

"Yes." Stella's heart hammered painfully. She wasn't sure she could work for this guy.

"You in any trouble? Why you looking?"

"I just moved to Jefferson."

"Where you leave from?"

Stella's eyes skittered from his face to across the cafe. "Holly."

"Whooeee!" The young waitress was lingering, still holding the pitchers. "Now that town there's a hole in the wall."

"You waitress there?"

"My last job was actually in a shop." Stella reached for her purse and the recommendation letter, but he went on.

"You got a license?"

"To waitress?" Did you need one?

"Nah, to drive." His face never changed expression, just a deep frown and hard eyes.

"Yes." She didn't want to reach for her purse again.

"Can I see it?"

This time she did unzip her bag and tug her wallet out. Her hotel key was caught on the clasp and skidded across the table.

He picked it up. "You ain't got a place to stay yet?"

"Just got in town today."

He turned around. "Rennie!"

She looked up from her pad. "Just a sec."

"Rennie can help you find a place. You should get settled in before you start, unless you're super hard up for money." He looked at the key again. "But I guess not, if you're there." He slid the key across to her and took the license, squinted at it, then set it back on the table. "You okay to start Monday?"

The hours. She needed to know the hours. "I think. When?"

"We would want to start you on days."

She frowned. "I'm not sure I have a whole lot of flexibility."

Rennie walked up, her gait a little off, like she was hurting. She wore soft white shoes with thick soles, like nurses did. "What she need?"

"A place. Your cousin got a list?"

"She does."

Corgie turned back to Stella. "So what's your issue?"

Stella's face burned. She couldn't tell them her boyfriend was in prison. "I get phone calls in the middle of the day. I like to be able to take them."

The young waitress poked her head in beside Rennie. "Ya got somebody on the inside, eh?" She shoved her way into the booth next to Stella, setting the dripping pitchers on the table. "Who it is? Your pa? Brother?" She assessed Stella's face. "Nah, a man. Your man is on the inside."

Stella turned back to Corgie. "Your ad said night shifts."

He rubbed his neck. "Trouble is, that can be a rough crowd. Someone young and pretty like you'd have a time of it."

Stella sat up straighter. "I can handle rough."

The young waitress turned to face Stella, revealing her own name tag that said "Cayenne." She saw Stella looking at it. "Yeah, like the pepper." She smacked her hand on the table. "Some of the boys that come in late are tough critters. Come up to see inmates, just like yourself, then seem to hang around to stir up trouble. Corgie's brilliant idea for a cafe attracts every lowlife west of the Mississippi."

"When did he go in?" Rennie asked. "He got privileges?"

Stella figured there wasn't much use hiding anything now. "A month ago. He called yesterday."

Cayenne wiped the dripping pitchers with her rag. "Then you can go see him. You got your papers square?"

Stella shook her head. "No visitor's forms yet. That's been slow. And now I've moved."

Rennie ripped an order from her pad and handed it to Corgie. "You get on back there and cook this up. We'll take her from here."

Corgie slid out of the booth. "I still say she ain't right for the night rounds."

"We'll watch out for her," Rennie said. "I can stay a bit late for her first few."

Apparently she had the job. The women were nosy, but seemed to want to help.

Rennie slid into the booth and picked up the license. "You got to get this changed right off, as soon as you have a place. Everything's gotta match. Your ID, your papers. Come by tomorrow morning, and I'll get you a list of places. You got a budget?" She handed the license to Stella. "Never mind, you work here, your man is in the pen, you got a budget. We'll see what we got."

"I don't have any furniture."

"Okay. I'll see what's around. Not much furnished. But there's garage sales. Certain parts of town got lots of people comin' and goin', due to transfers and paroles. We'll get you set."

Cayenne got up from the booth. "All right, fun's over. See you tomorrow. What's your name?"

"Stella."

"Well, all right, Stella." She lifted the pitchers like a toast and then turned back to the other tables.

Rennie stuck her pen behind her ear. "Come 'round about ten. When is his rec time?"

"I don't know."

"When did he call you?"

"Oh. About two."

"So that's his rec time. There's phone booths downstairs in every block. He won't get to 'em every day. There's not many, and he won't have much pull yet. But he got to you once. He will again."

"How long is rec time?"

"An hour, generally."

"So you know someone inside?"

Rennie pushed herself along the booth, painfully, to stand up. "My son. Been in since he was nineteen."

"Oh. Will he get out soon?"

Rennie's features fell a notch. "Not while I'm still livin'." She forced a smile. "Yours a short-timer?"

Stella didn't know what qualified as short or long. "Twelve to fifteen."

"Oh." Rennie smoothed her apron. "Young thing like you."

Stella knew what she meant. "We'll have to see."

Rennie nodded. "See you tomorrow."

Stella slid out from under the table, feeling more than a little lightheaded as she shoved her way out the door and into the cool early evening. She needed something to eat. And to drive around some more. She'd just gotten lucky, and she knew it. Somebody was watching out for her. Her bracelet slid down her arm, the amethyst one she'd broken on the tower, pieced back together in the long days of waiting at Beatrice's house. Of course. She glanced up into the evening sky, awash with blues. "Thanks, Grandma. You always did take care of me."

37

ALEX

"INSPECTION." The guard banged on the bars, waking Dane. He sat up. It was dark.

Alex rolled over on his bed as the guard shined a light on him. "What the hell?"

The door swung open. Dane wasn't as familiar with the night guards, but he recognized the stance, the set of the jaw. An ass-kicker. He'd have to play this really cool.

The bruiser guard stepped aside. "Cuff them."

Two other men entered the cell, jerking Dane and Alex up from their beds and locking their hands behind their backs. They were pushed forward until they stood outside their cell on the walkway.

The guard jerked the bedding off the steel frames, tossing it on the floor. He felt along all the seams, then got on the floor and shone the flashlight underneath. He reached up under Alex's bed and tugged something down. Shit. What was that boy up to?

Alex acted like he might step forward, but the guard bellowed, "Turn them around," so they were forced to face the railing. He could see some stirring in the cells on the walk across the way.

Dane tried to keep his demeanor calm as the guard tore through the cell. He could hear the table screeching as it was moved, the drawer opening and closing. He began reciting numbers in his head. His inmate number. His phone code. The perfume-shop phone. The hotel-room phone Beatrice had given him a few days ago. Stella was looking for a place in Jefferson. His heart surged, just thinking how close she was. He'd already had the forms sent, but Beatrice planned to drive them straight up to Stella, who had gotten a job already.

He clamped his jaw tight. Keep it cool. Finally, the guard came out. He held up a piece of mop handle, sharpened to a point, and shoved it in Alex's face. "Who's this for?"

Dane kept his head turned away, just barely able to see. So far the guard was only interested in Alex.

"Never seen that b'fore. Must've been there when I got there."

"I wasn't looking for the hell of it. You've been waving it around." The guard kneed Alex in the gut. "Still don't recognize it?"

"Not…mine." Alex could barely grunt out a sound.

Dane wished he would just admit it and move on. He'd watched him rubbing the damn stick on his bedpost for weeks.

The guard landed a fist to Alex's jaw next. "You look to me like you're resisting a search. I'm afraid I'm going to have to report how you attacked us with this broom handle." He chuckled. "Hope you weren't hoping for early release on good behavior."

The guard pocketed the makeshift weapon. "Back in your cell. Think about it."

Alex was shoved roughly back inside, still handcuffed. The other guard released Dane without comment and led him through the door.

Dane immediately sat down on the metal frame, head bowed, hands between his knees, to wait out what was going to happen, but careful not get involved.

"You gonna uncuff me?" Alex demanded.

"Nah, I think I'm going to have a momentary lapse of memory," the guard said, closing and locking the cell. "Have fun picking up in the dark."

He killed the light, washing them in semi-darkness.

They sat there, silently, then Alex kicked the bedding on the floor. "You narc on me?"

Dane shook his head. "Nope."

"God damn it!" Alex stood up, pushing aside the papers and clothes littering the floor.

Dane got up and shoved his mattress back on his bed. He turned and replaced Alex's as well.

"Thanks, man. I'm in deep shit now."

Dane didn't want to know anything. To get involved was to court trouble. He just grunted and set to getting his sheets back on, feeling his way around in the dark corners. When it was close enough, he fell back on the bed. Alex still paced. "I'm going to get my ass killed over this."

Dane turned to the wall. Alex had been desperate for credit, trying to get into the trade. He had night sweats and slept fitfully. Probably withdrawal. He'd do something stupid soon, something worse. Dane hoped he wasn't around as part of the fall. He only had so much he could feel for anyone. And all that he reserved for Stella and staying focused on not getting any more time.

38

First Day on the Job

STELLA pulled up to the Sinners' Cafe, hoping her first evening on the job went well. Her back ached from cleaning the crappy little apartment she'd managed to finally rent. It was filthy inside, but everything worked and the neighborhood wasn't bad. It sat halfway between the prison and the diner, no more than ten minutes to either one. And it was an address. She'd already applied for a change to her license and had the printout showing her new place. By the time her visitor's form arrived at the prison and the background check was done, she'd have a new ID and clearance to see Dane. Most importantly, she already had the phone installed.

Beatrice had been a huge help, driving up with the form, bringing news of Dane, and helping her set up. Beatrice also connived with Joe to get Stella's father to let them into Grandma Angie's house, so her new place had a couple of pieces from there—the bedside table where Grandma had stored the bracelets and her night things, plus a small rocking chair that had sat in the living room for as long as Stella could remember. It had exactly fit in the back of Beatrice's Oldsmobile.

Things were going about as well as they could go.

Dinner appeared to be in full swing. Stella froze at the door, shocked at the din and clattering of ice and plates and scraping chairs and the ring

ring ring of the cash register.

"What are you looking at?" Cayenne shouted from behind the counter. "Put this on." She tossed a heavy white apron. "You can get the rest of your uniform when things settle down." Stella caught the apron but still stood there, watching the crazy blur of mouths, hands, and food.

Three huge men in faded brown-stained overalls sat at the first table by the door, devouring plates of some mixed-up mash of green things, potatoes, gravy, and what might have once been a chicken-fried steak. The threesome worked almost in rhythm—knife cutting, fork stabbing, shoveling, wiping, gulping, then doing it all over again.

"Hey, you, take some water and menus to the Randolfs over there," Cayenne shouted again. She pointed at a group pushing tables together in the back. Dodging tables and tying the apron frantically, Stella hurried toward the family. Someone grabbed her arm.

"What?" Stella asked.

A burly man with "Butch" stenciled on his shirt pocket pointed to his glass. "I need some more tea, pretty miss." Stella grabbed the glass and headed back to the waitressing station, a long, high counter piled up with menus and rolled silverware near the back. Cayenne was behind it, hastily pouring water into red plastic cups. She didn't even lift the pitcher as she moved around the circle of glasses, dumping water all over the tray and counter.

Rennie hobbled past, her leg clearly giving her more trouble than a few days ago. "It's a rough one. Picked a helluva day to start."

"It is always like this?"

"Just on Fridays. We wouldn't have brought you on at a time like this, but Corgie's short a girl."

"I'll manage," Stella said, snatching up the pitcher of tea and filling the glass. "It's not rocket science."

"That it ain't," Rennie said. "Just holler if you get in a bind."

"Where's my tea?" shouted Butch. "A man's got to have something to choke down this steak!"

"Shut your trap!" Stella shouted. "It's coming."

The room quieted, and Corgie stuck his head through the service window. "Who was that?"

"The new girl," Cayenne said.

Stella set the tea in front of Butch, feeling chagrined. She should try harder. Rennie had been so nice to her, helping her find a place.

But Corgie roared with laughter. "Guess she can handle herself after all."

Stella snatched a couple of menus from the stand and headed back to the corner and the big table. She was going to fit in here just fine.

When the cafe settled down about nine, Rennie took Stella to the back to pick out a couple of the navy uniforms. She changed in the office, then stopped to look at a menu so she knew what the cafe served. For hours she had been writing down orders, assuming the customers knew what they were talking about. Rennie signed off for the evening. "I'm going to leave it to you and Cayenne. It'll be a tough crowd from here on out, but not busy."

Cayenne turned out to be terminally lazy. As Stella started cleaning off tables, Cayenne leaned against the counter and chatted with Corgie through the window.

An excruciatingly thin man with a fuzzy gray beard walked into the restaurant and sat at a booth piled high with dirty dishes. Stella looked at the rows of clean tables and sighed. Cayenne seemed to be ignoring him, so Stella headed for the station to get a menu and a glass of water.

Corgie gestured for Stella to come closer. "You'd better tell her about Crazy Charlie," he said. Cayenne laughed.

"What?" Stella asked.

Cayenne twisted a bit of scrunchy hair in her finger. "You'd better take him a big glass and an entire pitcher of water with lots of ice. And don't bother with the menu. He'll either order a ham-and-onion omelet with extra toast or a chili burger with ketchup." Cayenne leaned her elbows back on the counter.

Stella filled a pitcher with ice and water and headed to the table. There wasn't any room for the tray, so she set it on a clean table nearby.

"I'm going to sit here," Charlie said.

"That's fine. I just need to clean this off first."

His bushy eyebrows moved together. "Why isn't Cayenne waiting on me? She knows what to do."

"She's on break."

He sat with his arms crossed over his narrow chest and frowned.

Stella took the pitcher off the tray and piled the dirty dishes onto it. The load was heavy, though, and Stella's arms were ready to give out after the long day. As she turned to take the tray away, she knocked over the pitcher of water. Cayenne, who was watching with Corgie from behind the counter, burst out with a piggish snort.

Charlie sighed loudly. "I'm thirsty," he said.

Stella set down the tray and mopped at the water with her rag. "I'm sorry. I'll get another pitcher."

"No, I'll do it." He stood up, picked up the plastic pitcher, and headed toward the waitress station. Stella scooped the ice onto her tray and carried the whole lot back into the kitchen.

Corgie met her by the sinks. "You'd better be careful with Crazy Charlie. He's gotten his driver's license suspended three times for trying to run people over. They finally took it away last year. Keeps on driving, though."

Stella left the tray by the sink and turned to face him. "What are you talking about?"

Corgie leaned against the doorframe, picking at his fingernails. "When Charlie gets mad, he tries to wipe out people with his truck. This one man wouldn't buy one of his chairs—he makes chairs for a living—so he got in his truck, revved the motor, and headed right for him."

Cayenne blew through the swinging doors. "Did you tell her what Crazy Charlie did to you?"

Corgie tipped his hat back and scratched his head. "Once I charged him ten cents for the extra piece of toast, and he tried to run me over in the parking lot on my way home."

"And you guys want me to wait on him?" Stella tucked a dry rag into her apron waist.

Cayenne laughed. "He's all yours."

Great. Stella slipped past Cayenne and went through the swinging doors to the tables.

Charlie was already seated again, wiping off his table with Stella's rag. She pulled the order pad from her apron, took the pen out from over her ear, and slid into the booth across from him.

He was visibly startled. He stopped moving the towel and laced his fingers together, staring at his hands.

These people thought they already had her beat. No way, no how. Stella leaned forward against the table. "OK, Charlie. Let's get something straight. I'm your waitress today, and you're going to tell me what you want. Then I'm going to give it to you. So what will it be—ham-and-onion omelet with extra toast or chili burger with ketchup?"

When he didn't answer right away, she tapped her finger on the table. "Did you drive over here, Charlie? I thought they wouldn't let you drive anymore."

His head began to shake back and forth as he bent over. All she could see was the top of his gray hair.

"So Charlie, what is it? Omelet or burger?"

"Omelet." Charlie kept his head down.

"With extra toast," Stella said.

He glanced up. "Don't forget three grape jellies." Head down again.

"OK."

"And an extra napkin."

"OK."

"And I like to have my jellies early so I can peel off the foil."

"Sure. I'm here to give you what you order."

He looked up again, and Stella saw that he had startling light-blue eyes, the sort that made young girls melt. She wondered about him, how he came to be Crazy Charlie and not just Charlie. She had a feeling there were a lot of damaged souls in this town.

"Is that all?" Stella asked.

"Yes."

She slid out of the booth and ripped the order off her pad. She waved it at Cayenne and marched to the window to stick it on the metal wheel.

"You're a dead woman," said Corgie.

"Amen," said Cayenne.

Stella crossed her arms and stood firm. "I am not. Where's the grape jelly?"

Cayenne snorted again. "That's what I'm trying to tell you. We're out."

***

Stella sat in Grandma's rocking chair at the end of her first day, carefully removing her shoes. She'd have to buy something more practical, and soon.

Her feet were purple and red, squinched up at the toes. Even her most comfortable flats couldn't hold up to eight hours of hustling.

Her butt had been pinched, her waist had been squeezed, and her hair touched more times than she could count. The whole evening had been like playing dodgeball, but the missiles hurtling at her were all male appendages. Corgie had been right about rough. Charlie had ended up being the easiest part of the day, although the bellow he made when she'd told him about the jelly could have been heard across three states. He was long gone before she got off, so she didn't have to worry about a collision with his unlicensed vehicle.

The ones who'd scared her the most all had the same tattoo—a shamrock with "AB" on the leaves. She'd asked Cayenne about it, but she wouldn't talk, saying some things should just stay unspoken. But Stella had understood from their talk that they had brothers on the inside, and they planned retaliations against other inmates, or went after people on the outside based on what was said at visits. The whole business made her fear all the more for Dane.

She didn't have a bed yet. It would be delivered the next day. Stella glanced through the door of her bedroom at the pile of blankets that would serve as her sleeping place yet another night and couldn't make herself walk over to it. She rocked instead, a steady soothing movement that undoubtedly calmed 'most anybody who'd ever been held in one as a child.

Stella heard the alarm and knew it came from the watchtower on the corner of a prison. Men scrambled inside the walls across dirt and cement, some falling. She ran among them and searched for Dane. Everywhere inmates piled up, sandbars in the sea of people. She called and called for

Dane, but she couldn't find him. All of the prisoners looked the same.

Finally she startled awake and realized her phone was ringing. She hadn't known the ring.

She lunged for it. "Hello?"

A whiny voice came on. "You have a collect call from inmate Dane Scuffield from the Missouri State Penitentiary. Do you accept the charges?"

"Yes! Yes!" Stella gripped the phone tight now. He'd never called this early. She squinted at the clock. Actually, it wasn't early. She'd slept on the rocking chair clear through lunch.

"Stella?" Dane's voice made her legs feel wobbly, so she sat on the floor by the little table that held the phone. "You there?"

"I'm here." Her words were rough with sleep.

"You feeling okay?"

"I worked the night shift. I was just getting up."

"You got a job?"

"I did. I work at the Sinners' Cafe." She attempted a laugh. "It's fitting."

"How is your new place? Beatrice said you found one."

Stella looked around the gray peeling walls and stained carpet. "It's great. Sort of empty still, but there aren't too many furnished places around."

"I miss you. It's hard to imagine that I can't touch you."

Stella was glad to already be on the floor. "I know. I don't know how to do this."

"I don't either. You got the forms, right?"

"Yes, Beatrice brought them. I sent them in the minute I had an address here."

"It takes a couple weeks, but Maggie—the caseworker—she's good. She might get it done faster."

Stella squeezed her eyes closed, trying to remember his face, the angle of his jaw. She only had the one set of pictures, and he had already begun to fade in her memory. They'd had so little time. "I hope she does."

A loud banging came through the line. Stella tensed. "You okay?"

Dane's voice was strained. "Just time to go to the yard."

"Okay. I'm glad you called."

"Bye, Stella."

By the time she choked out her own "Bye," the line had gone dead. Stella set the phone back on its cradle. What was she doing here? Did she really intend to wait for him?

She lay back on the floor, staring up at the popcorn ceiling streaked with dirt and stained from leaks. Life handed you all sorts of things. She wasn't going to let her life go sour too. No way. No how.

39

MAGGIE HAS NEWS

THE guard slid the door open after the daily inmate count.

Dane and Alex got up from their beds to head down for rec time. Dane hoped to call Stella again. The more he could talk to her, the better he felt. He still didn't want her to wait for him, but he couldn't let her go. Maybe when they saw each other in person it would help. He was getting the drill down. As long as he didn't get into any fights or let Alex get him sucked into a scheme, he would get contact visits straight off, sitting across a table from Stella in a big room with dozens of other families. If he screwed up, he would have to stay in the room with phone booths and glass, or lose visitation privileges completely.

This weighed on his mind every hour, with each approach of another inmate, every conversation with Alex where his cellmate planned some other attempt to move contraband. He withdrew into the smallest, darkest part of himself, hoping to attract no attention, forging no alliances, and keeping to the fringe. He saw others doing the same, looking furtively from corners of the rec room or along the walls of the yard, trying to become invisible.

He got in line with the other men on the five walk, but the guard jerked him aside. "You got a meeting." He kept Dane with him as the other white-shirted men crossed over the bridge away from the cells to go downstairs.

A second guard led Dane out of the housing unit, through the metal cage, and back across to the administration buildings. Dane kept his head down, watching his own feet move across the concrete paths. He had no idea if what was happening was routine or something out of the ordinary.

They went down a corridor he recognized from his first day. The guard pushed him through a door. Inside, Maggie waited for him at her desk. She still wore her coke-bottle glasses, and her hair still looked like taxidermy. But she had on a more normal dress, not the one with big shoulders. She smiled with light-pink lips and gestured to the gray chair. "I'm glad to see you, Mr. Scoffield. We have a matter to discuss."

He sat in the chair, and the guard moved to the door. Maggie got up and closed it. Dane kept his hands on the desk, folded together. When she came back around, she sat on the corner rather than in her chair.

"You've been contacted by your father."

Dane's head snapped up. "Who?"

Maggie picked up an index card. "Bud Scoffield."

"I haven't seen him in twenty years." Nor did he want to. Ran off and left his mom with two rough boys. Married some other woman.

"He said you two talked regular."

"You talked to him?"

"When ex-cons try to get in for visitation, it gets noticed." Maggie returned to her chair. "Did you know he did time?"

"No. I haven't heard from him much. Phone calls on Father's Day. Sometimes he sent something on a birthday. Not often."

"Well, he spent five years in prison for armed robbery."

So much for Ryker being cut from the same cloth. Dane was looking more like his dad every minute. "When?"

Maggie scanned the card. "Looks like 1966 to 1971." She read on silently. "He wasn't allowed to leave Florida for another three years of probation." She looked up at Dane. "That's why he couldn't see you all that time."

"Nobody ever told us."

"He probably didn't want you to know."

"How did he find out about me?"

"I'm not sure. But you got two requests for visitation at the same time. The first was your dad. The other was a Joe Fontaine. Your old boss?"

Old Joe. He must have tracked down his dad. "So now what?"

"Well, if you want a form to go to Joe, we can send that out. But your dad is a problem. We have to get special clearance to allow previous offenders to visit inmates."

"You think he'd do something?"

"Just a formality. We have trouble with gangs sending messages to the inside. I'm sure you've seen some of that."

He hadn't, but then he talked to no one but Alex. "So you won't let him in?"

"It'll take some extra paperwork. I brought you here to ask if you even wanted it. You have to initiate the forms."

"Hell, I don't know."

Maggie pushed a letter toward him. "He was straightforward about his record and included his discharge papers. That's why we knew who he was. He seems like he's got your interests at heart. Take this, read it. See how you feel. I'll send the papers tomorrow, and you can fill them out or not."

Dane stood up with the letter, glancing cursorily at the words. The handwriting looked like his own, which bugged him. As he stepped out the door and the guard walked him down the corridor, he read a few lines.

I know what you're going through, son. I wasn't there for you growing up, and now you'll know why. But I'd like to see you now, if you're willing. I know you're keeping your head low and not talking to anyone, if you were like me. It can get mighty lonely. If you won't see me, I get that. It's what I deserve. But I hope you'll consider it. I'm right sorry about your mom dying. She was a good woman. Too good for someone sorry like the man I was back then.

Dane crumpled the note in his hand. He would have chucked it, except there was no place for it to go. The hallway was bare, the doors closed firm. Outside was just dirt blowing in the wind. He didn't have pockets. The guard led him out into the yard where the five walk was milling about with the rest of Housing Unit 4. He climbed the crumbling steps to the highest point near the wall, and sat down to tear the letter into tiny pieces, barely confetti dots that sailed into the air and drifted out toward the river that he could smell but had never seen.

40

HIGH EXPECTATIONS

STELLA pulled the plastic off the dress and hung it on the closet door. She stepped back to her bed and sat down, studying it from every angle. Plenty long to meet the length requirements at the prison. Nothing transparent. No cleavage. The emerald green would offset her hair perfectly. Cap sleeves. Cinched waist. The skirt swirled when she turned, as she had done plenty of times at the store. She kept imagining how she would walk up to Dane, seated at a little table, he had explained on the phone, and they could sit across from each other.

He'd be allowed one brief kiss, then they could hold hands and talk. If the room wasn't too busy, the visit could go on as long as they wanted. He didn't have work duty, so nothing would cut them off until the visitation hours ended.

Stella couldn't believe this day had finally arrived. Six agonizing weeks had passed since she'd last seen him at the hearing. Thanksgiving was just a few days away, so she'd get to see him yet again. She was working at the Sinners' Cafe most of the day, but Rennie was working part of her shift, and Stella part of hers, so they could each get a chance to go up there.

She glanced at the clock. One hour until visitation began. Last time she'd been there, it had been easy to walk up and sign in. Now that she had her papers, it would be a breeze. Stella would smile brightly at the cranky old biddy at the desk, then wait her turn on the benches to be called back.

She grabbed the dress and held it in front of her, spinning around the room. Seeing him this way wasn't perfect. It wasn't what she wanted. But it was something. After weeks of waiting, long hours at the cafe, dodging the pinches of strange men and leers of late-night hoodlums, she would get to do something entirely for herself.

***

Stella pulled up to the gates in her green dress. Her hair in the new scrunched style. She checked the matching eyeliner and bright eye shadow. Hopefully Dane would like it. It wasn't a look she'd had before. She'd gone from eternal teenager to adult while he was away. No doubt he'd changed too.

The guard noted her ID on the clipboard and let her through. Instead of the half-empty parking lot she remembered, though, cars were jam-packed, parking along the ends of the rows and up against the walls.

"What in the world?" Stella cruised slowly along the edges, dodging people thronging toward the door. Why were there so many people here? Her heart began thumping painfully, worried that their perfect visit would be thwarted.

She squeezed the Mustang between two trucks, a spot larger cars couldn't manage, and could barely open the door enough to slide out. She hid her purse under the seat, removing only her papers, her ID, and a plastic bag with change in it for the vending machines, just as the instructions had told her.

The line forming up to the door was long, snaking along the building for a hundred yards.

Stella walked to the end of it. Everyone seemed jovial and chatty, dressed more nicely than her last visit. She stood behind an elderly woman leaning on a cane. "What's going on?" Stella asked. "It's never this busy."

"Thanksgiving!" the woman said. "The out-of-towners come the weekend ahead, as they can't make it up on the holiday."

Well, hell. Stella glanced at her watch. She'd promised Dane she would be there right when they opened, but with so many people in front of her, it would be a long wait. She hoped he didn't mind.

A chill wind blew through, and she tightened her sweater around her. She could feel the scrunchiness coming out of her hair already. Damn. None of this was going according to plan.

"Might as well settle in," the woman said. "It'll take an hour or more just to get in the door."

"Will they limit everyone's visits?" she asked.

"Oh, certainly. I'd be surprised if anyone gets more than twenty minutes."

Twenty! Stella could already feel her good mood deflate. Why couldn't this have been a week ago? Their horrid luck that she would get approved right before a major holiday.

"Chin up, girl. He'll be right glad to see you." The old woman smiled, showing great gaps in her teeth. "My boy is always happy to get a visitor. Breaks up the day."

Stella leaned against the wall of the building. They hadn't moved an inch yet. She knew she should be happy with anything she got, but still, she felt miserable.

41

First Visit

DANE paced the length and width of his cell.

"Take a chill pill, dude," Alex said. "You're making me crazy."

Dane leaned his hands on either side of the window, sun slatting through the bars. It looked directly into another window just like it in the next building over. He couldn't see anything, but still he peered out, as if his line of sight could turn corners and follow paths, down to wherever Stella might be waiting.

Or maybe she hadn't come.

The guards had been busy, escorting inmates down the walk in a steady stream. Visitation had begun hours ago, and it had to be getting close to the end.

She wasn't coming.

He'd just talked to her yesterday, and she'd seemed keen on coming to visit. But she also talked about all the men at the cafe. He hadn't told her how their tattoos marked them as gangs. But maybe she knew. Maybe she liked one of them. Maybe all this was some sort of front to get to him. Maybe he'd pissed off the wrong person inside, and they were planning something.

He smashed his hands against the frame of the window, once, then twice. The pain in his palms felt good.

"Hey, if you're going to go mental, I want out of here." Alex backed up against the bars of the door.

Dane spun around. "I'm just waiting. That's all." He forced himself to lean on the wall, kick up a leg, cross his arms. Casual. Low-key.

"For what? Santa Claus? Think the Macy Day Parade is gonna march right up the five walk?" Alex laughed to himself and lay back down on the bed. "You expecting someone? Visitation is nearly over."

Dane clenched his jaw. "No."

"I never seen you act this way. You must be expecting something."

God, he could not get away, could not escape talking. He felt the walls acutely now. Stay calm, he told himself. You have to keep it down.

A guard approached, and Dane tensed. He didn't slow down, though, and Dane turned back to the window. Looking out was the only way he could keep it together.

But the bars behind him screeched. "Scoffield. Visitor."

Alex kicked the wall, sending loose paint raining on his bed. "I knew it! Damn, I never seen anybody."

Dane turned around and followed the guard out and down the corridor. He forced his shoulders to relax. She was here. By God, after all this time, she was here.

"'Bout time someone came to see you, Scoffield," the guard said. He was a bruiser, one of the real assholes.

Dane ignored him.

They exited the unit, and the guard unlocked the cage that led out to the other buildings. "Thought maybe you never talked to no one on the outside neither." He laughed, and they entered the cage.

"Still not talking, are you? So who is it? Your sister? Your mama?"

Dane kept his eyes on the ground.

"You're a fucked-up piece of work, aren't you?" At the exit to the cage, the guard turned to him. "You want to see them, right? You don't want to get roughed up right here at the last lock and end up having to go back in?"

Dane set his jaw. "No, sir, I do not."

This seemed to placate the guard, so he opened the last door. "All right, let's go see what you've got."

They walked along the path past the other housing units, and Dane could see they were heading back toward the red-brick administration building. Visitation must be in the same place as he met Maggie. Made sense. He felt calmer knowing he'd been in the building. It wasn't too rough. Nothing that would frighten Stella, not like the cracking and peeling cells.

They passed through the usual entrance, but another guard waited with a metal detector. He waved the wand around Dane, then sent them on through. Instead of turning down the long hall where he'd met Maggie, they walked down a corridor, turning and twisting until Dane was sure he would never find his way back on his own. At last he heard some noise, and they approached a room where several guards waited. One held a clipboard. "Inmate?"

Dane rattled off his number. Back here, his name was irrelevant. Behind the man was a door with a window, and in the room dozens of round plastic tables with flimsy chairs were filled with inmates and families. Guards were posted every few feet to watch over the din. He'd had no idea there would be so many people.

The ceilings were low, made of those foam squares to absorb sound, with an occasional plastic section for the lights. Vending machines filled one entire wall, many of them with kids in front, hands splayed on the glass fronts.

"Saw your woman," another guard said. "Quite the looker."

Dane clenched his fist, willing himself not to listen.

"You hear me? Where'd a punk like you score a bimbo like her?" He laughed and turned toward the door. "Maybe I shouldn't let you in. Maybe I should keep her for myself."

He walked in the door, and Dane followed, trying to stifle his rage. He spotted her in the back corner, in a green dress that flowed around her like Marilyn Monroe. Her blond hair was different, but it was her. Some punk was trying to chat her up from the next table. "Looks like she's already found someone," the guard laughed, and shoved at Dane's shoulder.

Dane forgot everything about where he was and how he had to be. He shoved back at the guard, who twisted to avoid stepping on a kid sitting on the floor. The mother snatched up the child, sending the guard off balance, and he fell into an empty chair, knocking it aside with a crash. Two other guards rushed forward and grabbed Dane's arms. Stella turned to him as the room hushed.

"You're done here." The two guards whipped him around and cuffed his wrists before he could say anything else.

Stella moved forward. "Dane! What happened?"

The first guard found his balance and took her arm. "Back away, miss."

Dane craned his neck, trying to see her. He'd waited all day. He had to see her.

He dragged his heels to slow them down, but this infuriated the guards, who lifted him up by the shoulders and flung him through the door. "Administrative write-up," one said to the man with the clipboard.

Dane still tried to turn and look through the doorway. Stella stood in the room, her hands on her cheeks. Her hair stood out like a halo, the green dress bright and vibrant in the chaos of people.

A guard grabbed his arm and pulled him away. "That's going to cost you three months of visitation."

Dane wanted to argue. He hadn't meant anything. But this was how things kept going for him. This was just how things were.

42

DEFEAT

CAYENNE entered the kitchen as Stella stuck her purse and jacket on a shelf.

"So how'd it go with your man? The big reunion?"

Stella yanked the apron down and rapidly tied it around her waist. "Fine."

"You don't look fine."

Stella searched around for an order pad and shoved one in her front pocket. She wanted to lie about the whole thing, say it'd been perfect, ideal, and she couldn't wait for Thursday when she'd see him again. But truth was, she'd been crying for three hours and her face showed it.

Cayenne handed her a pen. "It's Thanksgiving week. It was probably a madhouse, right?"

Stella nodded, tucking the pen in her pocket.

"So you only got to see him for what, five minutes? That upset you?"

Stella walked over to the stack of clean dishrags, threading one through her waistband. "Yeah. Wasn't what I expected." She filled a pocket with sugar packets and Sweet'N Low, then a handful of paper-wrapped straws.

She could feel Cayenne's eyes on her as she walked past. Rennie pushed through the doors, eyes lighting up when she saw Stella. "You got to see him! How did it—"

She cut off, and Stella guessed Cayenne had done something behind her to tell her to.

Rennie enveloped Stella in an awkward hug, making her suddenly homesick for Beatrice. "I'm sorry it didn't go grand, lovey. Those visits. They aren't much."

Stella cleared her throat. "It'll be better next time. I'll know what to expect." She didn't want to tell them about the guard's stumble, and how Dane was blamed, dragged out by two security men in handcuffs. She still couldn't get over the sight of it, like the morning they'd taken him from Grandma Angie's house. Her heart squeezed so tightly she could scarcely breathe.

"Maybe she should get the evening off," Rennie said. "Do you think we can cover?"

Cayenne came up from behind, assessing Stella's face. "We could do that."

Stella shook her head. She'd spent all afternoon avoiding calls from Beatrice and Janine, wanting to know how the meeting had gone. "I'd rather be here. Work until I drop."

She pushed through the red doors and out into the din of the early dinner rush. There'd been a lot of people visiting the prison, which meant a lot of diners at the Sinners' Cafe.

43

Consequences

DANE paced the length and width of his cell. He'd been moved to Unit 2, which had all single-person cells. The smaller room suited him fine if that meant no Alex to put him at risk for contraband searches. No one had said anything to him about why he was moved, just to pack up his things and be ready to move out in ten minutes.

He had no idea how the schedule on this hall differed, if rec time was the same or if they had the same set of phone booths. He was closer to the yard now, and the window overlooked the sports field and the covered weight station. Prisoners milled around. With no clock or watch or schedule to keep time by, Dane had no idea what time of day it was.

A guard approached finally, slipping a sheet of paper between the bars. Dane took it and unfolded it slowly. Hopefully it wouldn't be worse news.

But it was. Across the top were the words "Suspension of Visitation."

He almost crumpled it. But he had to know the deal. He scanned the page.

Reason for suspension: Assault of security personnel.

Assault. That was going to cost him. He sat on his bed.

Six months' revocation of contact visitation.

Damn. Longer than they'd threatened. He'd have to call Stella, let her know. He read on.

Thirty days' suspension of phone privileges.

Hell. He couldn't call her either.

Removal from honor dorm.

He had been in an honor dorm? No one had told him that. The A-Hall was one of the oldest. Who would have guessed it was considered the best?

He lay back on his bed. The ceilings were low. Unit 2 was newer, the same red brick as the administration building, with typical plaster walls and a bed bolted to the wall, unlike Unit 4, with its domed ceilings and carved windows. Still, prison was prison, and if Unit 2 meant he could be alone, that was fine by him.

He'd write Stella a letter. It was time to cut her loose. Worrying about her, wanting her, this was his problem. She set off something in him that he couldn't control.

He had a niggling suspicion that the A-Hall had been easy on him. If a simple shove of a guard landed him here, his first unit was probably a walk in the park compared to what he'd find at rec time. His gut twisted, but he clamped down on his unease with resolve. He couldn't have anything to lose. Which meant Stella had to go. That was the only way he'd get through these twelve years in one piece. His only chance at it, anyway. Whether or not he succeeded had little more to do with circumstances than his determination. All he could do was make his life as simple as possible.

He jerked his box off the floor, looking for the sheets of paper Maggie had sent on his first day. The bit of hot pink flashed from inside a crumpled page. He allowed himself to pull it out for a moment and run the fabric through his fingers.

He should toss it, but he couldn't make himself do it. He crumpled it back inside the paper and shoved the wad in the corner of the box. The writing papers were stuck together, and it took some concentration to separate a single page. He stared at the blank sheet. On it, he had to tell Stella good-bye. He dug around for the pen and hoped the right words would come.

44

FINALITY

STELLA dropped the letter to the floor. Tomorrow was Thanksgiving Day. She'd hoped to go back to the prison, see if she could get in to Dane. At least she'd have information if she went up there. He hadn't called since the botched visit.

But the silence had been better than this. Dane didn't want her to visit anymore. He'd told her to leave. Not to wait.

She let her arm hang over the edge of the bed, fingers grazing the carpet. She had to work a double shift to help cover for Rennie, who had family coming. She didn't think she could get up.

The phone rang, but she knew it wasn't Dane, so she let it ring. Probably Beatrice. Or Janine. Nobody else had her number. She didn't want to talk to anybody.

The frame with the strip of pictures sat on Grandma's table by her bed. She lifted it up, rolling onto her back to peer at it. Dane stared at her, but in the black-and-white version, she still couldn't see the color of his eyes. Two weeks. She'd only been with him two weeks. How many times had she even seen him in that time?

She sat up and grabbed the order pad from the apron she'd forgotten to take off the night before. She made a list.

Good Scents
Garage
Car delivered
Tower (!)
When he got cut (!)
Meeting Grandma

She paused. Grandma had met him. They'd made the bracelet together. She picked up the triple strand from the table. Dane's beads, the earth tones for his gentle side. But then the bright-orange bones. His danger strand. Seems like that should have been her warning.

She dropped her legs over the side of the bed. She tore the partial list of their time together off the pad and laid it on top of the frame. Then she placed the bracelet on top of that. She was wearing the Show-Me State shirt, so she pulled it over her head and folded it around the bundle. Everything they ever had together was in this one meager pile. Dane was right. It wasn't enough. Not for twelve years.

She opened the drawer of Grandma's table, the one that had secretly held Joe's bracelet all those years. She stuffed the things inside and forced it closed.

She was done.

45

UNEXPECTED GUEST

February 1985
Three months later

STELLA burst through the doors at the Sinners' Cafe. She was late.

"Corgie's fit to be tied," Cayenne warned.

"I couldn't care less," Stella said. She had four months of perfect attendance at this hellhole. He could stuff it.

She flashed a smile at a group of college boys. Valentine's Day was tomorrow, and she had no intention of spending it alone. Jefferson City was starting to feel like home, and although she should get off her butt and find a better job, she'd begun to think of Rennie as a mother, Corgie as some incorrigible uncle, and Cayenne as the bitchy sister she couldn't stand but missed when she wasn't around.

And the boys were plentiful. She didn't have her old spark, but months of difficulty had kept her lean, and her long blond hair, now almost to her waist and ironed straight, got her the attention she needed when she felt particularly blue.

She hurried back to snag her apron and dump her jacket and purse. Corgie stepped in front of her.

"Oh, stuff it," she said. "I'm not even ten minutes late."

"You got visitors."

Stella turned back to the red doors, still swinging. "Really? I didn't see anyone I would know."

"Said you wouldn't recognize them. A couple. All dressed up, like a funeral or something. You'll see them." He waved a spatula at her. "And don't make this a habit."

"Visitors?" Stella stuffed her things on the shelf and snatched up the apron.

"Being late."

Stella shrugged. She was more interested in the table of college boys than the visitors. The last man who had interested her had lasted only three dates, and they'd never even gotten in the sack. Like the rest of them, no fireworks, no go. She was reconciled that what she felt with Dane wasn't going to be easy to replace, and so she avoided entanglements. The five men in her life these past three months since Dane's letter had lasted no more than a week. But Valentine's Day was different. She'd put a rush order on this one. She hadn't had any real action since the day before Dane's arrest.

And a table full of prime suspects had just arrived.

Cayenne already had them cornered, but Stella could stop by anyway. There were plenty to choose from.

The couple Corgie was talking about sat in the back booth. The man was tall and straight-backed, with wiry gray hair, his black suit well fitted. The woman had a kind face, sort of church-ladyish, and a bun the size of a beehive on her head. Stella decided to get this part over with.

But when she got near the table, the man turned his face to her and she stopped short. He was Dane all over again, albeit older. That same nose the brothers had shared. And his hands. They rested on the table, and Stella's knees wobbled. His hands were most certainly Dane's.

The man stood. "You must be Stella." His eyes fixed on her, sparkly and gray. Gray! Dane's eyes had been gray!

She didn't extend a hand, shocked as she was, but he reached for her and took it. "You are as beautiful as Joe said."

"Joe?" She managed to choke out the name.

"Dane's old boss. He told us how to find you."

"You're Dane's—"

"Father. I'm Bud Scoffield." He walked her closer to the table. "And this is my wife Clarice. Dane's stepmother, although he's never met her."

Clarice took Stella's hand from Bud and grasped it firmly between her own. "Stella, I'm so glad to know you. Joe told us how you'd moved here to be near Dane. What devotion." She pulled Stella to sit in the booth beside her.

Stella could hear the boys laughing, flirting with Cayenne, and her face flushed. "I haven't seen him in three months," she said.

"Oh, I know," Clarice said. "They suspended his visitation. We hired a lawyer for him. It's been reinstated. They had video surveillance. The whole thing was really just a misunderstanding."

"But Dane did push the guy." Stella had been there. She knew what happened.

Bud sat down opposite them. "They overreacted."

"So," Clarice said. "We have a wonderful surprise." She glanced over at Bud. "Shall you tell her, or shall I?"

Stella wanted to escape. She didn't know these people. And obviously they didn't know Dane.

"You do it, sweetheart."

Clarice still held firm on Stella's hand. "We talked to Dane's caseworker, Maggie. In light of his wrongful suspension and the fact that tomorrow is Valentine's Day, we got him a special dispensation to have a visitor tomorrow evening."

Bud leaned forward. "Normally it's only for the married inmates, but we convinced them you were close enough."

Stella pulled her hand from Clarice. "But—you don't know me."

"Joe told us all about you," Clarice said. "He clearly adores you."

"Have you talked to Dane? Have you seen him?"

Both Bud and Clarice looked down at the table.

"You haven't!" Stella slid away from Clarice. "He asked me not to come anymore. How can I go see him?"

Bud rubbed his temple. "We only wanted to help. Of course you shouldn't see him if you don't feel like you should."

They both looked so disappointed that Stella could hardly stand it. They certainly weren't pushy. Dane obviously got a lot of temperament from his father, even if he hadn't been raised by him. She remembered Dane on the tower and his willingness to back away. Stella flooded with heat just remembering how he'd come up behind her, how powerful that had been. Suddenly the partial list in her drawer called to her. She wanted to finish it, to remember everything. "I'll go," she said. "I'll see him."

The couple smiled so broadly that Stella couldn't help but be happy for them. Clarice pulled a form from her purse. "Here's the special paperwork. It will get you in. Tomorrow at seven."

Stella was glad she had traded Rennie for the night off. The older waitress had readily agreed, saying the young pups needed that day, not the old cows like her. She glanced over at the boys, all gazing up at Cayenne. She'd be spending her evening at the State Pen.

"One thing," Clarice said.

Stella stiffened. She'd figured there would be strings attached.

"Ryker isn't on the list yet," Clarice said. "Dane has to initiate the forms."

"Ryker? Where is he?" God, she'd love to see him.

"Back in Texas. But he's willing to come up."

"Have you talked to him, then?"

Bud cleared his throat. "He won't speak to me. But we tracked him down. If you give Dane his address, he can send a form to him to visit."

That Stella could do. "I will."

Clarice pointed to the paper. "And this is our address here in Jefferson City. We're going to stay around a little while, to see if Dane will be willing to see Bud." She squeezed Stella's hand. "Don't worry about putting in a good word or anything. Bud has been writing Dane, trying to soften him up."

"Has he written back?" Stella suddenly hungered for news of him, proof that he was okay.

Bud shook his head. "No. I'm not sure he even reads them. He has cause to hate me. But I did get clearance to visit him, if he'll just send me the form. Wasn't easy." He grimaced at Clarice.

"What? Why?" Stella looked between them. They were hiding something.

"Dane didn't know that the reason his father didn't contact him all those years was—" Clarice faltered. "He was in prison himself."

Stella shot out of the booth. "What? Does it run in the family?"

Bud rested his head in his hands. "When I heard, I was devastated."

Clarice pushed the form back across the table. "Never mind about us, Stella. It's not about us. It's about Dane. We wanted to do something for him, anything we could. If this is all we can do, then it will be enough. We love him, and it doesn't matter if he won't see us. We're still his family."

Stella picked up the form, folded it, and tucked it in her apron. Family. It had been a long set of holidays for her, even though Beatrice and Joe had come up to see her. She wondered if family was something she just wasn't cut out for.

46

VISITATION

THE door rattled as the guard slid back the lock. "Visitation."

Dane looked up from his book. "You got the wrong con." He still had three months of suspension to go, and Stella was the only one on his list anyway. She had not contacted him after the letter, just as he'd asked.

"Stand up for escort."

Dane turned the book upside-down on his bed. Apparently, he was going somewhere.

They followed the rail of the Two Walk down. Other inmates watched from their cells as they passed. Someone leaving the unit at this hour was pretty rare. It usually meant something bad was going down. Maybe visitation was a code word for something else this time.

But as they passed through the cage and out into the night, Dane could see a few other inmates led toward the administration building from other units. Light splashed on the walkways as they webbed toward the red-brick building.

The other prisoners were jovial and bright, most holding cards or woodworking projects. Dane hadn't earned hobby or craft privileges and had been moved from laundry to the plate factory only a few days prior.

They lined up along the corridor he recognized from the failed visit with Stella. "What gives?" he whispered to the man in front of him, who clutched a papier-mâché heart that had been painted red.

"Special privilege," the man said. "First time? You'll love it. The guards are all laid back at this one." He ran his hand along the edge of the heart, smoothing a loose bit of newspaper.

It was Valentine's Day, Dane realized. He hadn't kept up with the dates. He didn't have anything to look forward to. His blood pressure rose a notch. This had to be a mistake. He couldn't be given a special privilege. He was on suspension.

The door to visitation opened, and the inmates were led inside without all the usual wanding and warnings. They walked inside, orderly despite the urgency he sensed among them. Four guards stood in the room, and each table had a woman at it. Only a few of them also had children. The scene was completely different from his last experience.

The room erupted in hugs and brief kisses, then everyone settled into chairs. Dane hung near the door, not sure why he was there, then he saw her.

Stella sat alone at a table in the center of the room, resting her chin on her hands and watching him. She wore the green Show-Me State T-shirt they'd bought at the truck stop and a pair of jeans. Her hair was longer, spilling over her arms to her elbows. She was the most beautiful thing he had ever seen, and he was momentarily dumbstruck, wondering wildly if he'd been shanked in his cell and this was some sort of death dream.

He forced his legs to move forward, and suddenly she was standing, waiting for him. He knew there were rules, and that he was really suspended, but that just meant he had even less to lose. He pulled her in an embrace so tight that he could feel every rib against his chest. He kept her close as long as he dared. She felt thinner, but good, so good, like he'd come home.

She sobbed against him, and he knew what that meant. She'd been holding things in too. Emotion throbbed between them. He couldn't believe he'd let her go. "I was wrong," he whispered. "I shouldn't have told you to go away."

She held on to his arms like a lifeline. "I shouldn't have listened."

He pulled back and knew they would allow one kiss, and in it he had to say everything he wanted to say, that he loved her, which he'd never said, and that he hadn't wanted to get angry, not at the bar, nor at her first visit, and that certainly he hadn't wanted what happened to his father, to be forced into a cell and to think that it was better to drop out of someone's life than to cause them any pain. He got it now. He understood completely how wrong his father had been, and how he'd been, and that something to lose was indeed better than nothing.

But he couldn't rely on the kiss. "I love you, Stella," he said. "I don't deserve you, not any part of you, but I love you."

She clutched at his shirt, that stupid convict's uniform. "I have loved you all along. I can't love anyone else."

All around them men and women embraced, exchanging Valentines and happy laughter. He hadn't wanted to feel this here, not now, but this was what life had dealt them. He'd see it out, if she would.

The guards were looking elsewhere, so he kissed her and kissed her, lips on hers and hands on her neck and she seemed to understand, as she was crying, and Stella never cried, and by the time a guard finally cleared his throat, he could let her go. He could sit opposite her at that plastic table and hold her hands, her pale strong hands, rougher from hard work, but still hers, and the bracelet. She was wearing the bracelet. He felt swallowed up by everything he'd missed about her and allowed into his heart the thing he hadn't let get to him in many long months. He felt hope.

47

WEDDING

Spring 1985

THE little girl in the white dress had gone far astray, flinging pink rose petals in wild chunks at everyone sitting along the aisle. Stella stifled the urge to run up behind her and set her straight, watching instead the photographer snap shot after shot, especially when a fistful of pink shot straight into Janine's uptight mother's face.

The music changed, and Stella stepped forward, met by Nick's brother, the best man, and together they walked along the carpet, trying not to laugh at the woman tugging errant petals from her ample cleavage. At the altar she blew a little kiss to Nick, looking nervous and red-faced as he waited for his bride to appear.

Stella turned to face the back. The music surged, and the guests all stood. Two ushers opened the church doors wide, and Janine appeared in her flowing white gown, face covered in a shimmery veil, arm linked through her father's.

Stella bit her lip, hoping she wasn't wrecking her makeup. Janine had eyes only for Nick. Stella glanced at the groom, amazed at the incredible smile that had erased his look of anxiety. They were both transformed in this moment, as happy as she'd ever seen them.

Stella glanced down at the bracelet resting against the bone of her

241

wrist. Gentle. Danger. Her in between.

They'd both changed. She'd grown up. He'd calmed down. Dane had even allowed Bud in to see him—the father he'd hated so long. It seemed impossible, but their lives were still growing and changing even while Dane was imprisoned.

The organ music wound down. The flower girl was tossing petals straight into the air. Stella had to work not to laugh.

She would get this day. And now, after five wonderful visits with Dane, each Sunday when they talked and held hands and even joked a little, she knew this was the one thing she wanted. This kind of day. With him. None of those other boys had worked. Only Dane.

As Janine's father stepped away, and Nick lifted Janine's veil, Stella realized what she had to do.

Wait.

PART THREE: *Decision*

48

RELEASE

Fall 1996
Twelve years later

STELLA pushed aside the yellow curtain. Midday had already struck, and it was time to get up.

She should have given up the night shift years ago, when Rennie retired with her bad leg and Corgie told Stella she could switch to days. But over the years, Dane had moved from one unit to another, and to make sure she could be home for his daily calls, she stuck with nights, glad for a job that more or less paid the bills.

Dane's parole hearing had already happened, and she'd slept right through it. They didn't expect anything to go wrong, but she didn't know exactly when he'd get out, either. Might be today. Might be a few days' worth of paperwork. She told Corgie that when it happened, she was taking a vacation. He'd shaken a spatula at her, but he knew she was as good as gone. Once the work committee assigned Dane his first job, they'd be moving wherever that might be, and her years at the Sinners' Cafe would end.

She stretched, looking out the window at the covered bulge of Grandma Angie's white Mustang. The old thing had given up the ghost three years ago, too much to fix. But she hadn't let go of it. Dane could work on it in his spare time, and it meant a lot to them. Now she drove a little Ford Escort, easy on the gas and not hard to keep up with.

But she had a big surprise for Dane. Bud had brought Dane's old Harley by last week, cleaned up and ready. Stella wanted to look at it one more time, rushing to the door of the garage but leaving it open so she could hear the phone ring. Stella had gotten her own motorcycle license last year, practicing on Corgie's beat-up Yamaha until she felt like she could handle the Harley. No other way to pick him up from prison than that.

She skipped back through the house she'd been renting the past year, tucked onto a little street only a few blocks from the prison. She loved going out on the porch where she could see the watchtower on the corner closest to her, an area that Dane had explained included the lower yard. He sat there most afternoons, and some days she felt closer to him just by looking up at that glassed tower and knowing he was looking at it too.

Bud and Clarice would be waiting to hear from her. Dane would call her with the news, then she'd relay it to them, then Beatrice, whom she still talked to every week to keep up with the gossip in Holly. After Janine had given birth to twins, they'd lost touch, although Stella always sent the babies gifts on their birthday. She patted her own stomach, still lean and firm at 34. She'd never been sucked into eating the grease-laden dishes at the cafe, which had turned poor Cayenne into a puffball before she'd finally quit around the time Rennie retired.

With any luck, they'd have their own baby before too much more time passed. They planned their own simple wedding ceremony at a chapel nearby, just waiting on the date for Dane's release. They could have done it while he was in, but in the end, Stella wanted to wait. She still remembered Janine's wedding day, and she wanted something of her own, without the peeling walls and guards standing in the back.

Just thinking of Dane being free to hold her without people watching loosened Stella inside, that part of herself she'd held so tightly reined for over a decade. A lot of catching up to do. The four times she and Dane had been together were moments she often pulled forward into her memory and held on to. The water tower, Ryker's sofa, the woods, and the phone booth. She was ready to be an old lady now and try a real bed.

The phone rang, and Stella tripped over the rug trying to lunge for it. She grasped the receiver, shaking her foot free. "Hello?"

She expected the recorded message that she was receiving a call from an inmate, a system that had replaced the operator-controlled collect calls years ago, but instead, a curt woman came on the line. "Stella Ashton?"

"Yes." Stella freed her foot and sat on a chair, fear curdling in her.

"This is Violet Humphrey from the Reentry Transition Team."

Stella breathed a little easier. "Hello, Violet."

"I have instructions for you for the release of Daniel Scoffield."

Stella snatched a note pad from the shelf. "I'm ready."

"He'll be released from the administrative building at two o'clock tomorrow afternoon. He has indicated that you will be here to receive him."

"Yes."

"All right. He must report to his new workplace, the Joplin Refinery, in three days, at eight o'clock on Monday, for training."

"Got it."

"You know the location?"

"Yes."

"It's vitally important he make it on time."

"Will do."

The woman rustled some papers. "His parole officer will be in contact about his weekly check-ins. Those are also vitally important."

"I understand."

"Is this the phone number the officer should call?"

"It is."

"And you'll be at the prison gates tomorrow at two?"

"Yes."

"Thank you. That is all."

"Okay. Thank you."

Stella hung up the phone. It was happening. Tomorrow, Dane would be out. He'd be free.

49

FRESH START

DECKER, one of the guards who had been on Unit 2 as long as Dane had, stepped up to the cell door. "You ready to get out of this cage?"

Dane stood up, looked around one more time, and picked up the cardboard box that held the few things he had accumulated in twelve years. Some pictures. Letters. The hot-pink bit of fabric from Stella's torn shirt.

Having a cell to himself all this time had helped keep him isolated from the other prisoners. He had few friends on the inside, not that anyone could really be called friends. He learned to seek out the lifers, the older ones who'd weathered decades of hotshots, gangs, and thugs. By the time Dane had been moved from the plate factory to the garage, which was outside the walls, he had a congenial relationship with a couple of the more skilled tradesmen, and had been able to work on newer models of cars as well as the machinery and trucks that belonged to the prison. This helped keep him employable for when he got out.

He never told Stella that his workplace was outside the gates. She wouldn't do anything, but she didn't realize that some of the regulars at the cafe were always seeking out the women of other inmates, pumping them for information, trying to see who might be an ally on the inside.

His position in the garage, while a step up from the factories, made him vulnerable, and by extension, her too. Still, they had made it.

Decker opened the iron door, slapping Dane on the back as he passed. "About time, old man, about time."

The other inmates on his walk came forward, waiting in their cells for the end of the midday count, to see him off.

"Nice threads!" one called.

"Your mama dress you?" asked another.

Dane smiled. He'd asked Stella to send him clothes, but Bud had insisted on providing the outfit, remembering his own day out, when Clarice had sent a brand-new suit.

And so his father had sent some pinstriped gray number, white shirt, tie, and all. Stella was going to bust out laughing when she saw it. But he could look forward to her stripping it off him, piece by piece.

They left the housing unit and took the path to the administrative offices, now as familiar a walk to him as the path to school as a kid. Today the red-and-white stripes of the squat building stood out bright and fine. He'd never be looking at the back side of those walls again.

They turned down a new corridor, one he'd never been on. Dane had expected to meet up with Stella in visitation. The hall was long and empty except for a figure at the end, a broad woman. As they approached, he recognized Maggie. No more shoulder pads or helmet hair, just a simple suit and a sleek head of gray. She still wore soft pink lipstick.

"Good-bye, Dane," she said. "I asked to be the one who brought you out."

Maggie had been kicked upstairs years ago, moving from caseworker to supervisor. Dane nodded at her. "Thank you."

"These are the best days." She laid a small box on top of the larger one he already held. "Your things from storage."

He remembered the spiked belt and watch chain. Things he'd worn the last day with Stella. They would enjoy looking at them again.

Maggie led him toward a doorway at the end, spilling light in through a bar-less window.

"Your paperwork is all in order," Maggie said. "Your new job starts on Monday." They reached the door, and she squeezed his arm. "I'm very glad to hear Stella is coming to get you."

Dane felt his throat thicken. If it weren't for Maggie, he might never have written Stella. Never gotten to this day. "Thank you" was all he could manage.

She pushed open the door. The light was blindingly bright. He blinked several times, trying to adjust, and he thought at first he might be seeing a mirage. His Harley, looking just as good as 1984, better probably, as they'd crashed it just before his arrest, and on it, Stella, in, of all things, a full-on wedding gown.

"You're looking kind of sissy for a ride like this," she said. She held one helmet in her lap, and a second one dangled from a handlebar.

"You're looking like you might get caught in the wheels."

She hitched up the dress, revealing how the hem was tucked into her underwear. "Not gonna happen."

"I'll just take those." Bud stepped forward and relieved Dane of his boxes. Clarice gave him a quick hug.

Dane scarcely noticed them as he slid a hand up Stella's thigh and tucked the dress more tightly up around her legs.

"Looks like we'd better get on to the church," Clarice said. "Then dinner to celebrate?"

Bud pulled her back, smiling broadly. "I think we'll take a rain check on the dinner. Tomorrow, maybe."

Dane paid them no mind. They could wait. He straddled the Harley behind Stella. His own license had expired years ago. "You know how to drive this thing?" he asked.

She shoved the helmet at him. "When I jump creeks, I don't end up in the dirt."

She stomped on the starter, revved the motor, and he held on to her slender waist in the beaded gown. Bud, Clarice, and Maggie waved as they cruised toward the guards, who opened the gate, and they sailed past the guard towers onto Capitol Avenue, ready for whatever came next.

Epilogue

THE hospital's maternity ward bustled with nurses and family, helium balloons and flower arrangements.

Stella grasped Dane's hand as they stood in the window of the nursery, waiting to see baby Angie.

"She'll be beautiful," Stella said. "The most beautiful child in the world."

Dane kissed her fingers. "Of course she will."

A nurse rolled in a clear plastic bassinet that read "Baby Girl Mays."

Stella clutched Dane harder. "There she is!"

The nurse saw them pointing and lifted the baby up, squalling and red-faced.

"She looks a bit like a pissed-off chicken to me," Dane said.

Stella elbowed him in the gut. Men. They watched as the nurse laid the baby under a heat lamp and undressed her for her first real bath. Kayleigh, the baby's mother and Stella's niece, was still in recovery after an emergency C-section.

Stella's back started to ache, so they watched a bit more then went back to the waiting area for word when Kayleigh would be sent to a regular room.

"I sure wish things were different for her," Stella said. "I know what it's like to not have family during hard times."

"She's got us," Dane said.

Stella laid her head on his shoulder. "This is hard, isn't it?"

"It is."

It had been twelve years since Stella's first pregnancy, and twelve years since she miscarried baby Angelica at a campsite in Missouri, just hours after the doctors told her the baby didn't have a heartbeat.

Eleven years since little Buddy died the same way, just a couple months into the pregnancy.

Four years since they gave up on the rounds of infertility treatments, as Stella had not been able to get pregnant again after Buddy. At forty, she had been tired, and done.

Kayleigh was Bud and Clarice's only grandchild, the daughter of the stepson Dane had been so jealous of as a boy. But Jamison had died in a car crash when Kayleigh was twelve, and Patty, his wife, had shut down on living, leaving Kayleigh to raise herself. By the time Dane and Stella moved to Texas, the girl was wild, running with older men and experienced beyond her years. When she turned up pregnant, the man had promised to marry her, and they even got so far as to have the date set and the wedding shower done.

Then he'd taken off. Dane and Bud were fit to be tied, swearing to hunt the man down. But Kayleigh had just gone right on, until a fight with Patty over giving the baby up for adoption led the girl to come to Stella's door, days away from delivery.

"Did you get the crib all set up?" Stella asked. They'd been working day and night to clear out the room they used for storage to be ready for the baby.

"Everything but the sheets. Couldn't figure the damn things out."

Tina, a friend of Kayleigh who had stayed with her during the surgery, popped into the waiting room, still wearing paper scrubs. "She's about to be moved," she said. "She's already got the baby with her in recovery, and they are about to roll her down."

Stella heaved herself up. "What room?"

"309," Tina said. "I'm going to go back. See how she's doing."

"Is she all right? How was surgery?"

"She threw up. But nothing else. I watched the whole thing. Wow!" Tina's eyes lit up. "They cut her belly right open, and then Angie's head popped right out!"

"You okay with all this?" Stella asked. Tina had lost a baby to preterm labor just two months before. She was only seventeen.

Tina tugged at one of her ponytail springs. "Well, it did remind me of when I had Peanut." She pressed her lips together. "But the baby is so cute. It's fine. I'll be fine."

"Well, get on back there and take care of my niece," Stella said.

Tina paused. "You sure you're okay with the baby being called Angie after all?"

Dane came up behind Stella and laid his chin on her shoulder. "We're okay with it."

Tina nodded and dashed back down the hall.

Stella turned in to Dane. "Are we?" Stella had had a bit of a nervous breakdown when she'd first learned Kayleigh would call her baby what Stella had named her own first child, after Stella's grandmother.

Dane held her close. "I think Angie would like this. Maybe it's our way of moving on from all that clutter in the past."

"Maybe so."

He led her out of the waiting room and into the hall. "You'll have to make a bracelet for her. What stones?"

Stella examined the signs to figure out which way to go. "Right now they'd be beet red to match that face."

Dane laughed. "Maybe we should wait until we see what little Angie's like."

They turned down a corridor, the doors lined with pink and blue ribbons. Stella bit her lip, grief coursing forward. She'd never gotten this day with Dane. So much love they had to share with a baby. And they couldn't have one, and with Dane's record, the adoption agencies had turned them down.

She was so proud that sweet Kayleigh was keeping her baby despite everything. She didn't mind at all having them live with her for a while. It was like Beatrice taking Stella in when she had nowhere else to go. Time for her to return all the favors in the world. Beatrice was not doing well enough to come down, but maybe when the baby was bigger, they could go up and see her. Maybe she'd even stop in on her own mom and dad. Maybe.

Old Joe had Alzheimer's and wouldn't recognize them. But maybe they would stop by the nursing home in Branson, the same one Grandma Angie had been in decades ago. He lived under the delusion that Stella was Angie, and Stella let it be. She tried to make it up every few months or so. He always thought it had been just yesterday that Stella had visited last.

"This is it." Dane stood in front of room 309.

Stella rapped on the door, then pushed it open. Tina sat on a chair by the bed.

Kayleigh lay propped up, looking pale and tired but holding the baby to her shoulder.

"Look, Angie, it's Auntie Stell!" Kayleigh turned the baby out. She was sleeping now, her little fist curled tight against her chin.

Stella washed her hands at the sink by the door and approached the bed.

"You ready for this?" Kayleigh asked. "She's going to keep all of us up at night." She carefully passed the bundle to Stella.

Stella cradled the baby's head in one hand, tucking her tightly swaddled body up against her chest. Too much emotion coursed through her to answer. She knew now that everything she'd been through had led to this moment, just so she'd know exactly what to do when her niece knocked on her front door, asking for help. And now this, baby Angie, sweet and perfect.

"It's going to be just fine," Dane said.

Stella finally got her voice back. "It'll be more than fine." She gazed down on Angie's face as the baby yawned with a gummy little toothless mouth. "It's going to be wonderful."

Watch for **Kayleigh & Jude**, the continuation of the broken love story of Stella's niece, in 2013.

To be notified when it will be released and to read sneak peeks, join Deanna's subscriber list at www.deannaroy.com.

To read some of the missing years of Stella and Dane's story, including their difficulties in starting a family, read

Baby Dust

But realize this difficult book is not for everyone. Read the first chapter online before you buy it at www.deannaroy.com/babydust.

Your review on Amazon or BN.com is appreciated—it makes a huge difference to authors when readers provide their reactions to a work.

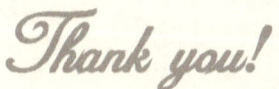

www.ingramcontent.com/pod-product-compliance
Lightning Source LLC
Chambersburg PA
CBHW032031240626
47154CB00003B/868